Praise for the novels

"Lawyer Kate Lange is back with another case that will test her courtroom skills, judgment and nerves. The suspense is intense, the action shocking and the plot intriguing. The insidious villain destroys a life, a reputation and a family, all as part of a chilling plan."
— RT Book Reviews on *Indefensible*

"*Indefensible* is a superbly plotted and suspenseful thriller, with…a riveting, dynamic storyline."
— Omnimystery, Mysterious Reviews

"Do yourself a favor and jump in the middle of these amazing books. You won't be able to put them down until the final page."
—Fresh Fiction

"Extremely well plotted, Callow's debut novel is a hybrid of a police procedural and medical thriller. Heroine Kate Lange is a standout character, and readers will certainly look forward to reading her further adventures."
— RT Book Reviews on *Damaged*

"Pamela Callow's debut thriller *Damaged* reminded me of the best of Robin Cook: lightning paced, innovative, topical…and most of all, frightening. Part medical mystery, part bloody thriller, here is a debut that had me flipping pages until the wee hours of the morning."
—James Rollins, #1 *New York Times* bestselling author

"*Damaged* is a taut, edge-of-the-seat thriller with strong characters and a driving plot that's inspired by emerging health technologies that may end up being, well, very bad for certain people's health. Pamela Callow is Halifax's answer to both John Grisham and Tess Gerritsen."
— Linwood Barclay, internationally bestselling author

"*Damaged* is a chilling and darkly compelling tale that will grip you from the very first page. Pam Callow delivers a complex and spine-tingling thriller. She is definitely an author to watch."
— *USA TODAY* bestselling author Julianne MacLean

"A compelling page-turner… Pamela Callow is a rising star."
— Bestselling author Rick Mofina on *Damaged*

EXPLOITED

BOOK 4 IN THE KATE LANGE THRILLER SERIES

PAMELA CALLOW

EXPLOITED

ISBN: 978-0-9951543-6-0

Published by Pamela Callow
Cover Design by Design for Writers
Digital Formatting by Author E.M.S

No man is an island.

*This book is dedicated with my deepest love and gratitude
to my brother, Steve Callow, who gave this book lift off,
to my husband, Dan, and my daughters, Julia and Katrina,
who keep me going,
and to Linda Brooks, an unparalleled friend.*

Prologue

1:58 a.m.

IT WAS THE DEAD of night.

Dead.

Night.

The two words circled in the mind of Leah Roberts.

Which would strike first: death—or darkness?

You are being paranoid. This has been all planned out. No one will be home.

But her gut screamed: *Have you lost your mind?*

Aiden gestured to her from where he crouched under a large window at the back of the Owen house. *Come on.*

Even across the length of the back yard, she sensed his urgency. It was now or never. If they succeeded in pulling this off, the truth would be known.

Hadn't her father always told her that she should do what she believed was right? *Do it, Leah.*

Do it.

She bent as low as her six-foot frame would allow and sprinted across the unkempt backyard of the Owen house. A hosta screened the cracked concrete foundation. She crouched behind the splayed perennial, aware of how inadequately the leaves hid her. Her heart thudded so hard that she thought it might break through the bone and skin that protected it.

Aiden rose to peer into the window. No lights were on. That reassured her. As did the overly long grass. The Owens must be away.

This will work.

She heard the window slide open. "We're in!" Aiden hissed.

That was easy.

Too easy.

If the Owens were away, would they have left their window unlocked?

Aiden nudged her with his boot. "Come on!"

Leah half-rose, half-froze as her brain tried to analyze the situation.

Aiden reached down and grabbed her arm. "Remember why we're here. It'll be over in a few minutes."

"I've changed my mind—"

A car door slammed a few houses over. They both jumped, scanning the street. "You have to do this, Leah. It's important," Aiden whispered. "I'm here for you, remember?"

Aiden's face was covered in a balaclava. Only his eyes were visible. Those eyes had shone with love, gleamed with promise, and given her strength when she needed it most. "You won't be able to live with yourself if you don't do this."

He knew her so well.

He yanked her to her feet and hoisted her onto the windowsill, pushing her from behind, and then leapt over the windowsill into the house.

Once inside, they stood by the window. Searching.

The house was dark, but with the help of the moon and a bare window, they were able to make out the basic features of the room.

A large sofa, with a throw folded on one end, dominated the room. A side table stood on the other side, cluttered with a television remote control, tea mug, and a stack of newspapers.

None of those inanimate objects explained the strange odor that hit Leah's nose.

It was a very human smell. But it was overlaid with the scent of decay.

It was the smell of life gone amiss.

Was this an old odor, perhaps of a mouse that had died in the walls?

Goosebumps skittered up the back of Leah's neck. It didn't matter how simple and fast this break-in was supposed to be, standing in someone else's house in the dead of night felt so terribly wrong.

Dead.

Night.

Those words would not stop stalking her mind.

She threw a glance over her shoulder at the window.

It's not too late, Leah.

Aiden tapped her arm and pointed.

She put one foot ahead of her.

No.

I can't do this. It doesn't matter if this is for the greater good.

It's wrong.

Aiden gestured again, impatiently pointing to the desk. *Do it,* his eyes said.

Her heart pounded so hard that she thought it would flee and leave her stranded in this house.

She inched backward until her hip connected with the windowsill. She could just slip through the window right now, and no one would be the wiser.

Her hands gripped the wooden frame.

Aiden spun around and grabbed her arm. Through the thick knit of her hoody, she felt a sharp point press into her side.

It was a knife.

She froze.

What the hell is he doing?

Those eyes that had gazed at her with love, tenderness, passion, and promise, now drilled into her with a threat.

He jerked his head toward the desk.

She tried to ease away. "What are you doing?" she hissed.

"Just do it."

She shook her head. "It's wrong."

His gaze narrowed. "Don't think I won't use this." He pushed the knife harder into her side. She felt the tip penetrate her skin. "It will only take a minute. And then you're home free, Leah."

"No." She tried to ease away from his knife. But the blade followed the curve of her flesh. She was strong, but Aiden was stronger. "Let go of me, Aiden!"

His thickly fringed eyes did not blink. "Joey will be next if you don't do this."

The words were uttered softly, but it made the threat all the more real.

She stumbled forward, her lover's knife pushing her toward the desk.

Do it, his eyes said.

Do it, the knife said.

The dark of the Owens' living room shifted around her.

It closed in with the unmistakable smell of death.

1

Two hours earlier.
11:54 p.m.

THE OLD FRONT DOOR was a better barometer than the weather forecast. When the weather was damp, Kate Lange's door let her know. And judging by the door's orneriness, it had been very damp while she was away.

Kate gave the door an extra push. It yielded with a lurch. She half-fell into the house, the rolling suitcase crashing into the back of her heels.

Seventy-five pounds of jubilant husky threw himself against her.

"Alaska! Hey, boy!" She dropped her purse, wrapping her arms around the dog that she had rescued when she first moved into this house. Clear blue husky eyes gazed at her with frantic relief that she had returned home. "I missed you." She kissed his silky fur.

A blur of black barreled off the sofa, launching against her hip in an explosion of pug excitement. His paws scrabbled for her attention. "Hello, Foo!" With one arm around the husky—who delicately nibbled his devotion on her ear lobe—she scratched the velvety head of the pug.

This was a welcome that would never get old.

Even if she was still bemused that the pug Foo Dog temporarily resided in her house.

A week before her departure for Italy, Finn Scott—dog walker and home renovator extraordinaire—had arrived on her doorstep with a hammer in his back pocket, two coffees on a takeout tray, and a drowsy looking black pug under one arm.

Kate recognized the dog. He belonged to Kenzie Sloane, celebrity tattoo artist to the masses, Finn's former lover—and the woman who had almost killed Kate just days before.

Kate had eyed man and pug warily. "Why are you bringing Kenzie's dog here?"

Finn's gaze was pained, but unapologetic. "She asked me to look after him while she was in jail."

Kate's interpretation of Kenzie's request was a little less charitable: Kenzie, never one to miss taking advantage, had zeroed in on Finn's soft heart.

And now Finn had to choose between his apartment or the pug, because his landlord threatened to evict him due to the building's 'no pets' policy. Naturally, Finn chose the pug. Kate hoped it was because of his feelings for the dog and not the owner. What else could she do but offer him one of the empty bedrooms in her house? She had the space.

She reluctantly had to concede that the timing had been perfect down to the hour. She had just had tea with her elderly neighbor Enid Richardson. "You need a change of scene," she'd said to Kate. "I've been worried about you. You seem to be a ghost of yourself."

Ha. A ghost. How true. But it was the ghost of others from her life that kept her up at night. The Body Butcher. Her sister Imogen. John McNally.

Kenzie Sloane. Those eyes...daring Kate to kill her.

She shivered.

Enid's bright blue gaze had narrowed. "You see? A warm Italian sun will do wonders for you." She patted Kate's hand

"But what about you, Enid? You haven't been well. I don't want to leave you." *In case anything happens*, she mentally added. She didn't think she could bear to lose Enid. Not yet.

Not ever.

"I'm feeling better." She gave Kate a reassuring smile. She *did* look a bit better. She had some color in her cheeks. "And I've got Corazon to help me. You, on the other hand, look like you need to get away from Halifax. Italy will be good for your soul."

Goodness knows that her soul had needed a little help. It had been thrown into darkness. Over and over again. She didn't know why her life had become so closely entwined with death. But when she had pointed that revolver at Kenzie Sloane and gloried in the urge to pull the trigger…

"It takes guts to do this, Kate. Not everyone can be a killer."

That memory sickened her. Terrified her.

And knowing that Alaska would be more than happy to have Finn look after him, she had decided to extend her initial two weeks' vacation to four, and go for broke. It was Italy or bust—for her soul. Especially after Nina Woods, the Managing Partner of McGrath Woods, had told her that the firm was concerned about all the salacious media attention that Kate had been receiving as a result of her teenage history with Kenzie Sloane.

Kate had flown from Halifax on a drizzly June day, her head pounding from the concussion she'd suffered at Kenzie Sloane's merciless, masterful hands. She had turned off her phone and her computer, allowing her concussed brain a chance to recover from the trauma it had suffered. Italy was a perfect distraction. Gorgeous architecture, a delight around every corner. She allowed herself to be caught entirely in the present, with no thought of the past, and no cares about the future.

And now, four weeks later, she was back. The question was whether the healing from the warm Italian sun had penetrated deeply enough. Or whether being back in the bedroom where her dead sister's box of mementoes sat in the closet would make her Italian sojourn a gelato-flavored dream.

"Finn? Are you home?" she called.

Foo Dog licked her hand. She had to admit, he was a cute yin to Alaska's majestic yang.

"Hey, you're back!" Finn's sun-streaked head appeared around the doorway to the kitchen. "I'm cleaning up the dishes. Just a sec." He hurried from the kitchen, wiping his hands on a dishcloth, which he tossed onto his shoulder to free his arms for a hug. "How was your flight?"

She returned the hug, and then kicked off her shoes. "It was long. It's good to be home."

"You look good. Better than you've looked for a while." He grinned. "And you've finally put on some weight."

Kate gave a rueful smile. "Who could resist all that pasta? And the gelato? And the bread…"

"You only live once, Kate." He reached down and scooped up Foo.

"Ha! You're preaching to the choir. And I think my body has decided that it wants to live life to its fullest, if you get my drift." Her pants felt a little too snug for comfort on the flight home from Italy.

"Trust me, a man likes a little something to hold on to."

Had he said that to Kenzie Sloane?

She banished the memory of the tattoo artist from her mind. "Speaking of gaining weight, you could use a little extra meat on your bones." His Florence + The Machine t-shirt hung loosely from his broad shoulders. "I might have to send you to Italy."

"I have to set a good example for Food Dog." Finn scratched under the pug's chin. "No one told me that pugs are on perpetual diets." Foo yawned contentedly in Finn's arms. Finn jerked his chin toward the wall behind Kate's head. "What do you think of the paint job?"

"I love it!" Kate gazed around her. The walls of the foyer had been painted sea foam blue. And the formerly dark-stained wood trim gleamed with crisp white paint. The entry looked fresh and inviting. "It came out better than I imagined. It makes the place look modern."

Pride gleamed in Finn's eyes. "Yeah, this old house is beginning to get a spring in her step."

"And the roses are gorgeous." A bouquet of exquisite pink roses that captured the sunrise in their velvety depths added an elegant note. "Are these from Muriel's garden?" Muriel was the other half of the dynamic elderly Richardson sister duo. Although Alzheimer's disease robbed Muriel of cognitive function and memory, it had not yet devastated her ability to create beauty from the earth. She maintained her garden with dogged devotion, occasionally over-pruning when she had forgotten she had pruned something just minutes before. But her garden bloomed under her care. Sometimes Kate wondered if the plants knew their caretaker needed them as much as they needed her. For there was no question that Muriel's garden was the most glorious on the street.

"Yes. Enid and Muriel have been awaiting your return. They invited you to tea this weekend."

"Has Enid been well?"

Finn nodded. "Yeah, she seems back to her old self."

"Thank goodness." Her smile quickly turned into a yawn. "Sorry. It's five a.m. in Italy."

"You need to get to bed. Do you want help with the bag?"

Kate shook her head. "I'm good, thanks." She climbed the stairs, grateful that Finn had turned on the light in the hallway. She opened the door to her bedroom. It looked cozy and serene.

She kicked off her shoes.

Her bed, pillows fluffed, invited her to lie down. She dropped her purse by the foot of the bed, and unzipped her carry-on. She knew she would regret not unpacking her suitcase, but one look at her closed closet door made her heart sink.

She wasn't ready to re-examine Imogen's box of belongings, not yet. The one and only time she had examined them, Kenzie had tried to kill her. There was too much trauma trapped in that document box. She was not ready to revisit it.

It took only a few minutes to brush her teeth and climb into bed. Alaska waited for her, an expression of sheer bliss in his eyes as he circled his large white frame on the fur-covered dog bed.

"Ah…" She slid between the sheets with a sigh of contentment. Alaska echoed her sigh, tucking his head on his paws. He gazed at her with such love that her throat tightened.

"I missed you, boy," she murmured.

His tail slowly swished.

Her laptop, deep within her purse, chimed.

With a groan, she slid out the computer, and flipped it open. The inbox had an alarmingly high count.

Her gaze scanned the list of senders. Exhaustion blurred her vision.

But then she saw the name that had been on her mind since she boarded her flight home. He had responded to her email quickly. She had only sent it in the departure lounge of the Milan airport.

"Hallelujah!" she murmured.

John Hillcroft had agreed to meet with her tomorrow morning.

2

11:58 p.m.

THE HOUSE WAS SUFFOCATINGLY dark.

Or maybe it was just dark.

And he felt suffocated.

Harry Owen pushed the door a little wider, hoping that the night air would disperse the dread that rushed to meet him. But the night air refused to cross the threshold of his parents' house.

He stepped inside.

There was an odor that made his throat catch. It had grown stronger as the weeks passed.

It was the odor of a dying body.

It was the odor of his mother.

He longed to keep the door open. He longed to turn on his heel and leave.

And not have to deal with what lay in the bedroom in the back of the house.

But he couldn't leave. In fact, he had come home a day early because he knew that time was running out.

His ears strained for any sound from the back of the house. No late-night canned laughter from the television. So, his parents were already asleep.

Sweat dampened his forehead as relief rushed through him. He was off the hook.

For tonight.

He could have a nightcap, check his emails, and get some sleep. God knows he needed it. Too many 06:25 a.m. flights to Ottawa, too many late night flights back to Halifax.

His mother had been worried that he would get sick from exhaustion, but he downplayed her concerns. *I need to be here, Ma.* She thought it was because of her. But really, it was because of him. He had squeezed her hand, the bones as brittle as twigs of saffron.

Would she allow him to hold her hand after he told her what he had come to confess?

His father had left on the light in the foyer, a small chandelier that had yellowed with age. Light shone blearily through the dusty pendants. He closed the front door, pushed the deadbolt above the knob into place, and then slid the bottom deadbolt. The yellow warning light glowed from the alarm panel. Once again, the alarm was offline. He wondered if his father had remembered to call the security company.

He doubted it. He and his father were in crisis mode now, the days stretching out as daily responsibilities were abandoned to focus on his mother's last moments.

He switched off the overhead light and hurried upstairs. His childhood bedroom, which had lost its ability to comfort years ago, sat to the right. Despite the fact he had stayed at his parents' house off and on for the past few months, the top level of the house had the unmistakable miasma of neglect to it. For years, his parents had slept on the main floor to accommodate his father's lack of mobility. But his mother had converted their old bedroom upstairs to a library, and she had once enjoyed spending a few hours a day in there while his father napped.

He hung his garment bag on a hook mounted on the back of his bedroom door. The bag covered the little lines that marched proudly up the doorframe. Next to each milestone

12

the date and his height had been inscribed, first in his father's bold penmanship. Then, after his ninth birthday, in his mother's neat printing.

His phone vibrated in his breast pocket. It was almost like a second, electronic heartbeat, it vibrated so often. But the phone calls no longer caused his pulse to accelerate, as it had when he was first elected. Back then it had been exhilarating: was it a constituent, a senator, the Prime Minister himself? He had answered the calls proudly, the youngest MP from his region, a junior lawyer with the halo of potential over his head.

After a few seconds, the vibration stopped. He sat on the edge of his bed and reached down to untie the laces of his shoes. The moon gleamed on the highly polished leather. He wanted nothing more than to kick his shoes away and flop onto the bed. But the hold of his childhood room was too great. With a sigh, he padded in his socks over to the bureau and placed the shoes on the mat as he had done since he was four.

He slipped his laptop from his briefcase, and logged onto his parents' Wi-Fi. He had upgraded it when he realized he would be spending weekends there. Fifty-three new emails since he boarded his flight, almost all of them flagged as urgent. "Goddamn it," he muttered. Everything was always urgent. Nothing could wait in the minds of the senders, even though Parliament moved at a glacial pace.

He scanned his inbox. He was searching for one name, one email that would ensure a good night's sleep.

But it wasn't there.

He knew it wouldn't be. The Prime Minister wasn't one to take no-shows at key fundraising events lightly. It didn't matter that Harry's mother was ill. The election cycle was about to begin and all hands were needed on deck. Harry was one of the few bright stars in an administration that had been plagued by spending scandals, a sluggish economy and voter fatigue.

He snapped the lid of his laptop shut. He couldn't bear to

look at the emails. He had cleared his weekend, so he could respond to the emails tomorrow—and hope that the report he had chaired for the Committee of Public Safety would redeem himself in his boss's eyes. Rumor had it that Minister of Public Safety Lindsay Muir-Brown was stepping down from Cabinet, for 'personal' reasons. They all knew it was because the PM had ordered her to resign after an embarrassing misuse of taxpayers' dollars. And now the Minister of Public Safety portfolio was finally within Harry's grasp. There had been encouraging backroom rumors. Diversity and the region he represented were in his favor. It had killed him to skip the fundraising dinner. And in fact, he was ashamed to admit, he almost didn't.

But the tremulous voice of his mother on the phone had pulled him home.

And the weight of his own shame.

He unscrewed a slim metal flask that had once been a weekend indulgence. A few long pulls, and his phone's vibration against his chest simmered into a fiery burn through his veins. Screw his emails. Screw his boss.

It took only a few minutes to change into a t-shirt and boxer shorts. He untucked the blanket at the end of his mattress so that he could straighten his legs. With a low sigh of relief, he slid under the sheets of his childhood bed. He turned on the television.

Later, when he tried to unjumble the nightmare of that night in his memory, he could not for the life of him remember what he had watched on TV.

3

2:06 a.m.

AIDEN LEANED OVER HER, his breathing fast and excited. Revulsion added to Leah's anxiety. She had heard him pant in the exact same manner when he climaxed. The knife pressed against her rib cage—even though she was doing exactly what he wanted her to do.

She straightened. "Done," she whispered.

He had manipulated her as thoroughly as a man could manipulate a woman who saw what only she wanted to see, whose academic record confirmed her brilliance, whose emotional vulnerability invited control—and whose naïveté assured exploitation. She saw it with breathtaking clarity now. When it was too late.

Like most women who had been screwed over.

But she knew this: he may have won this battle, but she would win the war.

Now it was time to get out of here and end this nightmare.

She swung away from the desk. Aiden, who still peered over her shoulder, didn't react in time. She stepped right into him.

And he backed into the side table.

The tea mug clattered onto the wooden floor.

15

They froze at the sound.

A light abruptly flickered through the crack of a door near the back of the house.

And Leah knew that Aiden had deceived her yet again.

The Owens weren't away.

They had been asleep.

And now, one of them had just woken up.

4

MEL OWEN'S FINGERS SCRABBLED for the light switch pinned to the side of his mattress. Damned raccoon. The random noises of its nocturnal prowling cut through his painkillers like nobody's business. He had been jolted awake, his heart pounding, cold sweat already emitting a rank smell under his pajamas.

The rank smell of fear.

It would never leave him. It defined him, just as the wheelchair now defined him.

Goddamned raccoon.

It was time to teach it a lesson. The bucket of water sat by his patio door, ready to be dumped on the animal that had destroyed his reprieve from pain for the past three nights. He rolled to the edge of the bed and pulled himself upright.

"Mel, can I get you something?" Salma murmured, her voice thready. The question was asked out of habit. She needed more help getting up than he did.

"Just some peace and quiet. I'm gonna get rid of that raccoon once and for all." He pushed his legs sideways, and set a sliding board on the edge of his mattress. He balanced the other end of the board on the seat of his wheelchair.

With his fist planted in the mattress, he inched his hips along the board toward the wheelchair.

The sound of a body connecting with a piece of furniture made him freeze. Salma gasped. "Is that the raccoon?" she whispered.

The sweat under his pajamas became a geyser. "If it isn't, whoever it is will sure as hell regret ever meeting me," he whispered. His fingers found the light switch and flipped it off.

Darkness fell over him and his dying wife of thirty-seven years.

Was there someone in the living room, watching these two old, frail-before-their-time bodies, waiting to strike? Regret hit him hard in the gut. Salma could have been safe upstairs, but pride had made him refuse Harry's suggestion that they sleep apart. They had never spent one night apart, he had told his son, except when he had his spinal surgery.

"Don't be so selfish," Harry had spat at him. "Can't you see Ma is exhausted?"

Yes, he had seen it. In the gaunt face, the way the weight had dropped from her softly rounded middle until the flesh shrank into strange folds, the tremor of her hands.

Perhaps it had not been pride. Perhaps it had been fear that made him refuse Harry's suggestion that they sleep apart. Not for himself. But that the cancer would steal her away, in her sleep, on the upper floor of their house, where he couldn't reach her.

And now, all there was between her and the intruder who stood so silently watchful in the living room was him.

And his gun.

Twisting awkwardly, he leaned toward his pillow and slid his hand under it. The sensation of the cold, smooth metal of his revolver eased his pent-up breath. He closed the gun into the palm of his hand. Using it to support his weight, he slid along the board into the wheelchair.

"No. Mel. Don't." The fear in Salma's voice was palpable. They both knew the price he had paid the last time he had confronted a robber.

God, please don't let this kill her. She is so weak.

One more push, and he was in the chair. He slid the board across the bed, careful to make no noise. "Stay in here. Don't come out," he whispered. "Call 911."

He disengaged the safety latch on his revolver. He kept it loaded. He cleaned it every week. It gleamed, thickly solid, on those legs so shriveled from disuse. But he didn't need his legs when he had a gun. He reached down to the wheels on his chair and disengaged the brakes.

Behind him, he heard Salma lift the phone receiver.

And then a floorboard creaked. Right by their bedroom door.

Salma heard it, too. Her breathing became high-pitched, a strange whistle in her throat that he had never heard before.

The phone thudded to the floor.

The footsteps stopped.

But where? Was the intruder waiting for him to exit the room, poised to attack?

He could hear nothing but the blood rushing through his ears, punctuated by his wife's breathy whistle. It scared him. *Salma.*

He dared a quick glance over his shoulder. His wife leaned precariously over the side of their bed, scrabbling for the phone.

Then she crashed to the ground, taking the bedside lamp with her.

"Salma!"

His heart racing, his hands so sweaty he could barely guide the wheels, he spun away from the door and rushed to the end of the bed.

His wife lay crumpled on the ground. Glass from the shattered light bulb covered her once beautiful black mane of hair, cold and jagged on the translucent skin of her face.

He guided the wheelchair next to her prone body, and leaned toward her.

She didn't move.

Her chest didn't move.

Oh, God. Where was the phone?

Then he saw the black receiver—it lay just under the edge of the bedframe. He reached over his wife and snatched the phone.

9 - 1 -

Hell, goddammit, he hit a 2!

His fingers would not stop trembling.

9 - 1 - 1.

He pushed the phone hard against his ear, as if the pressure would force someone to answer.

"911. What is the nature of your emergency?"

"Someone is in my house. And my wife fell—"

His eyes desperately traced her features under its mask of shattered glass.

There was no sign of the fear that had propelled her to the ground.

She looked so serene.

So still.

5

2:08 a.m.

A LARGE THUD AND the sound of breaking glass startled Harry out of his scotch-induced sleep. He jolted upright, threw the tangle of sheets off his body and leapt out of the twin-sized bed of his childhood. His knees buckled when his feet slammed into the floor. He kept forgetting that he was not sleeping in his own bed. He staggered forward, catching his balance, and ran out of the bedroom.

Later, when questioned by police, he could not say why he hadn't called down to his parents and asked if everything was all right. After all, his first thought when he had been awoken by the crashing noise was that his father had fallen out of bed.

But instinct kept him quiet.

Or was it memory?

He could barely see over the counter. "Get down!" His father's urgent whisper was quickly followed by his father's hand pushing his head down from view. He sat, his knees to his chin, curled into himself like the snail on the mysterious hosta in the garden. But he heard everything. The rage-filled, nasty words the men called his father. His father's angry response. The gun discharging. Once. Twice. Three times. The gurgled moan from somewhere inside his father's chest when he collapsed onto the counter. The cash register clanging furiously as the drawer was emptied. Then, frantic footsteps…

Footsteps.

He had heard footsteps. In the living room.

_____

The light under the door had abruptly disappeared.

Aiden gestured at Leah with his knife. *Come on.*

She crept toward him.

The silence was broken by a loud crash and the sound of glass shattering from inside the closed bedroom.

Then: a man's cry of anguish. It must be Mel Owen.

Leah's heart threw itself against her chest wall. *What happened in there?*

Aiden's gaze was fixed on the closed door, knife at the ready to deal with whoever came out of the bedroom.

Don't come out, Mr. Owen.

Please, don't come out.

_____

Harry crept down the stairs, his heart pounding. But his bare feet were steady. He kept his breath soft, crouching low and hugging the shadows in the corners as he crossed the foyer. The house was built on a center hall plan. On the right side of the foyer lay the formal dining room. The dining room led to the eighties' era country-style kitchen that had never been renovated for a paraplegic, because his father never cooked.

The living room was on the other side of the foyer. For years, it had been a formal room, and the study in the back had been used as the TV room. But after Mel's paralysis, the study had been converted to a bedroom, and the broom closet off the kitchen had been renovated into a bathroom.

Which way should he go? Into the living room, where he was sure he had heard the intruder?

Or go the back way through the dining room, into the kitchen, and then around through his parents' bedroom?

The thought of his father lying on the floor and his mother hiding in the bed propelled him through the dining room. He needed to make sure they were safe.

Don't think about what happened before.

He turned the corner into the kitchen, and slipped through the back entrance into his parents' bedroom.

He froze in the doorway.

"Oh, my God." His mother lay covered in glass, a lampshade tumbled drunkenly to one side as if it had fallen off her head.

His calm deserted him. He threw himself down by her side. "*Ma*—" His voice blocked his throat.

Fear chilled him.

Oh my God. No!

She couldn't be dead. Not his mother.

Not his mother!

Then it hit him.

I never got to tell her.

The realization he would never be blessed with his mother's forgiveness stopped his heart.

"Stop! You bastard!"

Harry saw his father, in his wheelchair, his back to them, yelling at a black-clad intruder in the living room. The intruder sprinted across the living room toward the back window.

It was wide open.

But had it been locked?

Before Harry could react, his father propelled his wheelchair directly toward a second intruder.

Dear God. He sprang to his feet and, with a final, frantic look at his mother, ran out of the bedroom. "Dad! Stop!"

"The bastard killed your mother, Harry!" His father snatched the revolver from his lap and pointed it at the intruder. "He killed her!

"Dad, no! Stay away from him!" Harry Owen lunged

23

behind his father. He reached for the back of his father's wheelchair.

———————

Mel Owen propelled toward Leah so fast that she was unable to get out of the way in time. His wheelchair slammed into her knees.

Her elbow smashed into Mel Owen's face.

"Leave my father alone!" Harry screamed at her, his voice hoarse with anger.

And fear.

She got her feet under her and staggered sideways toward the window. Harry's words echoed in her ears. God, he thought she wanted to hurt Mel Owen.

She held out her hands. "I'm—"

A shot filled her ears.

Her leg stung. And then exploded into fiery pain.

She gasped as another shot slammed into her shoulder.

She pitched to the floor. It was hard. It was warm. It was wet. Hot, metallic liquid slipped under her body.

She was floating in hot liquid mercury.

"Oh, my God!"

Through the blackness that flooded her brain, she heard the shock in Harry's voice.

Through the agony screaming through her nerves, she felt remorse crush her chest.

6

2:29 a.m.

THE PHONE HAD BARELY rung when Cooper Ellis snatched it from the bedside table, slid out of bed, and answered it with a soft, "Ellis." He hurried into the hallway, closing the bedroom door behind him.

"It's Pearson." Detective Sergeant Mike Pearson was the head of General Investigative Services—and Cooper's new boss. "We have a B&E, possible robbery involving prohibited firearms. We need you and Lamond at the scene."

"What happened?"

"The husband was woken up at approximately 02:08 by a noise. His wife fell out of bed while calling 9-1-1. She's dead."

"How?"

"Not sure. She was ill. But the homeowner claims that the suspects killed her. One got out through the window."

"Why aren't you calling in Homicide?"

"They are tied up with the Baker case." A gang-fuelled multiple homicide had occurred last night.

"How many were there?"

"We don't know."

He heard sheets rustling. Then the bedroom door opened.

25

"Coop?" Steph blinked at him.

He felt a rush of irritation, then guilt that she felt she had to check on him. He held up a hand and mouthed, "work."

She nodded and padded back to bed. But he sensed her alertness in darkness.

"Cooper? Did you hear what I said?"

"Sorry, Sergeant. My wife—" *was checking on me.* He swallowed the words. "—woke up. I'll be there in twenty minutes." He walked into the bedroom. Steph made no pretense of sleep. She watched him as he reached for his chinos, phone still pressed to his ear.

Pearson continued, "The place will be crawling with media."

Cooper zipped his fly. "Slow news night?"

"No. The house belongs to the parents of Halifax's MP."

Cooper lowered his voice. "Harry Owen?"

"The one and only." Pearson's tone would have been dry if it weren't for the situation.

"Jesus. Isn't he in Ottawa?" And then the pieces fell into place. "He was staying at his parents' house."

"Yes."

"Isn't he the mouthpiece for the Minister whose head is on the chopping block?"

There was slight pause. "Do you feel up to handling this case?"

Cooper closed his eyes. Adrenalin pumped through him. The case was meaty. Intriguing. Exactly what he needed to launch this new chapter in his career.

But this was a different kind of police work than what he had been doing for the past seven years. In Vice, he had worked his cases on the Internet, luring child predators and lurking on forums.

It had marked him in ways he never would have believed when he was assigned to that unit.

"Yes. I've reviewed all the procedures." He injected his voice with calm confidence. After years working undercover, he knew how to project the image that others expected. "I can handle it."

The chill miasma of Steph's doubt drifted over him. Turning his back, he reached for a shirt from his closet.

"This is critical, Ellis. I wouldn't even be putting you on such a high-profile case yet if Bruce and Mercer weren't tied up. But you came highly recommended."

All those commendations had paid off. The price had been high in his personal life, but it had given him a chance when he desperately needed it. "I'll report back to you when I'm done."

He dressed quietly, his mind preoccupied with the case. He turned to the door.

"Are you going to be gone long?" Steph called.

"I won't be back before you go to work." He shrugged on his jacket as he strode over to where she lay in bed, and pressed a quick kiss on her cheek. "I've got to go. Sorry I woke you up."

"It's okay."

What had he been hoping for? *Good luck on your first case with GIS?*

Or even… "I love you."

He picked up Lamond within sixteen minutes. Thirty minutes after he had taken the call from his new boss, he drove into the maelstrom that enveloped the Owen property. He approached the house at reduced speed, observing the scene. It had already been taped off, and the people clustering on the sidewalk had been pushed back by the street patrol.

They both heard the low mosquito-buzz of a drone as they neared the Owen neighborhood.

"It's a bird, it's a plane…" Lamond joked as Cooper turned onto the quiet North end street. A small smile lifted the corners of Cooper's mouth. From what he could tell, his new partner was on a permanent high. Even at 3:01 in the morning.

And even at 3:01 in the morning, pajama-clad neighbors

huddled in small groups—held back from the Owen's house by the patrol constables manning the scene—and pointed to the sky.

"Glad that Pearson ordered extra patrol to keep the scene tight."

Large halogen lights, set up by the fire department, illuminated the house and grounds. It was a modest, two-story center hall-plan home. Vinyl siding, shutters on the window frames, and a wheelchair ramp that connected a side entry to the driveway were the main design elements. Several large maple trees and a collection of evergreen shrubs accounted for the landscaping in the front of the property. No fence, not much privacy.

That was good. Hopefully, someone saw something.

An ambulance had been backed into the driveway. Cooper parked his car behind a squad car and jumped out, Lamond right behind him as they entered the house.

"Lamond, good to see you." Patrol Sergeant Sue MacLeod strode over to them. Small, broad, with open, freckled features, she gave off a farm-girl vibe. Until you looked into her eyes. "How's Ethan making out in Vice?"

Lamond grinned. "He's right at home."

MacLeod smiled. "A change is as good as a rest." She eyed Cooper. "You must be Ellis. Sorry to get you guys out of bed, but this isn't your garden variety house robbery."

Cooper nodded. "Did your team find the weapon?"

"It's over here in the living room." MacLeod led them in single file to the living room. They were careful to follow her direct path. No one wanted to be responsible for contaminating evidence.

Near the back of the living room, two paramedics crouched over a woman. Was this the victim or the suspect? When he got close enough to see her features, he ruled out victim. The woman was alive—but barely. And she was much younger than the age of Harry Owen's parents.

Pale white blond hair had been pulled back from her forehead with a black headband covering her hairline. Her eyes were closed. The lashes were invisible on her eyelids. She reminded him of a freshly hatched bird. Yet her eyebrows were strangely dark. With her fair skin turning grey from blood loss, the brows were grotesque. He revised his impression of her: she looked like an alien that had been shot from the sky.

Then he realized that she had darkened her brows so their unusually pale shade would not be visible. Just as the hairband had been used to cover her hairline.

She was smart.

The woman's upper body lay in a large pool of blood, her neck stabilized in a cervical collar. A black balaclava lay on the floor.

Calmly, but quickly, one of the paramedics cut the hoody and pants from the woman while the other paramedic kept a gloved hand over the bubbling wound in her chest. The woman was soaked in blood, her skin becoming alarmingly blue beneath the gleaming red fluid.

Cooper noted the tear in the upper shoulder of her jacket where the bullet had penetrated.

"What's her status?" Cooper asked one of the paramedics.

"Critical." The paramedic tore open a chest seal. Her partner secured an oxygen mask over the suspect's face, while the other paramedic applied the seal. "She has an open pneumothorax and needs to be intubated."

Lamond walked over to him. Cooper pointed at the pieces of sheared clothing that lay scattered on the floor. "I don't see FIS anywhere."

"Pearson said they were held up at a different scene." Lamond eyed the balaclava. "I'll see if FIS has an updated status."

"We need to get her on a spinal board and to the ER stat," the first paramedic said to her partner. "Is the IV in?"

Cooper watched them roll the woman onto the spinal board. She was in bad shape. He mentally gave her 20-25% chance of survival as they wheeled her to the ambulance.

"I hope she makes it," Lamond said.

Cooper stepped around the large pool of blood. "Doesn't look so good."

"Was she carrying a gun?" Lamond looked around the living room.

"Harry Owen told Warren that he thought she had a gun," MacLeod said, her tone neutral. Cooper couldn't tell if MacLeod believed the MP or not. "But the suspect had nothing on her, not even a phone."

"And Mel Owen shot her, anyway?"

"It wasn't Mel Owen who shot her. It was Harry Owen."

"Jesus," Cooper murmured. "Our wannabe Minister of Public Safety is a good shot."

One of the constables from street patrol approached them. "Sergeant, the Ident guys have arrived."

They both turned to the door. Two officers in bunny suits approached carefully, carrying their evidence collection kits. From the height of one of the detectives, he guessed that Riley was here. Everyone in the department knew Riley: she was the best Forensic Identification Services detective east of Montreal. Some said in all of Canada. She was renowned for her laser-like focus. And he knew she applied the same discipline to her body—she competed in triathlons in her spare time.

"Sorry for the hold up," Riley said, her hazel eyes barely acknowledging them before scanning the room. "Pearson specifically asked me to come. I had to go down to the station and restock the van."

"Glad to finally meet you, Detective," Cooper said. "I've heard a lot about you."

Her gaze zeroed in on his face. "Are you the transfer from Vice?"

"Yes. Detective Drake and I made a switch."

She nodded. "You guys did some good work. That kiddie porn ring you broke up was massive."

And it had almost killed him. "Thanks."

"Do you know whose house this is, Riley?" Lamond

asked. He looked as if he had a delicious secret he couldn't wait to tell.

Her gaze scanned the walls—searching for spatter, Cooper guessed—and then swung back to Lamond. "Damn," she breathed on a long exhale. "It's Harry Owen's parents'?"

Cooper nodded. "You know that means he will have the best team of lawyers on his case. Pearson made a point of reminding me that our evidence collection needs to be pristine."

She flashed a look at him. "Ellis, let's get one thing straight—it doesn't matter to me who the lawyers are, I follow every single protocol, every single fucking time."

He smiled. Geez, she was intense. "I know. Your reputation precedes you. I was passing on the Sergeant's instructions."

She crouched down by her kit. "He already spoke to me. And I'll tell you the same thing I said to him: you do your job. And I'll do mine." She pulled the white hood over her auburn hair. Conversation over.

Lamond tapped his shoulder. "Come on, the father and son are over there."

Cooper turned around. Mel Owen, the father, sat in his wheelchair, his eyes moving restlessly across the scene. Once in a while, his lips would move, and he would nod. But if he was speaking to his son, Harry Owen was oblivious. The younger Owen slumped in a chair, his dark head cradled in his hands.

He looked very different than the last time Cooper had seen him. It had been on television, where he flanked the Minister of Public Safety during the Minister's announcement of changes to the gun registry. Harry Owen, Juris Doctorate, Member of Parliament for Halifax, had stood confidently, his white shirt immaculate, his dark suit impeccably pressed, not a hair out of place.

Cooper studied the politician. His hair was mussed from the fingers that dug into his skull. Blood stained his plain grey crewneck t-shirt and navy-checked boxer shorts. If that was the blood of the suspect, the shot had been at close-range. His feet were bare. He assessed the man's feet and hands. No signs of scratches, cuts, or self-defense wounds. His feet were clean, the nails trimmed and tidy. No mud, dirt or bits of leaves caught in them.

Cooper strode over to the two men and cleared his throat. "Mr. Owen?" The older Mr. Owen's gaze swung to Cooper. It was expressionless. Empty. Like a pair of headlights, flickering dispassionately over the officers investigating the scene.

Harry Owen lifted his head. Dark bags under bloodshot eyes. "My father is not well enough to answer any questions. He's in shock."

Cooper studied the father more closely. "Does he require any medical assistance?"

"He has already been checked out." Harry rose to his feet. "He needs some rest." He edged his body so that he stood between Cooper and his father.

Cooper noted the son's protectiveness, vaguely remembering that Mr. Owen had been a victim of crime, years ago. He would have to dig out that case. "I am Detective Cooper Ellis, General Investigative Services. We would like you both to come to the station tomorrow for an interview, but there are a few questions—"

"I will not speak to you without exercising my right to speak to counsel. And neither will my father." The lids of Harry Owen's brown eyes were swollen. Had he been crying? Or had he been using drugs?

"I understand, Mr. Owen. But there are a few—"

"I will not speak to you, Detective—" there was a slight emphasis on 'Detective', "—until I have spoken to counsel. And nor will my father."

Mel Owen now watched them, his lips pursed. But he said nothing.

"Understood." Cooper's tone was polite, but firm. "We require your presence and your father's at 11 a.m. tomorrow at the station."

"I will see if my lawyer is avail—"

"Mr. Owen. We are investigating a major crime. One of the suspects is still at large and could be a threat to the public. You understand that your assistance is vital to this investigation."

Harry Owen's mouth tightened. He knew that the media would slaughter him if he, a member of the national public safety committee, failed to assist the police. "I understand, Detective. I will see you at 11 a.m."

"Thank you, Mr. Owen." Cooper turned away and spotted the white coat of the Medical Examiner. Detective MacLeod led the ME to the bedroom at the back of the house. Cooper glanced around. No sign of Homicide yet. He wouldn't be treading on any toes if he checked things out.

As soon as he entered the bedroom of Harry Owen's parents, his nose was hit by the smell of fear. Sweat, urine, blood.

Death.

A king-size bed dominated the room. The top sheet—in a floral pattern of green and yellow—hung in a twisted rope over the far side of the bed. A blanket huddled on the floor. Thin black skid marks parenthesized the floor at the bed's corners. Cooper guessed that they were caused by Mr. Owen's wheelchair.

The Medical Examiner crouched on the floor on the far side of the bed. He glanced up when he saw Cooper. "I am Dr. Guthro, Office of the Medical Examiner," he said, a warm resonance to his voice that bounced off the cold halogen lighting set up by the investigative team.

"Detective Cooper Ellis, General Investigative Services."

"A pleasure to meet you, Detective. An unfortunate case, it would appear. Poor woman." Harry Owen's mother lay in a tangle of wasted flesh on the floor. The twisted sheet had caught one of her emaciated legs in an ungainly position. Her nightdress appeared to have been pulled down, for her body angle suggested that gravity would have left her exposed when she fell.

Thin, fine shards of glass glittered in her black hair. A pale blue fabric lampshade lolled on its side by her head. Her hands, translucent from disease, now bore the distinctive dark blood clots of death.

"What do you think, Dr. Guthro?"

The doctor glanced up at him, his hand pressed against the elderly lady's throat.

"No pulse, no signs of breath." His Caribbean lilt bounced off the walls of the silent room. He discreetly raised Mrs. Owen's nightdress and inserted the rectal thermometer. After a few seconds, he pulled it out. "Body temperature is 34.5 degrees Celsius. Normal body temperature is 36.5 degrees, and the usual rate of heat loss post mortem is 1.5 degrees per hour. However, the decedent is elderly, and was reported to be at end-stage cancer, so I would expect her core body temperature to be lower. I estimate time of death approximately one hour ago."

Cooper checked his watch. "Two fifteen a.m.?"

"Correct."

"I know it's early to say, but do you think she died of natural causes?" The woman appeared to have been very ill.

The overhead light glinted on Dr. Guthro's wire-framed glasses. "It is a reasonable hypothesis at this stage, Detective. Of course, appearances can be deceiving." He reached for his camera. "I will take some pictures, complete the *in situ* examination, and let you know when the decedent is ready to be transported to the morgue."

"Thank you, doctor." Cooper turned to the door. "And when will you conduct the post-mortem?"

"First thing tomorrow morning."

"I will be conducting interviews from eleven onward. But please let me know ASAP if you find anything of note in terms of unusual marks, substances, et cetera. Anything helps."

"Understood, detective," Dr. Guthro calmly. "Business as usual, then," he added with a twinkle in his eye.

Cooper flushed. He had to remember he was the new kid on this block.

"Ellis!" Riley called him from the doorway, her voice muffled by the hood of her bunny suit. "You should take a look at this."

He hurried out of the bedroom and followed her to the television stand in the sitting area. A wooden case sat on the TV console. Three handguns lay in a row on a dark velvet cloth.

"Did you open that?"

Riley shook her head. "No. It was open. Looks like he had been cleaning them."

Cooper studied the guns. "Three handguns, two restricted, the other prohibited." They gleamed under the harsh halogen lights the team had set up. "We need to get a search warrant. And make sure the guns are all licensed."

Riley nodded. "The place is a friggin' arsenal."

Cooper shrugged. "Who can blame Mr. Owen? I think he was paralyzed from a robbery." His gaze fell on the window at the back of the room. "Was the window locked?" The bottom pane had been jammed all the way open, the window frames and panes covered in magna dust. A FIS detective meticulously applied tape to lift the prints revealed by the dust.

"No." Riley glanced at the bedroom door. The ME's head was just visible from where he crouched on the other side of the bed. "Mr. Owen's wife was very ill. Maybe he forgot."

"We'll have to ask him. Did you get any good prints?"

Riley's gaze shifted back to him. "Yes. But we're not sure if they belong to the homeowners or the suspect who got away." She twisted her mouth. "They haven't left much here to collect."

"No weapons?"

"Just the father's."

"So right now, all we have to go with is break and enter with intent?"

"Yup."

"And the million dollar question is why the hell did two

35

people break into the house of our MP's parents? Was it a robbery? Or was it something more?"

"Let's not make it more complicated than it is, Ellis. My money is on theft, plain and simple." They watched Dr. Guthro hurry out of the room, phone to his ear. "With unintended consequences."

Ellis scanned the room. It was an ordinary house, in a middle-class neighborhood, occupied by two people who appeared to live very ordinary lives. It could be that intruders' motive was uncomplicated.

But after spending years lurking on shadowy forums hunting for even more shadowy predators, his gut was telling him that the intent in this crime wasn't as simple as it seemed.

He shrugged. "Maybe."

7

2:41 a.m.

THE DOG BARKED.

Jesus Christ!

It had found him again. Aiden Boyne aka AggroBoy aka whatever-identity-was-convenient-for-the-situation pressed closer to the ground, shrinking his lanky form behind a shrub. The damp soaked into his work pants. He hoped that the dew would wash away his scent. That the K-9 team would not pick up his trail. He was terrified of getting caught. Especially by a dog. Those German Shepherds were trained to take him down. The thought of the dog's teeth made him want to puke.

And now one was after him.

The speed with which they had zeroed in on him had scared the crap out of him. They almost got him in one of the backyards he'd been zigzagging through, but he'd managed to squeeze through a broken board in a fence and get to the other side. Once he'd cleared the railroad tracks, he had thought he'd shaken them.

But now the goddamned dog was barking.

He knew what that meant.

It had found his scent.

He didn't have much time.

Or he would be serving time for the rest of his life.

And what the hell had happened in the Owen house?

It was supposed to be easy.

Instead, it turned into a fucking nightmare.

The old guy was screaming that he'd killed the old lady. He wished he'd just stuck the knife in Mel Owen's heart and ended it right there. Goddamned bastard.

And Leah...

She had chickened out on him. So much for her idealistic principles. He had thought Leah's convictions were stronger than fear of a simple break-and-enter. He had thought he had convinced her of the greater good of their plan. But when she crouched below the window, he could see in her eyes that she wasn't going to go through with it.

And he could not allow her to back out.

It was a lesson to him: you could not rely on women. Even when they tell you they love you. They were too fickle, too easily swayed by what they thought was right.

Just look at his mother. She had backed his father's demand that Aiden move out three months ago. He could have forgiven her if she had said, "It's out of my control. Your father pays the mortgage."

But no, she had said to him, "Tyson, it's time for you to take responsibility. You need to earn a living. And if you do that, if you prove to your father that you are reliable and trustworthy, then the door will be wide open for you at Green Matheson Security."

Screw Green Matheson Security. He was sick of hearing that his father had built it with only his two hands and it was worth millions. Things were different now. Aiden was their son. They had so much money. Why did he have to do something he hated just to make his goddamned father happy?

So he disowned them. From the minute they kicked him out of the house, he was no longer Tyson Green. He breathed life into Aiden Boyne, the online identity he had created months ago.

This exploit with Leah would give Aiden Boyne the freedom to do what he wanted, would allow him to prove to his parents that he didn't need to do some crap job just to make them happy. And it would make him a millionaire. Not too bad for a night's work—and six months of pretending to be in love with a woman who was the polar opposite of what he found attractive.

He hoped Leah was dead. She had done what they needed her to do.

If she were still alive, she would be arrested. No question about that.

What an effing screw up. He and Tr0lz had planned this out to the exact detail.

He hadn't expected that Mel Owen's house would be a friggin' arsenal. Although that had worked out to his benefit, if Leah was actually shot.

But he also hadn't anticipated that Harry Owen would come home tonight. They expected him to arrive tomorrow evening. It put a major time crunch on him and Tr0lz.

The dog barked again, a high-pitched whine of excitement.

Oh, shit.

Sweat rolled down his neck under his balaclava. He needed to get the hell out of here. He'd be leaving his scent everywhere.

He peered around the edge of the bush. It was dark in this backyard, although the house had a porch light. He could see the cops—but they couldn't see him.

But that dog could smell him.

He darted to the back edge of the property, racing around a shed. The next few back yards would be the riskiest. They were open, with only a few trees between them. He ran along the back boundary of the first yard…then the next…

The dog barked.

It was higher pitched. It was excited.

It was closing in.

Jesus Christ!

He launched into a sprint and headed back down to the

railway tracks. It would take him longer to get to his room, but it was safer. The tracks ran through the South End, past the granary and down to the waterfront, where the Halterm shipping terminal operated.

He skidded down the slope to the tracks and then began to run, dodging empty bottles and twisted wire hangers. Several chimney bricks had been discarded just ahead of him. He could try to nail the dog with one.

But he was too scared to stop. The dog was a moving target. It was too risky.

A train approached, the tracks humming. He dared a glance over his shoulder. Should he hop it?

Fear battled with need. He was terrified of the dog. But he couldn't abandon everything he had so painstakingly set up. He needed to get what he had left behind in his room.

The train slowed. He darted into the shadows of the brush lining the track. He did not want the engineer to spot him.

The cars squeaked and rattled as they rounded a turn. The roar of the engine filled his ears. He could not hear the dog now.

He watched the train disappear into the darkness, safety winding its way out of his reach.

No risk, no reward, Aiden.

That's what his father had always said to him.

He had no idea how deeply Aiden had taken that to heart.

8

THE NIGHT AIR WAS humid, the air softly pressing on Matías Leon. He stood on the balcony of his Fort Lauderdale apartment. Palm trees framed the stars. It was a beautiful night.

It was a terrible night.

He had been unable to sleep, nerves chewed in equal part by fear and excitement.

Now it was just past three o'clock in the morning in Halifax.

Something had gone wrong. He felt it deep in his gut.

Where was Leah?

What had happened?

He stepped into the living room, his gaze flicking through the posts that scrolled down his computer monitor.

Any news yet?

WhiteDwarf, u logged in?

They should be done now.

Yeah, it's been over an hour.

Anyone checked the news?

But no post from WhiteDwarf. Something had definitely happened to Leah. She would have checked in to the Forum by now.

It was his fault. He should have stopped her.

41

But Leah had thrown her hat into the ring with AggroBoy, and there was nothing Matt could do about it. He had warned Leah about AggroBoy, had told her that he suspected the guy had a criminal record. He even pointed out that AggroBoy's screen name showed his true character. 'Aggro' was a truncated slang version of 'aggravation'. And AggroBoy had hinted of persecution and prosecution by Harry Owen. But Leah told Matt that she trusted AggroBoy. She said that AggroBoy's name reflected the thorn that he wanted to be in the side of government.

That's when he realized that Leah and AggroBoy had more than just an online connection.

The pain had been deep. It had always been deep. Leah had gotten under his skin in a way that he couldn't explain.

Was that what love was? Something that could never be quantified, something that could never be articulated?

Something that just was?

He had seen Leah walk by him on the way to the restroom. The Irish pub was jammed at this hour, but she was hard to miss. Her white-blond hair had been pulled into a messy topknot, adding at least two inches to her six-foot tall frame. She had changed out of the baggy flannel shirt she had worn to their physics lecture that afternoon, and now wore a clingy sweater in a shade of blue that reminded him of the Florida sky. He could barely concentrate on the conversation of his friends. When he saw Leah exit the restroom, he casually slid out from the booth. And then he just as casually bumped into her.

"Oh, sorry about that." He smiled. He had to look up to meet her gaze. "You're Leah, right? We're in Astrophysics 405 together."

There was a flash of recognition in her eyes. "Yeah." She smiled. "I'm sorry, I don't know your name…?"

"Matías. Matt for short."

"Oh, hi."

"Do you want to join me and my friends?" He pointed to the booth. Dev, one of the few who had actually observed Matt's attempt to flirt, waved at Leah.

She appeared confused by the sudden attention. "Uh, sorry, I was just leaving." She gestured vaguely to a table near the front.

"Oh. Okay. No problem." He smiled at her. "Maybe we can go for a drink sometime?"

She turned wonderfully, enchantingly pink. "Okay."

They exchanged numbers.

And he fell unequivocally, irrevocably in love.

His throat tightened at the memory. They had dated. But it had ended. She was Canadian and wanted to return home after her graduation from university. He had visa issues. The truth was, they were both too young to change the course of their lives for one another.

Since he was a young child, his forte had been solving puzzles, putting together the missing pieces, creating a brilliant whole out of a sum of unfathomable parts. And yet he had been unable to piece together the one puzzle that would have made him whole.

So, he focused his energy on what he knew he could do well. To those who knew him in his daily life, he was Matt the business consultant. The Latino guy with the mad computer skills.

But on the side, he created an online identity known as 'Condor'. Then he formed a hacktivist group. And named it the Forum. The origin of the word stemmed back to Roman times, when a forum was the place to conduct judicial and public business. Wasn't that what the consortium of white hat hackers were doing? And if they had a gladiator-like edge, more power to them. Literally.

The Forum's triumphs exposing social injustices and pressuring government organizations were edged with bittersweet. Matt had once dreamt of him and Leah righting wrongs together, modern-day cyber gladiators. So, after he launched the Forum, he invited Leah. His heart had leaped when she joined. He had hoped—foolishly, in retrospect—that working together on the Forum might bridge the distance between Halifax and Fort Lauderdale. It might just give them another chance.

Ironically, Leah met AggroBoy there. Matt didn't trust the guy. But he couldn't warn his ex-girlfriend because he knew Leah would guess that Matt still had feelings for her.

And he couldn't convince Leah that AggroBoy's scheme to break into the Owen house was rash, dangerous. She had pointed out there was no other choice. Not if they wanted the truth to come out. Look at what had happened to Edward Snowden. He had blown the whistle—and was forced to abandon his family, his career, his country. His own government viewed him as a traitor, and charged him under the Espionage Act, a criminal act that would not allow him to defend himself on the grounds of public interest.

So there it was. Do they keep quiet about Leah's discovery because she could be prosecuted as a traitor of the country she was trying to protect? Or do they try to do something that was in and of itself illegal—but with minimal harm—and keep Leah safe from criminal indictment? AggroBoy had assured them that no one would be home when Leah and he broke into the Owen house. It was a simple cyber exploit. They should be in and out in ten minutes, max, AggroBoy told them.

The other hackers on the Forum supported AggroBoy's crazy plan. In fact, they egged on AggroBoy and WhiteDwarf, excited that the online boundaries of the Forum were being pushed.

Matt lost the argument. Matt aka Condor had been overthrown by his own supporters. And the Forum had a new ruler.

His name was AggroBoy.

And the truth was that Matt wanted to expose the Honorable Harry Owen and his garbage buddies. What Leah had revealed to the Forum was too big a story—and too big a strike against everything they stood for.

But now he was scared that Leah had paid too big a price.

9

AIDEN STAGGERED UP THE fire escape of his rooming house. He lifted the window sash outside his room, slipped inside, and collapsed on the mattress on his floor.

Thank God.

The dog didn't get a piece of me. The cops can't find me.

Unless—or until—Leah tells them.

He shot up from the mattress, yanked off his balaclava, and forced his trembling fingers to search for the tiny flash drive that he had zipped inside his jacket pocket. It was smaller than his thumb. He knew it could easily fall out of his pocket. Even though it had served its purpose, he could not lose it. His digital fingerprints were all over it.

His hand relaxed. The small, U-shaped plastic stick was still there.

He perched on the edge of the moldy plastic lawn chair that served as his computer chair and booted up his system.

His computer network, stacked on two planks draped across sawhorses, had been patched together from a laptop his parents bought for him in violation of his sentencing conditions, and a router that he stole from a nursing home. His landlord had Wi-Fi that had been a no-brainer to hack into.

45

His fingers had finally stopped trembling. But his heart rate accelerated as he logged onto his computer.

Had the exploit worked?

All those months of meticulous planning. And it came down to this.

He hunched over the laptop, typing furiously.

Then he sat back and held his breath. He watched the script scrolling down the screen.

"Hack-a-fucking-lujah."

Leah really was brilliant.

Even if she was easily fooled. She had fallen for his persona of romantic rebel hacktivist Aiden Boyne without question. If Aiden had been able to grow beard scruff without it being all patchy, he would have ticked off every box of her ideal hacktivist fantasy lover.

It was Tr0lz who had suggested that he seek out Leah at a hacktivist conference six months ago. Tr0lz had somehow discovered that Leah worked for KryptoCyber, and suggested that she would be a good recruit for their team. They needed someone with better hacking skills than they possessed to make their Dark Web venture successful. And Leah would be perfect. Given her background, no one would suspect her.

It had taken a bit of work to penetrate Leah's reserve. But the fact that they both grew up in the same city was a good starting point, even though they hadn't crossed paths. Aiden explained that he had gone to a private boarding school outside of the city—when, in fact, he had been incarcerated.

The novelty of hooking up with Leah had been fun for about two months. He had enjoyed the identity he had created for her benefit: Aidan Boyne, telecommunications consultant. He had enjoyed populating his Facebook and Instagram feeds with childhood photos of him posing with Muffin, the family cat. He threw in inspirational quotes about truth and justice for good measure. Of course, his identity was only skin deep on the Internet. But he knew that Leah played by an old-fashioned code: trust. She wouldn't dig deeper if she had no reason to.

So he made sure she had no reason to.

The biggest hurdle for him was money. Leah made a very good income. He needed to be able to convince her of his own career success. But his income sucked. His parents had cut him off after they discovered a stash of stolen video games in his closet. It forced him to shut down a nice side business on eBay because his father threatened to call his parole officer.

He had just been hired to sell cellphones at a kiosk in the mall, but it barely covered his necessities. He was hurting for cash.

So he told Tr0lz that he wouldn't date Leah any more. He couldn't afford the lifestyle he needed to project, and her earnest, do-good nature got on his nerves. He knew she was too idealistic to get involved with the Dark Web. But Tr0lz offered to pay him to keep dating her. He laughed at the offer. Then the first electronic transfer arrived. It was $1000. With more promised for every week that he kept up the identity of romantic hacktivist Aiden Boyne for a little longer.

With his new source of income, Aiden had begun the search for a better apartment when Leah told him she had found out something really 'disturbing' about one of KryptoCyber's clients. And that she didn't know what to do—because the client was the department of the Honorable Harry Owen.

He knew that he alone could not pressure her to do anything about it, so Aiden had convinced Leah to share her discovery on the Forum.

The hacktivists jumped on it.

Doxx the effer like Dark Seoul did to Sony!

Yeah, doxx Harry Owen!

Doxx him!

The effers lied to us!

We could change the whole election!

It went on and on, everyone egging each other until Leah realized that she had opened Pandora's box. Even if she decided not to act on her discovery, someone else would expose the secret.

She was panicked. "The government will trace this back to me, Aiden! I'm going to be charged with treason! My family will be ostracized. Oh, God!"

He had gripped her shoulders. Had held her gaze. In his most reassuring voice, he had said, "Listen. I have a plan. We can doxx Harry Owen and no one will ever know that it was you who did it."

"It's too risky," she said. "I can't see how they won't trace this back to me. My boss would look at his team first."

"But what if we upload a virus on Harry Owen's laptop from a USB that can't be traced back to you?"

She stared at him. "How? The only way to access his laptop is through his office."

"You said you discovered that he logged on to his parents' Wi-Fi. That he breached every security protocol in his department. What if we use his parents' computer as a host? We upload the virus onto that computer with a USB stick, and then when Harry logs his laptop onto the Wi-Fi system, his parents' computer sends the virus to his laptop through the family Wi-Fi network."

Her gaze narrowed. "How are you proposing that we put the virus on to his parents' computer? It's not like we can just walk in to his parents' house."

This was the delicate part. And it was the most crucial part. He knew Leah well enough that she would reject any kind of illegal activity that didn't suit her higher purpose.

"We'll break in one night—"

"Break in? Have you lost your mind?"

"Leah!" He caught her gaze with his own. "His parents are away. It's no big deal. We just get in the house, upload the virus, and leave. It will take ten minutes, max."

He held his breath. If she didn't agree to his plan, he would never be able to convince her to do what he and Tr0lz really wanted her to do. This break-in was simply a means to a very different end than what Leah had in mind. Once they completed the break-in, he could threaten to expose her actions unless she wrote the computer code that they needed. It was a perfect trap. She just needed to step into it.

Her pulse fluttered in the vein in her neck. Behind him, her computer monitor filled with posts from the Forum.

"There's no going back, Leah. You've got to do this. If you do it, you'll be a friggin' hero."

"I don't want to be a hero." Her eyes searched his for understanding. "I just want to do what's right. And breaking into a house doesn't fit into that category."

He swallowed his impatience. *Play it cool, Aiden.* "Sometimes you have to sacrifice a small principle for a bigger one. And I promise you, no one will get hurt. Harry Owen only comes home on weekends. And his parents are away right now." He was pretty sure that Harry Owen's mother was in the hospital. Whatever.

And the only people who would get hurt in this scenario were the ones who had had it coming for years: Harry Owen and Bill Green—Aiden's father. Ironically, humiliating and destroying Harry Owen was the stepping stone to the ultimate humiliation and destruction of his father. But Leah was the catalyst. Without her, each plan would fail. So he had made sure that he hit every pressure point with Leah so that she would agree to the break-in.

What Leah didn't know was that the data filling Aiden's USB stick was more than the files that Leah had targeted.

It was the entire contents of Harry's laptop. Aiden had altered the code so that *everything* on Harry's laptop became his.

Harry's life was now in the palm of Aiden's hand.

Just like Aiden's life had been in the palm of Harry's hand seven years ago, when Harry had flicked away Aiden's future as if it was a piece of dirt.

"You stick it to me. I stick it to you," Aiden murmured.

Aiden would finally have his revenge on the Dishonorable Harry Owen. On the criminal justice system. On the effing governments that tried to control something that was uncontrollable. No one could control the undercurrents that flowed through the Internet.

His father would soon learn that lesson the hard way.

But first, he had to let Condor and the rest of the hacktivists in the Forum know that Leah's mission had been accomplished.

He logged in to the Forum. In reality, it was a private chat room on the Internet. Just a space in the ether that became a 'room' by virtue of wires, radio waves and arbitrary bits and bytes that kept unwanted visitors away.

He typed: *Hey. We did it.*

Within seconds, Tr0lz answered: *It worked, AggroBoy?*

Aiden could almost see the wink that went with Tr0lz's question. They had planned this out so that no one in the Forum knew that he and Tr0lz had executed an exploit within an exploit.

In fact, no one knew that it was really Tr0lz who controlled the Forum. Condor had no clue.

Aiden whistled softly under his breath and typed a response to Tr0lz's post: *Got myself a package.*

What kind of package? Tr0lz asked. Aiden could sense Tr0lz's smirk.

I got the files that WhiteDwarf was talking about.

Condor jumped in—just like Aiden knew he would: *Where's WhiteDwarf?*

The guy was in love with Leah. It had given Aiden great satisfaction to know that he had trumped the self-righteous prick and taken Leah for himself. And soon, Condor would discover that Aiden had trumped him again with this exploit.

But first he had to keep Condor happy. He couldn't raise any alarm bells about Leah until he and Tr0lz had time to finish their exploit. His fingers were damp with sweat as he typed: *Dunno.*

There was a pause. The cursor blinked at him.

Could Condor sense the lie? Then his words came in a flurry of accusation: *Isn't she with you?*

Aiden stared at the question. His lip curved in a smile. He

would just let that message sit there for a minute. Because he could. Finally, he typed with painstaking slowness: *Nah.*

He rubbed the back of his neck. It was slimy with sweat under his black hoody. Then, just to keep Condor from getting all fired up, he added: *She said her roommate would be looking for her. She went home.*

She's not responding to my messages, Condor typed.

Give her time, Aiden responded. *She had to go the long way home.*

As planned, Tr0lz asked: *When you gonna doxx Harry Owen?*

And as planned, he responded: *Tonight. Or tomorrow.*

Suddenly, a private message flashed across the screen from Tr0lz: *Did you get EVERYTHING?*

YES. But I gotta go into hiding. The cops are after me.

Where will we meet?

He hesitated. Was Halifax too dangerous for him now?

But he had no money. He'd blown through the last thousand that Tr0lz had sent him. And Tr0lz—the bastard—told Aiden that he would have to wait until after the break-in of the Owen house for his payday.

Where we planned. 10 tonight.

Aiden glanced at the clock on his computer screen. Damn. The police could have found his trail by now.

He grabbed his army surplus backpack and emptied the pockets. He had twenty-three dollars in cash. Shit.

He ran his fingers—grimy and rough—through his hair. He had grown it out after he was released from the juvenile detention center. It brushed his shoulders, a long, shaggy mane that masked his features when his head was lowered.

What did he have that he could pawn? He scanned his room. It was a shitty room, full of shitty things. Like his life. Thanks to his shitty mother. And his shitty father. He thought of his basement suite at home. The sixty-inch HD television. The tricked-out computer system. The video games center. The rainfall shower with the heated towel racks. The luxury SUV at his disposal whenever he wanted. The endless supply of gourmet food in his mother's chef's kitchen. His parents had kicked him out, cut him off.

But he would have the last laugh. They had no idea, no friggin' clue what he was capable of.

He ejected the USB stick from his computer. He slid his laptop into his backpack, pulled his hoody over his head, and climbed out of the window. It took only a minute to climb down the fire escape. He leapt onto the ground. By tonight he would be Master of the Cyber-fucking-Universe.

He broke into a jog and headed down to the railway tracks. He would have a nap and dream of the life that was about to be his.

10

8:23 a.m.

KATE HURRIED ALONG THE boardwalk that edged the waterfront.

She had slept through her alarm, only to be awakened by Alaska's warm tongue licking her hand. When she blearily opened her eye to check the time, she bolted out of bed.

A mere forty-five minutes later, she had managed to pull herself together, feed the dogs, and find a parking space in the parkade of her office tower. She was glad that John Hillcroft suggested they meet in a coffee shop close to the Law Courts, because her jet lag was in dire need of caffeine.

It was hard to believe she had been strolling through the Piazza San Marco only a few days before, the Venetian sun soaking into every pore. There was something about the sun in the Mediterranean. It had a full-bodied quality to it, a voluptuousness in every ray. It lulled one into a sensual state of relaxation. Perfect for a vacation.

Perfect for not thinking.

And yet, somewhere amongst the museum trips, leisurely meals, and early morning runs along cobblestoned streets, she had experienced an epiphany. Despite the pleasures of her trip, she had been eager to return home.

She hurried along the Halifax waterfront, the tang of the

sea air invigorating her. A blue and white ferry zipped across the harbor, emerging from the fog with a bounce of optimism. A smile curved her lips. She felt a small thrill of excitement about her meeting with John Hillcroft. The last time she had a job interview, she had been an inexperienced associate willing to take whatever John Lyons offered her for the prospect of working for a prestigious firm like Lyons McGrath Barrett.

Now, she had built a solid reputation as a lawyer, and had defended Randall Barrett in a case that had been viewed by many as unwinnable. Surely, John Hillcroft would recognize that she could bring a perspective that many other Crowns had not personally experienced.

The ferry unloaded as she strode by the ferry terminal. She was absorbed into the throng of disembarked passengers. It was morning rush hour and she allowed herself to be swept with the crowd. Within a few minutes she had reached her destination.

Here goes.

She pushed open the heavy wooden door of the coffee shop, pausing on the threshold. It was a popular spot on a Friday morning. There, in the corner, she glimpsed John Hillcroft. He was already robed for court. He gave her a quick wave as she ordered an Americano at the counter. Cup in hand, she strode over to where he sat.

"Kate!" He rose, extending his hand. Kate had crossed paths with him a few times in the courthouse, but she hadn't realized how tall he was until now.

Kate shook his hand, noting the firm, dry grip. "Thanks for meeting with me, John. I know how busy you are."

He settled back in his chair, folding his legs under the small table. "To be honest, I was a bit curious to meet you after Eddie called."

She had been curious—and nervous—to meet him, too. The Cambridge-educated prosecutor was renowned for his success in the courtroom. He wore his black robe with the ease of a man who was confident in his abilities.

Crisp. That was the word that Kate thought of as he faced her. Neatly trimmed hair—brown with a few sprinkles of silver, smoothly shaven face, gleaming black dress shoes, crisp barrister tabs under equally crisp white wing-tip shirt collar and a crisp English accent.

Crisply confident. Crisply intelligent.

"I can just imagine what Eddie said. Trust me, I have my good points." She smiled. But she could not miss John Hillcroft's allusion. He was curious to meet the woman who had come face to face with a serial killer—and survived. Would he judge her in the same manner that her firm had judged her?

"There's no question of that, Kate. You are a celebrity in this town. I know of your cases." He folded his hands on the table and leaned forward. "I would like nothing more than to trade war stories with you." He smiled. It was a startling transformation to his face, making it less severe and more boyish. "But I have to appear in court in half an hour. Let's cut to the chase. Eddie told me you are looking for work in the office of Public Prosecutions."

"Yes. I think it's a natural fit given my background."

He studied her for a moment, his expression impenetrable. "I agree."

Kate felt a hitch of anticipation. It must have showed on her face, because John held up a hand. "But. And there's a big 'but.' We have no openings."

"None? I'm willing to move out of the city." Her stomach tightened. There had to be a Crown job somewhere. "I can be flexible. I don't have any attach—" *Whoa, Kate, that's a bit too much information.*

And maybe not entirely accurate?

"I'm sorry, Kate. You know we would love to have you join Prosecutions. But with the cutbacks from the last budget, we have no positions available. We just filled our last opening."

She studied him, in that moment wanting nothing more than to be *him*. Becoming a prosecutor was what she was meant to do. She knew it. What Nina Woods had said to her before she left for Italy merely underscored the rightness of her decision.

Why else had she survived so many terrible things, but to help set the world right again?

"I understand." Kate forced a smile to match her words. "But do you foresee anything opening up soon?"

John Hillcroft's gaze was regretful. The man's face naturally fell into inscrutable lines, but his eyes were more expressive than he probably liked, given he was the Chief Crown Prosecutor for the region. "I'm afraid not. We just filled two other vacant positions last month, although we could use more hands on deck. Despite our efforts at lobbying the government for more positions, we have been unsuccessful. The government seems to think that fewer prosecutors will result in fewer crimes." His lips twisted. "But, all it means is that more criminals are getting released on constitutional grounds because of the delay in proceedings or insufficient time for our Crowns to adequately prepare." He drained his coffee cup and stood. "Sorry, I must go."

Kate pushed her chair away from the table and grabbed her briefcase. "I really appreciate you meeting with me, John."

"It was my pleasure. Why don't you walk with me to the Law Courts? We can discuss options for you."

He politely ushered her out of the coffee shop. Kate fell into step beside him. "If you want some unsolicited advice, Kate, ask McGrath Woods to take on more criminal defense work. You have a talent for it. I would surmise that Randall Barrett would be open to your request."

Kate's lips twisted in a smile. So, John Hillcroft had a sense of humor. A rather dry one, given his oblique reference to her successful defense of Randall Barrett a year ago. "Perhaps." She hesitated. Should she tell him that her firm wanted her to keep a low profile and stay out of trouble? No. That was between her and Nina. Instead, she said, "But I really don't want to do any more defense work. I only did one case, and it was by necessity. And——" she paused, reluctant to share a decision that was so fresh that she was still testing it. "I am tendering my resignation to McGrath Woods at the end of the month."

They arrived at the base of the steps leading to the Law Courts. Hillcroft raised a brow, but that was the extent of his reaction to Kate's revelation. "Well, if I were you, I would go to one of the boutique defense firms and get more criminal law experience under your belt. It will give your application weight when something opens up." He must have sensed her dismay, because he added, "Many prosecutors have worked on both sides, Kate. It is the best preparation for the job. A good defense is the best offence. And vice versa." His phone chimed. He turned toward the broad concrete stairwell that led to the Law Courts "You can call me any time if you have questions."

"Thanks, John. I appreciate your help. Maybe I will give Eddie Bent a call." Eddie Bent had been instrumental to her success in her very first criminal defense case. "He told me the door was always open."

John Hillcroft threw her a sideways glance. "I would suggest you look elsewhere, Kate."

Her stomach tightened. "Why?"

"Nothing specific. Just a sense that all might not be well." His phone chimed again. "Before I go, I wanted to touch base about the Kenzie Sloane case."

Kate forced herself to not react to the name. "Yes?"

"As you know, she was very unhappy that bail was denied." The judge had deemed her a flight risk, especially given the fact that there were no family members who had agreed to act as surety. "Her defense team has made a request to proceed with a preliminary inquiry." A preliminary inquiry was a special proceeding which determined whether there was enough evidence for the accused to stand trial.

Kate's stomach sank. "On what grounds?"

"She claims that you tried to attack her and that she had hit you by accident."

"I see. So I'm going to have to appear as a witness?" The thought of seeing the red-haired, blue-eyed, multi-hued tattoo artist who had tried to kill her made Kate nauseated.

She wished she hadn't left Venice.

"I'm afraid so. And the matter is scheduled next week."

"Next week?"

"We are trying to work around the judge's vacation schedule." He gave her a sympathetic look. "Sorry, Kate. I must run. Good luck. I'll call you when I need to prep for the Sloane matter." He sprinted up the stairs to the entrance of the Law Courts, his robe billowing behind him.

Kate watched his retreating back. What the hell…?

This meeting had not gone in the direction that Kate had hoped. At all.

She had planned—naïvely, it now seemed in retrospect—to find career fulfillment. Her work at McGrath Woods felt faceless. Empty. She didn't want to focus on billable hours, or defend large corporate interests. Especially when the partners for whom she worked no longer wanted her on their plum files.

She had done what she needed to do at McGrath Woods. She had proven herself and found her purpose. McGrath Woods, in turn, had grudgingly given her a chance. But it also had served up two cases that almost had her killed. And turned its back on its former Managing Partner when the stink of scandal wafted down its plush corridors. And now it seemed to be turning its back on her. Again.

She needed to defend justice.

And the face of justice was a victim's face.

But she couldn't resign without a plan in place. No, she was not spontaneous enough to walk away from a steady paycheck at a reputable firm.

She dialed Eddie's number. After four rings, his familiar gruff voice filled her ear, setting the unnamed fears stirred by John Hillcroft to rest. "Kate. Welcome home."

She strode down the boardwalk toward her office, swinging her briefcase. "Hi, Eddie. Rumor has it—" Her stomach tightened again. She gave John Hillcroft's rumor a mental kick to the curb. He was wrong. She knew Eddie better than he did. "—That you are looking for a partner to keep you on your toes."

He paused. Then laughed. "Should I be ordering new stationery?"

She grinned. "How does Lange & Bent sound to you?"

"Not as good as Bent & Lange." He laughed again, lapsing into his smoker's hack.

"Seriously. Do you have enough work for two until I can get my feet under me?"

"I'm overrun right now, Kate. I could definitely use another body. The chair is yours. But I'm a little surprised you want to do this. I had the impression from Hillcroft that prosecutions was more your thing."

"It was. It is. But there are no jobs. And I need to get some experience in criminal law. As you have told me many times, it's a totally different beast from civil law."

"That it is." He paused. "Seriously, Kate, do you really want to leave McGrath Woods? I thought things were going well for you. And Randall's back now."

She exhaled. "Actually, things weren't going well. Nina Woods dropped a bombshell on me just before I left. I am tired of my career being dictated by the whims of the partners. And I don't want to work in a firm where I feel like one mistake will throw me to the lions. Again."

"Randall will have your back."

"The point is that I don't want to work for a firm that treated him the way they treated him."

"Point taken. But have you thought about who your clientele will be if you work with me? They aren't what you are used to dealing with at McGrath Woods."

"Eddie, I've been to Provincial Court before."

"Kate, I'm not trying to patronize you. I'm just concerned that this move might not be good for your mental health. You will be defending people accused of crimes. Some of them are horrific. After everything you've been through, I'm not sure if you should do this."

Doubt crept around the edges of her resolve. "I want to be a prosecutor, Eddie. Hillcroft told me that unless I got some experience, it wasn't going to happen."

"Okay." He paused for a moment. "Listen. Here's the deal. You can be my partner, but I decide which cases you take. Okay?"

"You mean you want to screen them for content? I get the PG crimes and you get the X-rated?"

"Exactly."

It was tempting not having to confront the truly soul-searing cases. But… "No deal, Eddie. I appreciate your concern, but I need to take control of my career. If it turns out that I can't stomach the cases, then being a prosecutor is out. I wouldn't have much choice about my cases as Crown."

"True." He gave a resigned laugh. "Welcome aboard."

Kate thought of his shambling body, ash flecked on his desk, the warm light in his hazel eyes. "Where are you now?" She would bring him a coffee. Cement the deal.

"Not at the office. Why?"

"No reason." She kept her tone light. "I just thought I might bring us celebratory Americanos."

"I'm in court most of the day. Let's have dinner and get the details sorted out."

A seagull shot up from the wake of the ferry, carrying something in its beak. "Sounds good."

"I'd offer to have you over, but I'm still unpacking." Eddie had been house sitting for Randall Barrett while he and his family were in Manhattan for ten months. Randall had returned just a few weeks ago, and Eddie moved to a new flat.

"I know Alaska would love to see you. Come for seven." Kate smiled as she hung up the phone. The smile quickly faded as she neared her office. She hadn't expected that her first day back at work would be marked by joining forces with Eddie Bent, her mentor and friend. But it had a sense of inevitability to it.

She approached the large foyer of Purdy's Wharf Tower Two, catching her reflection in the mirrored elevator doors. She had worn a short-sleeved silk knit sweater in a deep indigo, and a dark pencil skirt that she had managed to zip up over the past month's vacation diet. She had dug around in her suitcase and found a silk scarf in blue, violet and magenta. She knotted the scarf around her neck, sleeked back her recalcitrant hair into a low ponytail, and threw on some lipstick and mascara. With her dark glasses and low heels, she had felt ready for the world when she rushed out of her house this morning.

Now, as the elevator stopped on the penthouse floor, she realized that the world for which she had felt ready had changed abruptly. She would no longer be working in a prime office tower, with leather furniture and sleek modern art. She would no longer have the breathtaking view of Halifax Harbour, or of Georges Island marking the Narrows, or of the fir-dusted McNabs Island with the lighthouse on the tip.

She would no longer have the security of a top-notch firm behind her.

But how secure was it? Every few months, the firm seemed to vacillate in whether it loved her or hated her. After being away for a month, she realized that she had never felt comfortable in the aura of prestige that McGrath Woods emanated.

She strode out of the elevators.

It's time to roll out Kate Version 2.0.

11

"ARE YOU ALL RIGHT, Harry?"

No, I am not all right. And I doubt I will ever be 'all right' again.

"I couldn't believe the news this morning." His publicist ignored his lack of response. "You should have called me. I can't keep the media on hold for much longer. You need to issue a statement."

Harry stared through his hotel window at the Halifax Harbour. The ferry frothed the deep blue of the water into a playful wake. On the open top deck, commuters enjoyed the sun and fresh air. The scene had an in-your-face cheeriness to it that made his head pound. "I'm sorry, Sophie. It was four-thirty in the morning before I even left my parents' house. I didn't want to wake you."

"It's my job to deflect the media for you, Harry." Her voice was tight.

"What difference does it make whether I called you in the middle of the night or not?"

There was a small hesitation, a tiny hitch in her breathing that made his gut clench. "Oh, God. Don't tell me you said something to them." He spun away from the window, reached for the remote and turned on the news.

His story was running. Of course, it would be. But he was

not expecting the headline. "Jesus Christ, Sophie! Have you seen how they've spun it?"

"I'm sorry! I didn't know what had happened. A reporter just called me and told me she was running a story on the government's position on self-defense. She asked me to confirm a quote. So I did." Her voice rose a notch. "You should have called me, Harry. I didn't know."

His breath came out in a low, weary sigh. "No. You did not know." He sank onto the hotel bed. "I should have called you." He repeated the words, his tone defeated, as he watched the headline scroll across the bottom of his television screen. *MP Harry Owen: "I believe my property is sacred. Shoot first, ask questions later."*

Could this day get any worse?

Finally he asked, "Did you at least tell them I said that years ago, before I was elected?"

"Of course. I even clarified the context." Sophie paused. "But you and I both know it doesn't matter in the eye of the public."

Every word must be parsed, reflected on and tested before a statement was made. He knew that. But he didn't know that rule when he uttered that statement in an interview about the robbery in his parents' store.

He exhaled. "I gotta go. I have a meeting with my lawyer in a few minutes."

"Harry, we need a statement from you. We have to deflect this. Emma Dumond is having a field day with this." Emma Dumond was a bright young lawyer who was running for his seat in Halifax. Ironically, she reminded him of himself just a few years back, before he had been forced to hide his cynicism from his constituents. Except she was much savvier with social media. Last month, she had milked his refusal to assist Frances Sloane's assisted suicide agenda. Frances Sloane might be dead, but public opinion was alive and well. It hadn't helped that the courts had performed a judicial about-face and had struck assisted suicide from the Criminal Code of Canada.

If only you knew the minefield I tread. "I don't even know if I will be charged with anything."

"But isn't that girl almost dead?"

"That girl is a criminal." The weight pressed on his chest. Those eyes...like a frightened doe when he shot her. "And so far, she is still alive."

"But they are saying the gun was a prohibited weapon—"

"I didn't know it was, Sophie. They can't prove intent."

"Harry," she said, her voice low, "they are going to want to know how a MP on the Public Safety Committee could not know that his father owned a prohibited weapon."

"Jesus, Sophie, do you know everything your father owns? I had no idea. He doesn't tell me everything, just like I don't tell him everything."

Even though that was supposed to be an innocent remark, it sounded strangely ominous. As if he had a secret to hide.

He did. And now that his mother was dead, he was going to keep it that way.

There was a pause on the other end of the phone.

He cleared his throat. "Look, I gotta go."

And then he hung up.

He left his phone by the bed as he took a shower. The warm water slid down his skin. His mind raced. He twisted the temperature knob to the cold setting. Icy drops pounded into his skin. He closed his eyes and let the water run over his face, his chest, his thighs.

Make it go away. Make it all go away.

That seemed to be his mantra for most of his life.

But no matter how cold the water, he could not numb himself from what had happened last night.

Too many old memories. Too much fear.

And too many questions.

He couldn't sort them out. His mind was jumbled, running from moment to moment. His memories of last night were bizarrely fragmented, darting behind columns of willful oblivion, hiding from the specter of truth.

It scared him that he could not piece it all together, that there was no logical sequence of events.

He stepped out of the shower and wrapped a towel around his hips. His reflection showed a man in his prime, one of Parliament Hill's 'hottest bachelors', a man with a reputation for discarding a slew of beautiful women.

It suited him fine. It made him happy, made his career work.

Until today.

The phone call he had received an hour ago from the Prime Minister had shaken him. The PM was distant. He demanded to know what Harry was doing to mitigate the situation. By 'situation', he meant the political fallout.

Harry promised his boss that he would take full responsibility for any mistakes made. He swore to keep the party out of it.

But it was a hollow promise in an election campaign.

He knew it. And the Prime Minister knew it.

If Harry brought the party to its knees with a scandal, his own career was finished.

His lips twisted.

He hurried from the bathroom when his hotel phone rang. He shrugged on a blue oxford cloth shirt and then picked up the receiver.

"Harry."

Relief flooded him that it wasn't yet another reporter. But just as quickly dread tightened his stomach when he heard the strangely flat, hoarse voice of his father. "Yes, Dad."

"Are you...are you...ready?"

His father's unfamiliar stumbling scared Harry. What would his father say during the police interview?

Would he remember to stay quiet?

"Yes, I'll be over in a few minutes." Harry put down the hotel phone, eyeing his cell phone from a safe distance.

It vibrated on the coffee table, badges flashing across the screen. He had been through enough news cycles to recognize that his phone was a harbinger of how his day would go. The hotel lobby would be a nightmare.

He called the front desk. "It's Harry Owen. How many media are outside?" His tone was polite, yet invited no questions.

"Good morning, Mr. Owen." Harry could not miss the front desk agent's suppressed excitement. "The street is lined with cars." Her voice dropped. "There are a number of reporters waiting in the lobby for you, Mr. Owen."

"Do you have a back exit we can take? One that I can wheel my father through?"

She paused. "You could use the staff exit. I will come to your room and take you there. You need a staff access card to unlock the door."

"Thank you. I will be in my father's room."

He finished dressing, combing his hair until it was smoothly swept back from his face. It was inky black, like his mother's, but silver threaded the thick strands. He did a quick sweep of his room to make sure that nothing personal was left out. He had brought very little with him except a change of clothes, his toiletries, and his laptop. He placed that in the room safe. Then he locked his room, double-checking the door.

He crossed the hallway and knocked on his father's door. The peephole was too high for his father to use. "It's me." He kept his voice low, and glanced over his shoulder. The corridor was empty.

The door finally swung open. Harry stepped inside his father's room, closing the door behind him.

His father wheeled himself toward Harry. To his relief, his father was dressed, his cheeks ruddy from his morning shave. But he had missed a small patch of grey stubble by the edge of his jaw. It made Harry want to weep.

"Hi Dad," he said, raising his voice over the sound of the television. A commercial blared in the dim room, the sunny voice of the announcer setting Harry's teeth on edge. "Why is the TV so loud?" He scanned the room for the remote.

"Because I want to hear everything they say. About

66

Salma. And how those bastards killed her." His father's lips trembled. Bloodless, thin, twisted with grief.

God, his father was a mess. Detective Ellis would take him down in minutes. "Look, Dad, we have a meeting this morning. With a lawyer. You need to listen to everything he says. And then we have to go to the police station."

His father swung his gaze away from the television. "Have they caught the guy that did this to her?"

Harry shook his head. "One suspect is still on the loose. The other is in the hospital."

"The hospital?" Mel Owen's finger twitched on his trousers. "Why is he in the hospital?"

"Because I shot her——"

A loud knock made them both jump.

Jesus Christ.

Harry flung open the door. The front desk agent smiled cautiously at him.

How thick were the goddamned doors? Had she heard what he said?

He grabbed the handgrips on his father's wheelchair. "Dad, we need to go see the lawyer now."

He hoped like hell that Randall Barrett could fix the nightmare. Because it seemed like everything Harry did just made it worse.

12

Pain.

It flared through Leah's cells, raced across every nerve, gathering energy, until the cells fused together into a hot core.

RED. YELLOW. PURPLE.

WHITE HOT.

A supernova of agony.

She moaned.

The supernova began to swirl, white, purple, pink streaked with black, funneling into a cosmos of pure pain.

"Stay with us!"

The supernova exploded.

The black hole rushed up to consume her.

13

KATE STRODE DOWN THE hallway to Managing Partner Nina Woods' corner office. On her way, she passed Randall's office.

The door was closed. Before she could decide whether to knock, Nina Woods appeared around the opposite corner.

"Kate!" Nina's bright silver hair gleamed in the light streaming through the glass building. "Welcome back." She smiled.

It was funny how things could change. Kate could not remember an instance when Nina Woods had given her a genuine smile last year. Nina was a rainmaker for McGrath Woods, the woman who had single-handedly kept the ship afloat when Randall Barrett was charged with murder. She was known as the Ice Queen, but she was, in fact, the White Queen on the chessboard of McGrath Woods. Nina never gave away her hand, always keeping her strategy quiet until the beginning of the endgame.

"How are you?" Nina's gaze flickered over Kate, and then back to her face. "Italy agreed with you."

Kate nodded. "Yes. It did."

"Could I have a word with you in my office, please?" It wasn't really a question. Not when the Managing Partner posed it.

"Of course." Kate cleared her throat. "Actually, I was on my way to speak with you."

"Oh?" Nina Woods walked into her office. "Have a seat, Kate."

Kate followed her soon-to-be ex-boss into her stunning corner office. It had once been John Lyons'. She shook off the chill that skittered along her arms at the thought of her former mentor.

She remembered that day when he first invited her into his office to work on the TransTissue case. She had been excited at the carrot he had dangled before her. Her future had suddenly held promise. And she had gazed through the commanding view of his twenty-second floor office and been in awe. Of his success, his power, all on show with his million-dollar view.

Even now, the view moved her. There was something about the deep, mysterious body of water that spoke to an elemental part of her. Perhaps it was the immutability of the ocean, how it reached beyond them all. It just went on forever. Nothing could stop it.

And at the horizon, silvery fog performed a sleight of hand with the long, flat lines of an incoming container ship.

"Coffee?" Nina Woods held out a thermal coffee jug.

Kate shook her head. "No, thanks. I just had one."

Nina nodded, the brisk movement swinging her smooth hair as she poured coffee into a mug with *McGrath Woods* emblazoned across it. At the sight of it, Kate remembered that she had one at home, in her cupboard. Would she and Eddie have mugs with the Bent & Lange moniker? She doubted it. That wasn't his style.

"Kate, I've been reflecting on the conversation we had before you left for Italy," Nina said. "I'm afraid I might have given you the wrong impression when I told you that clients were concerned about your reputation."

Before she left, Nina had told her that the partners were becoming uncomfortable with the attention being drawn to the firm. They wanted to put the John Lyons scandal behind them. At first, Kate's role in ending the Body Butcher's killing spree had given the firm a welcome sheen after Lyons' betrayal. Her defense of Randall Barrett had allowed the firm to tout its pro bono efforts, but there had been a lingering sour taste that another partner of the once-esteemed firm was embroiled in a case that made headlines.

When Kate became the target of a stalker who was connected to the Frances Sloane case, it was impossible for McGrath Woods to stay out of the news. There were too many newsworthy angles: MP Harry Owen's refusal to address assisted suicide, the death of a prominent female architect from a terrible disease, the high school connection of a celebrity tattoo artist to one of their associates, the discovery of a bog body, the cracking of a cold case...the list was long and well-exploited on slow news days. McGrath Woods' name appeared constantly in relation to Kate's name, and it was no longer the benefit it once was. Clients with large, confidential deals were concerned that their firm was dragged through the news cycle so frequently. They asked that Kate not be attached to their files.

It had angered Kate that her firm hadn't acknowledged that both the TransTissue and the Sloane files were cases that McGrath Woods had assigned to her. That she was the aggrieved party—not them.

But it all came down to billable hours. The firm couldn't succeed without clients.

And clients were beginning to look elsewhere.

Kate raised a brow. "I don't know how one could misinterpret that statement."

Nina gave her a cool look. "I should have qualified that statement. Clients in our litigation and corporate practices do not want the attention that your name attracts."

Maybe they were worried she'd uncover some unsavory practices and not look the other way.

Kate returned Nina's cool look with one of her own. "The firm used to bask in the media attention I received."

"It's gone on too long, Kate." Nina's tone was clipped.

But she softened it in the next breath. "In fact, we feel that your talents would be better utilized elsewhere."

Kate stared at Nina with mounting incredulity. She knew what Nina was about to say. And she couldn't believe Nina and the firm would kick her when she was down.

But then again, she could.

Kate knew exactly what would be Nina's next words. But she wanted to make the Managing Partner say them—so that she would never give Nina Woods the benefit of the doubt again. "And where do you think my 'talents' lie?"

Nina smiled. "In the Family and Probate practices."

A flush burned in Kate's chest.

She had come full circle. She had started out at McGrath Woods in family law, the pink ghetto. She had believed that if she worked hard enough, was fast enough on her feet, that her value would be recognized.

But, no. Her value was measured in the volume of billable hours she could bring in to the firm. And her reputation— solely the result of her experience at McGrath Woods—was now a liability. So she was being demoted. By a woman who knew full well the unfairness of the situation, but tried nonetheless to make Kate buy it.

The White Queen leaned back in her chair.

The endgame had been revealed.

And the pawn would now make its move.

"I am tendering my resignation, Nina." Kate stood. "I plan to leave today. I passed my files to the litigation team before I went to Italy." She remembered they had been more than happy for her to hand them over last month. Had this been in the works even when she was recovering from McNally's attack?

One look at Nina's face confirmed that it had.

She turned and strode out of Nina's office.

At nine in the morning, the firm hummed with energy, phones ringing, printers spewing documents. McGrath Woods was in fine form. Perhaps it sensed that its balance would soon be righted, that the splinter in its side would soon be extracted.

Had Randall known about this?

Kate crossed the foyer, her pulse racing, her mind focused on the thousand and one details necessary to wrap up her short and dramatic career at McGrath Woods. It was over. Everything she had worked toward—the civil litigation practice, the partnership, the corner office—was over. At least at McGrath Woods.

And she felt a sense of release that was unexpected. She hadn't realized the weight she carried from the work and trauma she had experienced here.

It had shaken her confidence. Destroyed her trust.

And almost killed her.

The elevator dinged.

She startled, her fight-or-flight reflex forever triggered after her fight to the death with the Body Butcher, her gaze flying to the opening doors.

An older man in a wheelchair stared past her. He was neatly dressed, but he radiated distress. Bloodshot eyes. Patchy grooming. A hand that convulsively gripped the crease in his trousers.

Poor man. He reminded her acutely of Frances Sloane. Kate had tried her best to advocate for her client's desire to change the assisted suicide laws. Harry Owen's refusal to even meet with Frances still stung. He had been so arrogant. So righteous in his views.

The man's caregiver propelled him forward.

Kate veered out of his path. His caregiver caught the corner of her eye.

Kate could not control her shock.

It was Harry Owen. He, too, appeared distressed. His eyes were bloodshot, his face gaunt.

His gaze met hers. She couldn't pretend she hadn't seen him, not after the way she had reacted.

She nodded. "Mr. Owen."

He could not control his shock, either. "Ms. Lange." He hurriedly pushed the elderly man toward the reception desk.

Kate continued walking, her face now expressionless, her mind racing. Why was Harry Owen here?

And on today of all days?

As she opened the glass door leading to her office, she heard the Honorable Harry Owen say, "Please tell Mr. Barrett that Harry and Mel Owen are here."

14

THE WAITING AREA OF McGrath Woods struck a note that was entirely familiar to Harry: power and privilege. Before he had been elected to Parliament, he had practiced law in a firm much like this one.

But the very atmosphere that comforted Harry unsettled his father.

"This is too rich for me, Harry," he whispered. "I can't afford a lawyer from here."

Harry patted his father's arm. "Dad, he promised to give you a reduced fee." That was a lie, but he'd say anything right now to allay his father's agitation.

"Why do we need a lawyer, anyway? We haven't done anything wrong." His father glared at the receptionist, as if she had pointed an accusatory finger at him. She turned to her computer monitor.

"We need to make sure the police understand that, Dad. And it's more complicated since I'm an elected official—"

"Harry, good to see you, although I am sorry about the circumstances." Randall Barrett strode to where Harry sat with his father. Harry hadn't seen Randall for several years. He had followed Barrett's criminal case closely. He should not have been surprised to see the toll it had taken on the

75

famed litigator: his once gleaming blond hair was dull, streaked with silver. Grooves—not just lines—marked his forehead and the sides of his mouth. Yet Barrett's in-your-face bullish masculinity had not diminished one iota. He still inspired confidence. And made any alpha male within throwing distance bristle.

Harry rose from his seat and shook Randall's hand. "This is my father, Mel Owen."

"Mr. Owen. My deepest sympathies on the loss of your wife," Randall said, his tone somber. "It has been a trying night for you both. Let's see what I can do to help you through this ordeal."

He led them to a conference room. A space at the table for Mel's wheelchair had already been cleared. Harry pushed his father to the table, and then sat in the leather chair next to him.

Randall held out a thermal coffee pot. "Coffee, Mr. Owen?"

"Yes. With cream." Mel Owen croaked out the request.

"Same for me," Harry said in response to Randall's querying look.

Randall handed a cup to each of them. Harry took an obligatory sip. It was above par, and it burned a welcome trail into his chest. It was the first time he had not felt numb this morning.

Mel cradled the white porcelain mug in both hands. He seemed bemused by his surroundings. His gaze darted from the mahogany-veneered boardroom table, the eight black swivel chairs that had been precisely positioned around the table's perimeter, and came to rest on the massive flat screen television that hung from the wall opposite them.

In that moment, Harry realized how small his father's world had become.

And how oblivious Harry had been to that fact.

Now, his life was inextricably connected to his father's demons.

As if he didn't have enough of his own.

He put down his coffee. It had left a burning trail from his esophagus to his gut.

"Let's talk about what happened last night," Randall said. "Mr. Owen, can you walk me through the events?"

Neither of them wanted to revisit last night. And today, they would be forced to remember it again and again.

The moment of Salma's death.

The moment of Harry's misjudgment.

Both were life-altering events. Both would haunt Harry for the rest of his life. But he'd be damned if he paid a political price for the criminal acts of some scum. His father had been a victim twenty-five years ago. Harry saw what it had done to his mental state. And the terrible price he had paid with the loss of the use of his legs. It had changed him, the anger slowly eating through the love of his family, more destructive than the bullet itself.

He wouldn't let that happen to him. That's why he had gone into politics, what fuelled him every morning when he stepped into the House. No petty burglars were going to stand in his way.

Yes, he shot the girl.

But she deserved every torn tissue, every bleeding vessel, every nerve screaming in pain.

"Go ahead and tell him, Dad," Harry said, his voice steady. "You did nothing wrong."

15

THE WAR ROOM BUZZED with energy. Cooper sat in the seat next to Lamond. God, this felt good. He absorbed the electricity in the air, felt it recharge his flagging brain. This was what he wanted.

To feel alive again.

"Get much sleep?" Lamond asked. They had left the Owen house at about 5:00 a.m. "I managed about two hours." He took a long pull from his coffee.

Cooper shook his head. "I didn't go home. Didn't want to wake the wife." He ignored Lamond's sideways glance and shrugged. "And I wanted to get those interviews prepped."

Riley hurried in and slid into the seat next to Brown.

She shot Cooper a look.

Had he been staring? He gulped his coffee.

Pearson strode into the meeting room. He dropped his folder on the table, and planted himself in front of the diagram of the crime scene. A man whose large proportions were slowly losing the fight against gravity, his presence commanded attention. He glanced around to make sure all eyes were on him. "Okay, team, we all here? I asked Detective Riley to attend the debriefing to give us a report on the FIS findings so far."

Riley stood. She had removed her bunny suit, but her HPD t-shirt and trousers were wrinkled. He was sure Riley had been at the crime scene all night. And hadn't she come directly to the Owen house from an earlier scene? She had probably been up for at least 24 hours. No wonder she looked so tired. But her gaze was focused.

"The crime scene is still under FIS control," she began. "To enter, you must report to me first." The team nodded. "In brief, we have found blood near the bedroom on the main floor. No other locations. We have tested under the floorboards and found no spatter except in that location. The samples have been sent to the lab to determine whether it belongs to more than one person—"

Pearson held up a hand. "Sorry to interrupt, but this is a good time to get an update on the suspect. Gabriel—" he turned to the most junior member of the GIS team. Cooper had not met Constable Angie Gabriel yet, but he had heard of her. She was one of the newest members of the force, a Mi'kmaq with a Master's degree in psychology. "Have you I.D.ed her yet?"

Gabriel put down her pen. He noticed she was a leftie. "Not yet. She had no wallet or phone in her clothing. The team has not recovered a bag or anything that appears to belong to her. Her prints are clean. No one has reported a missing person."

"Has our anonymous Jane Doe recovered consciousness?" Pearson's tone was brusque. Cooper could just imagine the pressure he was under.

"Again, negative. I spoke with the ER staff. She had surgery early this morning to remove bullet fragments from her chest. She is under sedation."

"What's her status?"

"Still serious."

"Has she said anything at all?"

"Not yet."

Pearson made a note. "I want you to stay at the hospital with her. See if any next of kin arrive looking for her. If no one shows up by noon, we need to get a photo out to the media." He swung back to Riley. "Continue, Detective."

Riley held up an evidence bag. It took a moment for Cooper to realize it wasn't empty. Several pale threads glinted beneath the plastic. "We found these hair strands. It is an unusually pale blonde shade."

Gabriel peered at the bag. "It looks like Jane Doe's. She is white blonde. Like a rabbit."

Cooper remembered the pink skull that showed beneath the fine white fluff at her temples. More like a chick's down than a rabbit's.

"Where did you find them, Riley?"

"One strand was found in the sitting area on the carpet. And the other hair was caught on the window frame in the living room." Where the suspect had fallen.

"Where exactly in the sitting area was the first strand found?" Cooper asked.

Riley walked over to the crime scene diagram. "Between the television console and the computer area," she said, pointing at a spot on the diagram with her pen.

"Anything to connect the suspect to the guns in the television console?" The recent changes to the Criminal Code increased the degree of punishment for anyone breaking in with intent to steal a firearm.

Riley shook her head. "No. The fingerprints did not match. And there were no hairs there. But she was wearing gloves. And it doesn't rule out that she hadn't the intent to take them."

"Nor does it tie her to them," Cooper said.

Her gaze narrowed. "Agreed." She pushed a wisp of hair away from her face. In that moment, her fatigue was obvious. If the entire team hadn't been watching, Cooper would have offered his coffee to her. But he wasn't sure she would take it. "In fact, we can find nothing in the house that suggests what they were doing there."

"What about Mel Owen's claim that the suspect who fled had killed his wife?" Cooper said. "Was there no sign of a struggle? Or weapon?"

Riley shook her head. "The scene is consistent with Mrs. Owen dropping the phone and falling out of bed. We don't think either of the suspects had entered the bedroom. The room had no prints, fibers, hairs or bodily fluids that belonged to anyone but Mr. and Mrs. Owen, and their son, Harry." She glanced down at her notes. "One thing, though. There was a large bottle of Oxy in the room, as well as Dilaudid."

"Was any of it missing?"

"No. The pill count was consistent with the date the prescription had been filled."

"Could be a possible motive, though," Cooper said. "They knew Mrs. Owen was seriously ill, they figured they could get some drugs to sell. But Mr. Owen chased them away."

Lamond nodded, made a note. "I'll check with the pharmacy and see what was prescribed for Mrs. Owen. Maybe the first suspect got away with some meds. They could have been in the living room."

"And if you find that there are missing meds, get a street canvass in operation, Lamond," Pearson said. Then he turned back to Riley. "And what about the upstairs?"

Riley shook her head again. "It was clean. No shoe treads, prints, hairs, fibers, spatters or any evidence to suggest that the suspects went up there."

"And Harry Owen's room? What did you find in there?"

"Nothing. He's not a suspect."

"What do you mean? He shot an unarmed woman."

She glanced at Pearson. "Sergeant, you want to tell him what you told me?" Her tone was flat, but there was an edge to it, as if the wrong word could trigger a tripwire.

Cooper's phone rang. He glanced at the number and jumped out of his chair. "It's the ME." Pearson nodded. He hurried out of the war room and into the hallway. "Ellis."

"Detective, it's Dr. Guthro. How are you this fine morning?"

Cooper swallowed a smile. "Wonderful. And you, doctor?"

"Just dandy. I have completed the autopsy on the decedent Salma Owen."

"And…" Cooper sipped his coffee. After Riley's debriefing, he doubted very much that she had died at the hands of the suspects.

"She suffered a myocardial infarct. It was very fast. Given the advanced stage of her lung cancer, she had little chance of survival."

"Was there any sign of struggle? Choking? Battery?"

"No, detective. There were no self-defense wounds. Her petechiae were normal. She had a contusion on one hip as well as her shoulder, but these are entirely consistent with the decedent falling out of bed." He paused. "There was a large tumor pushing into her right ventricle. The opioids in her system would have decreased her respiratory rate. She was actively dying."

"Actively dying?"

"Yes, she was palliative. In the final phase of disease. Her body was shutting down."

"I see. Thank you for calling." Cooper glanced at his watch. "And for calling so promptly."

"I started early today. I knew you were on a schedule."

"Thank you, Dr. Guthro. You go above and beyond."

"In more ways than one," he said, his tone amused. "Good day, Detective."

Cooper strode into the war room. Pearson stood at the crime scene diagram, pointing at a line marked on the property. "This is the probable path of the suspects' entry to the house—" he broke off when he saw Cooper. "What were the autopsy results?"

"Natural causes," Cooper said. "Mrs. Owen was very ill and had a heart attack."

Riley nodded. "Consistent with our findings."

Lamond bit into a bagel. "So Homicide is off the case, then."

"That will make this morning's interview of the two Mr. Owens very interesting," Cooper said. "Riley, you said that there were other weapons in the house. Are they all accounted for?"

"From what we can tell."

"When do you think you will be done processing the scene?"

Riley scanned her notes. "We should have the interior finished today."

"Okay, we will arrange to bring the Owens to the house tomorrow to conduct an inventory to see if anything else was taken."

"I will still be with the team working on the property. I'll make sure there is a dedicated path for them to access the house."

"Thanks. And it needs to include the wheelchair ramp. Mr. Owen is a paraplegic."

"Will do." Riley closed her notepad and began to rise from her chair.

"Just a sec. What're we doing about Harry Owen's bedroom?"

The Staff Sergeant threw Riley a look, and then said to Cooper, "Nothing."

Cooper straightened. "But he shot the accused. What if he knows her?"

Pearson's glance became impatient. "Even if he did, Harry Owen is a victim. Not a suspect. The intruder turned and confronted the father. Harry Owen believed she could have taken the gun from his father's hand."

Riley pushed back her chair, her face closed. "If you need to reach me, I will be at the site all day."

He had no doubt that Detective Riley would not go home until every blade of grass had been examined.

16

THE ICU UNIT REMINDED Detective Constable Angie Gabriel of a beehive, people with focused energy hovering in the rooms, monitoring vitals, adjusting meds. She watched the activity through the glass door of Jane Doe's room. The surgical team, headed by Dr. Rita Kapur, had just arrived, flanked by a group of residents. Everyone wanted to see Jane Doe.

Angie sipped her coffee, observing the family and friends who walked by, voices low, huddled together. It was interesting to watch what this foreign, sterile environment did to people. So far, none of these anxious family members belonged to the young woman with the distinctive white-blond hair.

Twenty minutes later, Dr. Kapur strode out of Jane Doe's room, her pager beeping. Angie sprang to her feet, blocking the surgeon's path. "Dr. Kapur, may I speak with you?"

Medium height, fiftyish, salt-and-pepper hair, Dr. Kapur radiated suppressed energy beneath a mask of calm. She glanced at her pager number, frowned, and looked up at Angie. "Will you be quick? I have an urgent call."

"Yes. I am Detective Gabriel, Halifax Police Department." She opened her badge. The surgeon's eyes flickered over it and then returned to Angie's face. "We are investigating the incident that resulted in the suspect's injuries."

That caught Dr. Kapur's attention. "What exactly did she do?"

"Break and enter. She was shot when she confronted the owner."

"By the police?" The surgeon frowned.

"No." Puzzlement flashed through Dr. Kapur's eyes. Not too many ordinary folk owned handguns in Halifax. "We need to know when she will be able to answer our questions."

"She is sedated at present. I expect the sedation will wear off in the next few hours. But she is on narcotics. I am not sure how well she will be able to respond to an interrogation."

"It's not an interrogation, Dr. Kapur—"

Dr. Kapur's pager beeped again. "Is she a danger to my staff?"

"Not as far as we are aware. We have two officers on guard."

The pager beeped. "I'm sorry, Detective. I must go."

Angie ignored the impatience in the surgeon's gaze. "When the suspect's family identify her, we need to be informed immediately. She may be visited by an accomplice, so we will have two members of the force stationed outside her room at all times. If her health status changes, we need to be informed. And, if she communicates in any way, verbal or physical, we need to know that, too. Please make sure this is written on her chart—" Dr. Kapur's pager beeped and she moved as if she was about to dart around Angie.

Angie shifted her weight so that Dr. Kapur could not leave before she was finished. "And do not share any information at all about Jane Doe with the media. The police will be providing updates. She is currently a suspect in a major crime."

"And a major news story," Dr. Kapur added. "We have already banned the media from this floor. They were way ahead of you, Detective. Now, I must go." She pivoted in a neat 180 and hurried away from Angie, checking her pager as she went.

Angie gazed at Jane Doe's inert form lying behind the glass window. The sheets were tucked neatly around the woman's upper body. Her upper torso and shoulder were heavily bandaged, presumably from the wound in her chest. Various drips and tubes were hooked up to her wrist, chest, and throat. With her translucent skin, white blond hair, and white bandages, she resembled a ghost.

Ghost in the machine. For surely it was a machine that was keeping this ghost woman's body going right now.

From the corner of her eye, Angie saw a woman in her fifties bolt out of the elevator and rush toward the nursing station. A man hurried behind her. "We are looking for our daughter. We were told she could be here." The woman's voice trembled as she glanced back at her husband. Wind— or anxious fingers—had caused his white-blond hair to stand in soft tufts on his head.

Bingo.

Jane Doe's family had just arrived.

"We have a patient who was carrying no identification," the nurse said. "Can you provide any details about your daughter?"

"She is six feet tall, weighs about one-seventy, hair the same color as mine," the man said, his voice staccato with urgency. "Is she here?"

"Yes."

Anxiety radiated from the two parents. The nurse gave them a reassuring smile, and asked, "Do you have any I.D.?"

The man pulled out his wallet and showed his driver's license. The nurse glanced at it, and said, "Mr. Roberts, what is your daughter's name?"

"Leah," her mother said. "Leah Roberts."

The nurse handed Mr. Roberts' driver's license back to him. "We will need her health card number and photo I.D. as soon as possible."

"Can we see her?" Mr. Roberts asked. "Will she be okay? The news reports said she was in critical condition."

The nurse rose and walked around the desk. "She is down the hall. I will take you to her room, and then I will page Dr. Kapur, her attending surgeon." The nurse strode toward Leah Roberts' room, the parents on her heels.

Angie hovered outside the glass window, watching Leah Roberts' parents huddle around the bed. She slid her phone from her pocket and dialed Cooper Ellis' number.

"Detective Ellis."

"Cooper, it's Angie. I just got an I.D. on Jane Doe."

"Let me grab a pen." He returned to the phone within seconds. "What's her name?"

"Leah Roberts. Her parents are with her right now."

"Is she conscious?"

Angie watched Leah's father lift the ghost woman's translucent hand and press it against his cheek.

"No. And I spoke to her surgeon. She is still sedated but they hope she will recover consciousness within a few hours."

"I'll run a check on her."

Through the glass window, Leah Robert's mother touched her daughter's darkened eyebrows.

In Angie's experience, three-quarters of the suspects of a crime had relatives who knew something was 'up' with their loved one.

But the other twenty-five per cent wore the exact same expression as Leah Roberts' parents: disbelief.

And a sense of impending doom.

"I'm going to talk to the parents."

17

THE SOUTH FLORIDA SUN poured through the window. Matt half-rose from his desk, and yanked the cord of the blind. The plastic edge bounced against the windowsill, the clatter breaking the stillness of the ripe, humid morning.

He sank back into his chair.

No message yet from WeepingGelsan. The hacktivist was relatively new to the Forum, and clearly a Dr. Who fan. Matt had immediately recognized that the two symbols of the word 'Angels' had been reversed to create 'Gelsan'. The Weeping Angels were one of the Doctor's more terrifying adversaries. They would strike when you blinked.

This particular Dr. Who fan seemed young, maybe in high school. He would not have been Matt's first choice to confide his concerns about Leah. But based on Weeping Gelsan's IP address, he lived in Halifax. And Matt needed to know what the hell was going on there. CNN had reported that a Canadian politician had gunned down an intruder in his parents' Halifax house. The politician could only be Harry Owen.

And he knew that Aggroboy hadn't been shot, because he'd already been bragging about the exploit on the Forum.

Matt jumped to his feet and began to pace around the

room. Why had AggroBoy lied about Leah's whereabouts?

Was she dead?

His phone buzzed. He snatched it from the desk. Relief rushed through him when he read the private message: *condor this is weepinggelsan*

He immediately typed: *What happened to Leah? Is she okay?*

she was shot in the chest

Fear made his usually quick fingers stumble over the letters as he typed: *How bad is it?*

He held his breath as he watched the gray text bubbles on his screen. They were little nuclear clouds of doom.

doctors say pretty bad. she's lucky to be alive

He frowned. *How do you know what the doctors said?*

i'm her brother joey

Of course.

It made perfect sense. He remembered that Leah had a kid brother. But he had never met him.

Matt texted: *Call me now.*

Within seconds, the phone rang. He sprang to his feet. "Condor." He didn't want to reveal his identity to Leah's brother yet. Just in case the police had set him up to this.

"It's Joey." From the break in his voice, it sounded like this kid was definitely still in school.

"Tell me what's going on down there."

"It's crazy. There are reporters and police everywhere."

"What about Leah? How bad is it?"

"She had surgery right away. They said she almost died." Joey's voice faltered.

Matt's grip on the phone tightened as if it was Leah's hand and he would never let go. "Has she said anything to you?"

"She isn't conscious yet."

Were Joey's parents trying to protect him from the truth? Was she in a coma? He needed to see her.

He cleared his throat. "Did she speak to the police before her surgery?"

Joey's voice lowered. "I don't think so. But they are guarding her room."

"Okay." Matt circled the room, trying to collect his thoughts. "Have they found AggroBoy?"

"I don't think so. They don't even know who he is. They were trying to find out his name from Leah before her surgery but she had a tube stuck in her throat."

Matt's thoughts jumped on top of one another. *Slow down.* He needed to think this through. "Did they find anything on her?"

"I don't know."

"Do you know where her laptop is?"

"She usually keeps it in her bedroom."

"Go get it."

Joey paused. "What do I do with it when I find it?"

"Hide it until I get there."

"You're coming to Halifax?" The kid's voice broke.

"Yes. This is a mess. And if the cops get hold of Leah's computer, the Forum could go down."

What he couldn't tell Joey was that he could not bear to think of Leah lying unconscious and near dead in that hospital bed, while he was thousands of miles away.

"Okay." Joey sounded scared. "What if the cops catch me?"

Matt stopped in front of the picture window. Out in the distance, a massive container ship slid past the horizon.

He needed to inspire confidence in the kid. "They won't catch you. Go now, before they execute a search warrant on Leah's apartment. And cover your head."

"Fuck, fuck, fuck," Joey said, his voice cracking. "I don't know if—"

"Joey, listen to me. We are all in this together. You will be charged with conspiracy if the cops get hold of Leah's computer. You need to get it before they do."

"I'll be charged as an accessory if they catch me."

The kid was smarter than Matt realized. He hated to do it, but it was time to twist the emotions.

"If you find her laptop and hide it, Leah will be safe. They won't know why she was in that house. But if they find her machine, the game's up."

"Fuck," Joey said again. "Okay, I'm going in."

"I'll be in Halifax tonight. Where should I meet you?"

"The library. Everyone brings laptops. No one will notice us."

Once again, the kid's smarts impressed Matt. "How about the astronomy stacks?"

"How did you know that it's Leah's fav—oh, right. *WhiteDwarf.*" A White Dwarf was a star that had expelled its outer layer, so that only the hot core remained. Almost 97% of the stars in the Milky Way eventually become White Dwarves. And of those, some become supernovas.

Leah had always viewed herself as a White Dwarf, but Matt had known from the moment he met her that she was a supernova.

"Got it," Matt said, with a twinge in his heart.

18

JOEY YANKED HIS HOOD over his head, and slouched a little deeper. He fished around in his pocket. Leah had given him a spare apartment key so he could feed the cat when she and Maddie were out of town.

He rounded the corner of her quiet, residential street. Leah's place was in a converted Victorian three-story house, the brown wood shingles faded and chipped. It was a step up from the student-only buildings right by the university campus, but not by much. Leah liked it because the rent was inexpensive, and Maddie could afford it while she attended med school. They had met in a science lab five years ago, and had been roommates off and on for the past several years. Maddie had just broken up with her boyfriend, so she moved back in with Leah for the year.

Joey sprinted up the porch stairs, and unlocked the front door. Mike, one of the grad students who lived below Leah, hurried down the stairs, fastening his bike helmet with one hand. "Hey, Joey," he called as he ran past him.

"Hey, Mike," Joey replied, trying to sound normal through the hammering of his heart.

As soon as Mike left, Joey took the stairs two at a time. He didn't want to encounter any more of Leah's neighbors.

The fewer people who saw him, the better.

Was Maddie still at home? It was a Friday morning. Did she have classes? His mind raced. He'd tell her that he needed the spare gaming console that Leah had in her closet.

His breathing restored, he knocked softly on Leah's apartment door.

No answer.

He quickly unlocked the door and slipped into the apartment.

"Hello?" he called. "Maddie?"

No answer. Judging by the empty lasagna tray by the sink, and the scarf that had been discarded by the door, he guessed that Maddie had been in a hurry when she left.

A black cat ran over to him and wound itself around his legs. "Hey, Spook," he said, scratching the cat's ears. It meowed in response.

He eyed the cat's bowl. Had Maddie remembered to feed him?

He doubted it.

He opened the fridge door and pulled out a half-empty can of food. Spook sat by the counter, tail twitching, as he dumped the remainder of the tin into the cat's bowl. "Here you go," Joey said. Out of habit, he rinsed the can and threw it into the recycling bin behind the pantry door.

Then he froze.

He heard footsteps. On the stairwell outside Leah's apartment. Was that the cops? If they found him in Leah's apartment...

The front door slammed. It was just another tenant. "Phew."

He hurried into Leah's bedroom. The blinds were still drawn, blocking the morning light. He flipped on the switch and looked around. The sight of Leah's bed—empty and unslept-in—and her old toy elephant stuffed behind a pillow, made tears prick behind his eyes. *Leah. What did you do?*

He knew why she did it. She didn't know that he knew. She had no idea he'd been creeping her hacktivist forum.

He'd discovered her secret a few months ago, when she'd left her laptop open and gone to answer the front door. A message scrolled across the top of her screen. Then another, and another. A group of hacktivists with screen names like Condor, PillBaby and MotherDoxxer were chatting idly about SQL, the software language that was used in data management systems. MotherDoxxer described in great detail the most recent successful doxxes posted on an online site called Pastebin. It was a well-known site favored by hacktivists because they could post online the text of the documents they had hacked.

It didn't take a rocket scientist to figure out these guys were all hacktivists. And that they were finding weak spots in the SQL data management programming software, and then creating hacks to illegally access files. Once they pasted the hacked documents on Pastebin, it was easy to tell the media where to find them.

When he realized that Leah was secretly a hacktivist, he joined the Forum as WeepingGelsan. He wasn't allowed to access the more exclusive chat rooms within the Forum, where the higher-up hacktivists plotted their exploits, but he pieced together enough information to know that Leah knew a secret about someone. One that outraged the Forum. And they wanted her to doxx the guy who was screwing around with so many people.

Joey knew that the exploit was going to be executed sometime soon, but he hadn't realized it had taken place last night until Maddie texted him this morning. She wondered if Leah had spent the night at the family home, because she hadn't returned to her apartment. Joey had begun to shake.

He told her that he thought Leah had stayed at work.

But he knew it had to do with the Forum.

When his parents had discovered that Leah was in the hospital, he'd still been in bed, luxuriating in his summer vacation. He almost puked from shock when his father told him that Leah—the older sister who had always been a model student—had broken into the house of a politician's parents and had been shot in the chest. What the hell?

Why would Leah do something that crazy?

And then Condor had sent him a message. The message that he knew could land him in a huge amount of trouble.

But what else could he do?

Leah was his sister.

He would do anything to protect her.

So he had agreed to Condor's plan. Even though in his heart of hearts, he knew it was almost as crazy as what his sister had been accused of doing.

And here he was. In Leah's bedroom. About to become an accessory to a crime committed by the girl who had always protected him.

His gaze fell on the bed with the old faded star quilt that Leah had had since she was a baby. How prescient their grandma had been, to make Leah a star quilt.

The astronomy posters on her wall.

The photo of him and her, arms around each other, grinning at the camera as Leah held out the starfish they had found on a beach in Prince Edward Island. Her white-blond hair, streaked with mud. He remembered after the photo was taken how she had waded out to the rocks, crouched down into the water, and carefully released the creature into a tide pool.

This couldn't be happening.

His sister was not a criminal.

She was good.

She was kind.

And now she was almost dead.

The drive in her laptop began to whir.

He strode over to her desk and flipped up the screen. Commands scrolled down the screen.

It was a data dump.

From someone else's computer.

"Holy crap," Joey murmured.

Leah's hack had worked.

Whatever she had done last night, she had succeeded in finding a vulnerability in the guy's computer, and the entire contents of his laptop had downloaded onto Leah's. She had obviously set up a timed data sequence to conduct the exploit. Had she guessed she might not be able to do it herself? Did she have a sense that this whole stupid break-in would go so terribly wrong?

Spook ran into the room and wound his body around Joey's legs. He quickly shut down Leah's computer and stuffed it into his backpack.

"Gotta run now, Spook," he said as he hurried from Leah's room.

Whatever Leah had done, she had done it because she believed it was the right thing to do.

That was good enough for him.

Spook jumped onto the back of the sofa. The cat began to groom his whiskers as Joey opened the door to the landing and checked to see if anyone was about.

He was glad he had fed the cat.

It might be a while before he could return to the apartment.

"Be good, Spook," he said, his throat tightening. "And catch some rats while I'm gone."

The cat's green eyes blinked at him.

19

IT HAD ONLY TAKEN a few minutes to resign, but it had taken most of the morning to clear any trace of Kate's presence at McGrath Woods.

A stack of document boxes sat on the floor by her credenza. She had slowly filled them while a steady stream of colleagues dropped by her office. The news had spread of her resignation. Some of her colleagues were bemused, some skeptical, a few genuinely sad to see her go. One openly hinted that she had suffered a nervous breakdown when he had learned that Kate planned to do criminal defense work.

Kate pasted a pleasant smile on her face, and accepted the well wishes. What else could she do? She was not the same person as when she began her career with something to prove and everything to lose. She had had a string of personal failures to her name when she was hired by then-Lyons McGrath Barrett. She had believed that success would be her ticket to happiness. That the stunning corner office occupied by John Lyons—and his successor Nina Woods—was the ultimate destination.

For some, maybe.

But not for her.

She picked up the battered silver clock that had followed

her everywhere since she was twelve. It ticked a steady beat against her hand. She set it next to a stack of folders. *Time for a new chapter.*

The photo of Alaska was the only item left on her bookcase. She remembered how she had placed it close to her desk after she had started her job. He had been an unexpected addition, a dog that had been orphaned when the previous owner of the house had died. She had had no idea how much love she had let into her life when she opened the door to the stray. And it had introduced her to Finn—one of her closest friends.

You see, Kate. It paid to take the chance.

A soft knock on the half-closed door made her glance up.

The gaze that met hers was the one she'd been waiting for all morning. In fact, it was one she had been waiting for the past ten months.

Randall Barrett. Former managing partner of McGrath Woods, former husband of the beautiful, unfaithful Elise Vanderzell, former accused in the murder of his ex-wife, former power broker who almost had her fired from her job just three months after she began.

Former almost-lover.

Randall's eyes were just as intense as she remembered. But there was a new expression added to the mix.

Wariness.

He waited in the doorway. "Can I come in?" Formal, polite, one colleague to another.

She placed the photo of Alaska in the box. "Yes. Of course."

He strode toward her, stopping by the chair. A safe distance.

But for whom?

His eyes—piercing, blue—searched her face. Drew her in.

She had forgotten what it was like to be in the same room with Randall. She had forgotten the effect his physical presence had on her. She was a mere electron in the magnetic field of his presence. Her heart raced. Her body flushed. Her nerves were pitched to an edge that teetered between pain and pleasure.

It was both thrilling and scary. A rollercoaster.

She had never liked rollercoasters.

She took a step back.

His gaze flickered at her withdrawal. "I heard from Nina that you resigned. Is that true?" There was a different question in his eyes. *Why didn't you tell me?*

"It only just happened."

"Why are you leaving?" She knew he wondered if it was because of them. Or, to be accurate, 'almost them.' Or, to be even more accurate, because things had been rapidly deteriorating between them since Kenzie Sloane had returned in her life.

Both of them had sensed it. Both of them had tried to stop the unraveling. In fact, the phone calls had become more frequent after John McNally stalked her. But the more Randall tried to reach her, the less Kate wanted to talk. Speaking about what happened was too difficult. She wanted to bury it and move forward with her life. Laugh, eat good food, go for a rejuvenating run, and have someone hold her close when the nightmares struck.

Not stumble through another phone call that only served to prove how widely their paths had diverged.

Texting didn't work, either. They could never communicate what they wanted to say. Both she and Randall were lawyers, after all. They both hated committing themselves to anything that left a digital footprint.

It was an occupational hazard when it came to matters of the heart.

Now, up close, she saw the deep lines around his mouth, the silver threaded through his dark blond hair, the shadows under his eyes. And in his eyes.

She wondered what changes he saw in her. Did he see a woman who had been pushed to her limits physically and emotionally one time too many?

"Did you know that I was being moved to the family law practice?" she asked.

The muscle by his eye twitched.

"Yes."

Silence didn't just fall between them.

It crash landed.

Kate's finger traced the edge of the frame holding Alaska's photo. "Why didn't you warn me?"

"The decision was made by the partners while you were away, Kate. You had a no-contact policy in place while you were in Italy, remember?"

She raised a brow. "What was your vote?"

"Kate, I can't tell you that. All partner votes are confidential."

She held his gaze. "I need to know, Randall."

Hurt, anger, pain flashed across his face. "I voted against it. But I have no sway here. This is Nina's firm now." He stepped toward her. "Is that why you are leaving?"

"Yes." Then she shook her head. "No. There are a lot of reasons."

"Is one of those reasons because you decided to take Eddie up on his offer to become his partner?" Randall knew that Eddie had made the offer a year ago, after Eddie had mentored Kate through her defense of Randall's criminal charge.

"Yes."

"I spoke to Eddie. You had made the decision before Nina broke the partners' decision to you."

"Nina gave me the heads up before I left for Italy that I was unpopular with clients. It doesn't take a rocket scientist to figure out that I should consider my options."

"The family practice move would only be temporary. It's just to give the firm some breathing room. The media has been relentless." He rubbed a hand over his jaw. "I shouldn't say anything, but the firm is struggling. We lost three big retainers in the past month, and never regained our footing after John Lyons threw us under the bus."

We. Was this McGrath Woods vs. Kate, Round Two?

"If the firm is trying to keep a low media profile, why did I see Harry Owen in the lobby? He asked for you."

Randall thrust his hands into his trouser pockets. "Harry was involved in an incident last night. He called me."

"What did he do? Get caught with a Cabinet minister's spouse?" Harry Owen was renowned as a ladies' man.

"He shot someone last night, Kate."

Kate thought of the smooth, confident Member of Parliament who had listened to her plea for empathy for Frances Sloane with little of his own. "Where? Why?"

"At his parents' home. He shot an intruder. With his father's unregistered, prohibited firearm."

Kate raised a brow. "But why is he coming to you? You don't do criminal defense."

"I'm deflecting for him. After the screw-up by his publicist this morning, it's obvious he needs someone to speak on his behalf." Randall gave a wry smile. "Having been through the media gauntlet myself in the not-too-distant past, I think I can help him. And I thought this case would be perfect for you to join as second chair."

Had jet lag made her brain stop functioning? She was having a hard time following this conversation. "You've lost me. First you tell me that the firm can't handle any more negative publicity, but you take on a client who is going to have international media coverage for shooting someone with a prohibited gun. And then you tell me that I'm going to be moved to family law but—"

"—This is most definitely not a family law case," Randall finished for her, with a small smile.

"So what gives?"

"First of all, Harry Owen is a popular Member of Parliament—except with you," Randall added, "—who will receive a considerable amount of sympathetic press coverage. He did shoot someone, but it was in self-defense. His father was being robbed."

"Again?" Despite Kate's aversion to Harry Owen, she

was horrified that his father had been victimized for a second time.

"Yes. It was a terrible situation. His mother died during the break-in attempt."

"She was murdered?" This was getting more awful by the minute.

Randall's gaze narrowed. "We aren't sure. The ME is doing the autopsy. She was very ill."

"Regardless, what a terrible way to die."

And judging by her horrified reaction, it was a wonderful case for McGrath Woods. The Honorable Harry Owen would be a sympathetic figure. And the firm would have its name associated with him, time and time again.

"It has been heart wrenching for Harry Owen."

"It's his father that I feel the most sympathy for. Regardless, why would you want me involved in this?" And then her stomach tightened. "Did you think adding me to the case would up the sympathy quotient? A crime victim defends another crime victim who was driven to killing his attacker, just like she was?" She raised a brow when she saw the confirmation in Randall's eyes. "Why does Harry need that? Isn't being a victim of a break-in enough to make the public sympathetic?" Her mind worked through the implications. There was only one reason that Randall would want to stack the defense team with someone with her kind of warped public profile. "He shot someone who shouldn't have been shot, right? The suspect was unarmed, I bet."

Randall gave her a steady look. "Until you are on the case, I can't comment, Kate."

"Touché. But I'm surprised Nina Woods would let you touch this. It definitely changes the complexion of the case."

"Nina Woods does not have sole control over our client list, Kate."

"And I'm surprised you would use me like that, Randall." She said the words as softly as she could, but he jerked back as if she had struck him with them.

"I thought it would help you, Kate."

"Help me!"

"Defending Harry Owen would make you a media darling."

"I thought the firm was tired of media darlings."

"No, they are just tired of media darlings who are associated with the wrong type of clients. Serial killers, violent ex-cons."

"Not handsome MPs."

"Exactly."

"He could be worse than a serial killer, Randall." She could not disguise the edge to her tone. And she did not want to. She was tired of the attitude in the firm. And she was becoming concerned that Randall was falling all too readily back into the firm mentality. Eddie had said Randall would have her back.

Eddie was wrong.

Randall's gaze narrowed. "Do you really believe that?"

"No." She shrugged. "But I don't trust him."

"I'm not sure I do, either. But right now he needs someone to help him." Randall's voice lowered. "I remember only too well what it felt like to have my colleagues and friends abandon me. I need to give him the benefit of the doubt. Just like you gave me the benefit of the doubt." His eyes became tender.

And it hit Kate right in the place she wanted nothing more than to ignore.

The heart has a mind of its own.

Randall stepped closer to her. "Do you believe that I would use you?"

Not anymore. "No."

His gaze held hers. "Do you trust me?"

What a loaded question.

And it obviously took her a fraction too long to respond.

A vein throbbed in Randall's neck. "We need to talk, Kate. You seem angry with me. Is that why you're leaving?"

"I'm not angry with you. And that's not why I'm leaving."

"You took longer and longer to return my calls. And then you went radio silent for a month. How do you think that made me feel?"

"I'm sorry. I just needed time."

"Time for what? You're supposed to talk to me, Kate. That's what people who lo—"

He stopped. Then he said, "You don't know how much it killed me when I heard about what happened with Kenzie Sloane and McNally. I wanted to be there for you. With you. But I couldn't just leave my kids."

"I know. I understood that—I *understand* that. I am not trying to punish you. But when all that stuff happened...I was scared." Tears stung her eyes. She willed them to go away. She would *not* cry in her office. "And you weren't there."

"But Ethan was." His eyes bore into hers as if he could divine the state of her heart by uttering her ex-fiancée's name.

Kate swallowed. "Yes." What had happened with Kenzie Sloane had given her more insight into Ethan's own struggles as a police detective than anything that had happened before. He had cared for her. And he had been there when she needed someone the most.

"Is that why you stopped calling me?"

"No." But it was hopeless. She could not look into Randall's eyes and not tell the truth. "Yes."

The muscles around his eyes twitched.

"But not for the reason you think. Ethan and I are not back together." She had turned him down as gently as she could. "Just before I left for Italy, he sent me an email..."

An email. It was so impersonal, and yet, she knew why he chose to tell her that way. Too much had already been said.

She had wept when she read it.

But it was the tears of release. Of a love that had been built on a deception, and not grounded enough in who they each were. And where they were going.

When they finally understood the other, too much had changed.

Kate stared at the man standing before her. If she was honest—and God knows, she'd been trying to avoid that painful truth for months—he was one of the reasons why Ethan had not been able to convince her to give them one more chance.

"So if you aren't back together with Ethan, then why are you leaving?"

Her fingers gripped the edge of Alaska's photo. She remembered how Marian MacAdam had stared at the picture of her dog's face. How Kate had wondered if her client had lied to her.

Her entire experience at McGrath Woods seemed based on lies.

But the biggest lie was the one she had told herself. "I have to." She swallowed. "You know, I've been through a lot because of McGrath Woods. I could be carrying a fatal disease in my cells. I suffer from nightmares almost every night. And I bear the guilt of not helping Marian MacAdam. But, I've never blamed the firm—I have always blamed myself. And I even let the firm use what happened with the Body Butcher to help rebuild their image. I did it because I was ambitious." Kate shook her head. "I feel used by the firm, Randall. But I also feel kind of dirty. Like I slept with someone to get ahead. And out of this whole crappy situation, I'm most disappointed in myself."

"Kate." Randall's tone was firm. "You've never compromised your principles to further your own agenda."

"Maybe not. But I didn't take a stand against the firm when they used me to promote their new brand after the John Lyons scandal. I could have said 'no'. But my ego was stroked. And I hoped it would give me some leverage with the partners. Instead, they've used my image when it suited their purposes. And they've discarded me when it hasn't. I'm now viewed as a liability." A rock had lodged in her throat. It was called truth. Why hadn't she seen this before?

"Why don't you think this over? You've been through so much. We don't want to lose you."

"I don't know about the 'we', Randall." Her tone was dry. "You are the only person who has tried to convince me to stay."

"I don't want to lose you." His voice was soft. But the words echoed in her ears.

And they scared her. He scared her.

She knew he wanted her.

And she knew she had wanted him.

Still wanted him.

But their desire for each other had sprung from a circumstance fraught with pain, loss, peril. It had forced them through tremendous lows and highs.

It had been a rollercoaster.

And she hated rollercoasters. The thrill was over before you could catch your breath.

"You haven't lost me." She kept her tone light. "I'm going to be a few blocks away at Eddie's office."

"Kate, you know I want to support whatever decision you make—"

But. She knew it was coming.

"—But have you really thought this through? What it would be like to mount a defense of people accused of terrible crimes? Are you really up for that?"

She took a deep breath. "I can't do this anymore—" she gestured to her now-empty desk "—and not have it mean something. I don't know why I ended up going through everything I did, but it changed me, Randall. In ways that I can't explain."

"I understand, Kate. Believe me, I've been changed, too."

She did believe it.

She just was afraid that they both had changed so much that there was nothing to keep them together.

Except sexual attraction.

And as tempting as that was—she inhaled the crisp cotton of Randall's shirt—it had ended disastrously for her and Ethan.

Her heart wasn't prepared to go through that again.

She pulled her attention back to his question. His concern touched her. He was afraid for her.

Even after she had tried to push him away.

"Everything that has happened to me at McGrath Woods has had one overriding theme: the need for justice for those who have been victims. I want to help people who have been harmed, Randall. I want to protect people so it won't happen again."

He exhaled. "So tell me again why you are joining Eddie's practice if you want to help victims?"

"I met with John Hillcroft this morning. He told me to get some criminal defense experience so that when a job becomes available, I'm in the running."

"But you could do that here."

"Not in the family practice."

The narrowing of his eyes acknowledged the truth of what she said.

"And Eddie offered me a partnership. It would take at least another five years to make partner here. And I can't trust any of them. They haven't had my back, and they haven't had yours." She threw him a challenging look. "Why are you staying with them?"

His lips twisted. "I can't afford to leave. Two kids, a mortgage and all that. I was almost bankrupted after the criminal charges. I even leased my yacht to a company in the Caribbean to cover the bills while I was away. Fortunately, the billables from the merger in Manhattan helped my short-term situation. If I switched firms, I'd have to buy in to a new partnership. And the partners at McGrath Woods sweetened the pot. They're hoping that my contacts in Manhattan will open up some new markets for them." He shrugged. "Also, they knew that I could have stayed with the firm in Manhattan if I'd wanted. But I wanted to bring the kids back here."

That was news to her. It hurt that Randall hadn't told her he'd been offered a permanent position in Manhattan. But then again, she hadn't given him the chance.

"Hillcroft didn't suggest I partner with Eddie. In fact, he warned me against it. Do you know why?" Eddie and Randall were very old friends.

Randall frowned. "No. I don't."

"Did you see him while I was away in Italy?"

"Yes, of course. He stayed with me for a week after the kids and I returned from New York. And then Nick and I helped him move into his new place."

"How was he?"

"He seemed fine." But they both knew that Eddie would always put a good-natured smile on the situation. The question was whether he would drown his sorrows later.

"I guess I'll know soon enough. I'm having dinner with him tonight."

Randall took a step toward her. And just like that, the air held its breath. "What about tomorrow night? My boat was sailed back last week and is tied up at the waterfront right now. We could have dinner at the Bicycle Thief and then go for a cruise on the harbor."

This was the moment. The rollercoaster was sitting, idle on the track. Waiting for her to jump onboard.

She knew if she turned it away, it would find another track.

She had never liked rollercoasters.

Ever.

She swallowed. "It sounds lovely, Randall. But I have to take a rain check."

Hurt darkened his eyes. "You have my number."

The rollercoaster sped away from the platform, leaving her standing by an empty desk.

20

SWEAT SEEPED INTO THE fine cotton of Harry's shirt. Even the strongest deodorant couldn't protect him from the shock of what Detective Cooper Ellis had just revealed.

Leah Roberts?

Jesus Christ.

Why the hell had she broken into his parents' house?

He tried to keep his expression neutral. "No, I don't know who she is," he said, his heart hammering at his lie. Detective Ellis had hit 'record' from the minute that Harry's and Mel's rights had been read to them. Everything he said would be on tape. And everything could be held against him. Time to change the subject. "Do you know who the other guy was?"

Harry noticed the look that Detective Ellis shot him. This guy was built like a linebacker, with a broken nose to suggest he might have once been a linebacker, but he was no fool. He had picked up Harry's reaction to his revelation.

Shrewd brown eyes surveyed him across the table. "No."

"She hasn't told you?"

"She is still unconscious, Mr. Owen."

The trigger was a smooth, hard, cold curve around his finger. Rage and fear surged from the very deepest part of his being. No. Fucking. Way. Not going to be a victim again. His finger yanked on the trigger.

109

The intruder staggered back as the bullet hit her leg. Her eyes—now, it was so obvious that she was a she—widened in shock. Fear.

Remorse.

She sank to the ground, strangely graceful.

Her eyes begged his.

Not for mercy.

But for forgiveness.

He closed his eyes.

And pulled the trigger again.

He glanced at his father. His father glared at the detective. Harry had instructed him to say nothing. "I mean *nothing*, Dad. Leave it to me." And Harry had entered the interview room knowing that his political career hinged on what he disclosed to the inscrutable detective sitting opposite him.

"Why do you think Leah Roberts was in your house last night, Mr. Owen?" The question was directed to Mel.

Harry shifted ever so slightly.

His father threw him a glance. "I don't know."

"Do you know her?" The detective slid the photograph of Leah Roberts toward Mel. The photo showed a young woman, with striking white blond hair and fair skin, holding a black cat to her face. It gazed at the camera lens with an expression of contentment.

Mel stared at Leah's photo. "This is the woman who killed my wife." He pushed the photo away. "No. I don't know her." Then he muttered, "But I'll never forgive her."

The detective pivoted the photo toward Harry. "How about you, Mr. Owen? Are you sure you don't recognize her?"

Harry pretended to search his memory. His only interaction with Leah Roberts was fresh in his mind.

"Mr. Owen," she said, her voice hesitant. "I've been asked to get your passwords."

He glanced up from his desk. The woman wore a navy suit, and a pale pink blouse. She was attractive in a Viking kind of way. Then he remembered: she was one of the cyber geeks hired by the Prime Minister to ensure the "integrity" of the data after they had discovered that their data had been hacked—months before. They needed to make sure it didn't happen again.

The decision had come from Cabinet to keep the breach secret. It would only raise alarm and encourage more hackers to exploit the system before it could be fixed.

But Harry knew the real reason. The government, plagued by scandals, couldn't afford to admit that it had allowed its citizens' identities to be stolen. Especially not in an election year.

So KryptoCyber was brought on board to patch the leaky ship.

"Oh, yes, I was expecting you," he had said, adding "Ms. Cyber Viking" silently. "Do you need my laptop?"

She shook her head. "Not right now. I just need your passwords."

And so, dutiful public servant that he was, he had given them to her.

Except the one that his boss had directed that no one reveal.

And one that he would never reveal for personal reasons.

If Leah Roberts had hacked into either of those secret email accounts, his career could be over. And he couldn't tell the police. They would seize the accounts to investigate Leah.

"No. I have no idea who she is." He threw the detective a challenging look. "Does she have a criminal record?"

Detective Ellis shook his head. "No. And this is where it gets troubling. She works for an information security firm. One that was hired by the government to review all the information technology systems. Including yours." He pushed the photo closer to Harry.

Harry had to force himself not to look away. But all he could do was remember the pleading in Leah's eyes when he pulled the trigger.

"Are you sure you don't know her? Maybe you asked her out on a date?"

Is that what the police were thinking? That he screwed this girl? He almost laughed at the ludicrousness of the question. "No. Why do you think that?"

The detective shrugged. "It's just one of the avenues we need to cross off our list. You're a well-known Member of

Parliament, Mr. Owen. One who has many female admirers. We know that Ms. Roberts had done work in your department. Do you think she might have fostered feelings for you that you didn't share?"

Mel twisted in his seat and looked at his son. Harry could read it in his father's eyes: did your philandering ways bring this woman into our lives and cause your mother's death?

Harry pushed back his chair. Sweat ran down his sides. "Look, I have no idea what this woman was thinking. I'm not responsible for whatever reasons she may have had for breaking into my parents' house. And I resent this line of questioning."

"I'm sorry, Mr. Owen." The detective's eyes were sympathetic. "We are merely trying to figure out why she was in the house of your parents. The circumstances are unusual."

The panic that had his heart in a chokehold loosened its grip. "Of course." *You need to calm down.* "My mother had narcotics. I suspect this woman was a drug addict."

"I understand your mother was very ill," Detective Ellis said.

"Yes." Harry swallowed. "She was palliative. She had days—"

"Weeks!" Mel spat the word so hard that saliva sprayed the smooth veneer of the table.

Harry exhaled. "She had been sent home to die, Dad."

And she had, indeed. Just not in the manner any of them had expected.

There was a moment of silence.

The detective cleared his throat. "I'd like you to take me through what happened in the living room, Harry."

Dread tightened Harry's stomach.

"You heard someone?"

Harry swallowed. "Yes. My dad chased after him—we thought the intruder was a man—and I ran after my dad." Harry closed his eyes. Then he opened them. "He caught up to the intruder. The man—goddammit, woman—hit him in the face."

"With a weapon?"

"No. Her fist."

Detective Ellis studied Mel's face. "Did she hurt you, Mr. Owen?"

"Yes. In the jaw." Mel pointed to the spot where Leah's elbow had connected with his face. A faint bruise tinged his flesh.

Harry leaned forward, palms on the table. "I thought she was going to grab Dad's gun."

"Which was where?"

"On my lap," Mel said.

"So what did you do?"

"I grabbed it first," Harry said, before his father could say anything more. *Leave this to me, Dad.* "But she turned on us. I had flashbacks to when my parents' store was robbed…"

The timing had to be perfect. Heat of the moment, flashbacks, justifiable reaction. "I remembered the moment my dad was shot by those robbers."

Mel threw his son a pained look.

"And I pulled the trigger." Harry's voice shook a little. "I wasn't trying to kill her." Wasn't he? Wasn't he trying to kill her when he fired that second shot?

No. I closed my eyes. If I had wanted to kill her, I would have kept them open. "I just wanted to stop her."

"Did she verbally threaten you, Harry?"

She had been trying to say something. But he didn't want to listen to this intruder who had terrified his mother to death. His voice hardened. "No. And she hit my father."

"Was she carrying a weapon?"

Harry frowned. "I don't know. I thought she might be armed…"

"Did you see anything in her hands, pocket, bag?"

Harry exhaled. "I'm not sure. It happened so fast."

"Understandably, you were terrified of being injured after your previous experience." Detective Ellis' gaze fell on Mel's wheelchair. "However, Mr. Owen, you were in possession of a prohibited weapon—"

"I was shot and paralyzed by a prohibited weapon!" Mel flung his arm toward his legs. "And I've lived a life sentence in this wheelchair!"

The detective's voice was calm. "I'm not judging you, Mr. Owen. But we have to look at the facts. And the law. I am advising you to expect charges to be laid."

Mel's face turned red. Harry shot him an alarmed look. His heart cried out at the injustice of what the detective said, but his lawyer's mind acknowledged that his father had been caught breaking the law.

"But I'm the victim!" Mel shouted. "Why should I be punished for defending my wife and my property?" He pounded his fist. "Goddamn our criminal justice system. It protects the guilty!"

The irony of the situation did not escape Harry. He was on the Committee of Public Safety. "It's a balance, Dad," he said, his voice trailing. Pathetic. The whole situation was pathetic. He turned to Ellis. He knew that the police were bound to lay charges given his father had been caught with an unregistered and prohibited gun, but he had to say something. "Detective, my father was the *victim*. Again. All he was trying to do was protect himself and my mother."

Mel threw Harry a fierce look. "I am tired of being the victim. I am tired of having my life ruined over and over again, and these goddamned criminals getting off the hook!"

Dad. No. His father was getting out of control. He would throw them both under the bus if he didn't stop him now.

Harry jumped to his feet and stood behind his father. A fresh round of sweat streamed from the back of his neck. What would the police do with his father's admissions? "Detective, we are exercising our right to remain silent." He placed his hands on his father's shoulders and gave them a warning squeeze. *No more, Dad.*

But he feared that too much had been said already.

21

THE PALE LAYER OF dust streaking the floor-to-ceiling windows of the Granville Street building gave the otherwise gracious architecture a shambling air. Rather like its occupant, Kate thought. She pulled open the glass door, noting the set of security locks, and the heavy wooden trim finished in glossy black paint. A bell chimed to announce her arrival.

Despite the dust, Eddie Bent's new digs were definitely an improvement over his communal office-share. Although built during the Victorian era, the building boasted the elegance of Georgian design. An old brick wall had been left exposed, providing a gritty textural contrast to the smooth wood floors and sleek office furnishings. In front of one large window, a leather sofa and two chairs had been neatly arranged around a neutral rug. There were two offices in the back.

Kate offered Eddie silent kudos. She walked over to the half-open office door on the right. "Hey there, pardner!"

Eddie laid down a sheaf of papers on a desk that was stacked with file folders, rising to greet her. "Kate! Thanks for coming on such short notice."

Kate held out two coffee cups. "I brought us Americanos to toast the new firm of Lange & Bent."

He reached out for a cup, grinning. "Bent & Lange, if you want me to stop smoking in the office."

Kate eyed him over the lid. "I knew you would play hard ball."

He raised his cup. "To Bent & Lange."

Kate tapped her cup against his. "To Bent & Lange, the pursuit of justice, and may the coffee shop on the corner never close."

They both swigged their coffee. Kate wiped her mouth with the back of her hand. "On second thought, may the coffee shop on the corner be bought by someone who knows how to make espresso."

"It all tastes the same at midnight." Eddie gestured to the file. "And I think this case will prove my point. I hadn't expected to put you on a case the same day we became partners, but welcome to the life of a criminal defense lawyer. I hope that Nina Woods didn't give you any grief for leaving so soon."

Kate gave a rueful smile. "None whatsoever. I think she was happy to put the Kate Lange chapter of McGrath Woods' storied existence behind them."

Eddie shrugged. "Their loss, Kate."

"Time will tell." She pushed down the hurt. No matter her reasons for leaving McGrath Woods, it rankled that they were so patently relieved to see her leave. "Where should I put my briefcase?"

"There is a second office. But it's unfurnished. I thought I would have time to order furniture for you when court was adjourned at lunch, but things got busy." He ran a hand through his shaggy salt-and-pepper hair. "Why don't you call my supplier and they'll send a desk and chair over for you on Monday." He grabbed one of the chairs facing his desk and pulled it closer. "Have a seat. I want to brief you on this file."

Kate sat down, dropping her briefcase to the floor. "Got something interesting?"

Eddie sank in the black leather executive chair behind his desk. He shuffled under the open file and produced a newspaper. "Very." He tossed the paper at Kate. "Have a look at the headlines."

She unfolded the newspaper and scanned the front page. *House Invader Shot by MP.* She gave a low whistle. "Good catch, Eddie." The Owen case was a good catch for Eddie— and for the firm she had joined. But her heart sank. She had just forced herself to walk away from the man who represented Harry Owen. And it hurt. She couldn't deny it. Now, instead of giving herself distance from the situation, she would be involved in a case where Randall Barrett was opposing counsel.

She glanced at Eddie. "Did you know that Randall is representing Harry Owen and his father?"

"No, but it doesn't surprise me. I knew they were acquaintances."

"So I'm assuming that you were retained by the suspect who was shot by Harry Owen?"

"Yes. Her family retained me until she is capable of giving consent. She's still under sedation."

"She?" Kate gave a low whistle. "Harry Owen shot a woman point-blank?"

"And with a prohibited, unregistered weapon."

"Jesus." So that's why Randall wanted her on Harry Owen's file. It would make Harry less of an ogre for shooting an unarmed woman if his defense counsel was a woman who had survived an attack. *Stop thinking about him.* She forced herself to scan the article. "But the media don't know the weapon was prohibited."

"Yet." Eddie picked up a yellow sticky note, on which a phone number was scrawled in his almost indecipherable handwriting. "Your friend Natalie Pitts called me."

Kate's journalist friend had landed a plum job as a television news anchor after unearthing a key piece of evidence during the investigation of Randall's criminal charge last year. "Nat's a terrier when it comes to digging for stories. But she respects boundaries." Kate sipped her coffee. "What did you tell her?"

"Nothing. I've got nothing to tell at this stage." He patted his shirt pocket. His hand trembled. He tucked it quickly under the desk.

"I'll review the file." She glanced through Eddie's office door toward the main reception area. "Over on the sofa."

She thought of her office—*former* office—in Purdy's Wharf, cool and professional, tidy. Sleek. Encased within a womb of power and security. For that was what McGrath Woods offered its clients and its staff. Power. Security. A safety net.

But the price had been too high.

The sofa it was.

Eddie gulped down the remaining dregs of his coffee. "Let's do the review together at my desk. It would be better if I briefed you."

She lowered herself onto the chair, her gaze flickering over her new partner. His eyes had bags under them, his skin grayish. A pang of concern for her mentor overrode her curiosity about the criminal file. "You should have come to Italy with me." She and Nat had originally planned to go together. But Nat had unexpectedly needed to replace her car, and could no longer afford the trip. So Kate went solo.

"Why is it I never take good advice?" Eddie's tone was wry.

There was a tinge of sadness to his gaze that gave Kate pause. What *was* going on with her new partner? "Don't worry. I plan to go back." She kept her tone light, slipping a notepad from her briefcase, and pushed away a pile of papers on Eddie's desk to clear a spot to take notes. "Okay, I'm dying to hear about our new client. What was she doing in Harry's house?"

"His parents' house," Eddie corrected. He leaned back in his chair and absently patted his shirt pocket again. "And her parents don't know why Leah was there."

"Have you spoken to her?" The news report indicated the suspect was in bad shape in the hospital.

Eddie shook his head. "Not yet. She was under sedation this morning."

"Does she have a criminal record?"

"Here's where it gets interesting, Kate. She is clean as a whistle. Top student, scholarship, has a good job in information security."

"Over-achieving millennial who turns to drug addiction and steals to finance her habit?"

"Either that…" Eddie leaned back in his chair. "Or she knew one of the Owens. And was in the house for a reason. She had darkened her eyebrows and hairline."

Kate tapped a pen against her bottom lip. Eddie reached over, took it from her fingers and flipped it around. Then he handed it back to her. "You were giving your lips an interesting tattoo." He gave it a critical eye. "Looks a bit like Alaska's paw print."

Just the mention of a tattoo made her skin crawl. Kenzie Sloane had left a permanent mark on her soul, even if it wasn't outlined in ink. "I'm still jet-lagged." She wiped her mouth with the back of her hand. "Leah Roberts must know Harry. It seems unlikely she would know the elderly parents. And she's in information security, right? He's the Chair of the national Public Safety Committee."

Eddie leaned toward her. "He is?"

"Ever since he gave Frances Sloane the brush-off, I've followed his career closely." Kate arched a brow. "It's amazing the kind of people who get ahead in politics."

Eddie shrugged. "No one else wants the job. The trolling and attacks have gotten so vicious. Case in point. Have you checked out the social media trending today for Harry Owen?"

Kate shook her head. "I try to avoid all that stuff. It clutters my brain."

"Social media is key for criminal defense. We need to know how our clients are being perceived, whether there is bias—and also whether we can use some of those perceptions to underpin an alternative theory of the case." He pointed to her smartphone that she had laid by her notepad. "Get thee a social media account ASAP."

Kate opened the app on her phone. "Hmmm…how about @JusticeQueen?" she asked with a small smile as she searched for Harry Owen's official Twitter account.

"I was thinking more along the lines of @Bent&Lange, although I like @JusticeQueen. Maybe save that one until you are elevated to the bench." He noticed her frown. "What's up?"

"Harry Owen is being trolled pretty hard by someone named @TruthAboutHarry."

"What's he saying?"

"He's accusing Harry of all kinds of things. Fraud, sexual harassment, shooting his own father."

THE BODY BUTCHER LEFT YOU FOR ME. The note had been left on her windshield by John McNally. And it was seared into her brain. Stalker, troll—the lines were blurred.

"Could be a typical troll. Or…may I?" Eddie held out his hand for Kate's smartphone.

Kate fought down the memory of McNally. His face, his anger, his pain.

His glee.

She glanced at Eddie. He waited, hand extended. She gave him her phone.

He quickly scrolled through @TruthAboutHarry's posts. "He hasn't posted anything for several days."

"Do you think he is connected with the break-in?"

"Perhaps. We'll see what the police come up with. But let's keep an eye on this account." He handed Kate's phone to her.

She nibbled on the end of her pen. "In the meantime, let me see if I can come up with a connection between our friend Harry and Leah. Perhaps he invited her to the house."

Eddie rubbed his jaw. "So, maybe he's a jilted lover and shot her when she refused his advances?"

"I could totally see why she would jilt him."

Eddie held up a cautionary hand. "I know your previous dealings with him have made you dislike him, Kate. But Harry Owen could be a victim of a crime. Plain and simple."

"I don't think there's anything plain or simple about our Member of Parliament, Eddie."

Eddie glanced at Harry Owen's face plastered across the front page of the paper. Kate had to admit, his expression was a study of shock in black-and-white.

"But this certainly will create tremendous sympathy for him," she said. McGrath Woods would be in seventh heaven. "Given his party was trailing in the polls, this is just what he needed. You don't think he shot Leah because he was trying to portray himself as the defender of his elderly parents?"

Eddie pushed the newspaper away. "Maybe he shot her because he believed they were under attack and he *was* trying to defend his parents."

"Or he was trying to prove that firearms shouldn't be banned."

"My, you did wake up on the cynical side of the bed this morning, didn't you? If that's what Italy does to a person, count me in." Eddie's gaze was amused. "In the meantime, let's see if we can figure out our client's true motive, before the government blindsides us with damage control."

"I think they blindsided themselves when Harry's publicist threw him under the bus this morning."

"I wonder if the government intended for Harry to become road kill, or if it was simple ineptitude." Eddie pushed himself to his feet and threw his creased barrister's robe over his arm. "I have a court hearing in twenty minutes. Make yourself at home."

He hurried out of the office. Kate flipped through the sparse file folder. Not much to go on. Yet.

She walked into the main reception area. The sun beat through the windows. It was warm. It was quiet. Jet lag slammed into her.

That sofa looked pretty darn inviting.

First day as partner...and she needed a nap.

What the hell.

She ignored the lure of the leather sofa and began a Google search of Leah Roberts. There weren't any references to her online except for the usual social media accounts: Facebook, Instagram, and LinkedIn. She began scrolling through Leah's Instagram account, as that seemed to be the most heavily populated with posts. There was a particularly striking photo of Leah cheek-to-cheek with a cat named Spook. Kate studied the young woman's face. If you didn't look too closely, you'd think she was sixteen, with her fresh, smooth skin and open features. But her eyes told another story. They were wary in the photo, not daring to reveal whatever secrets lay within.

Her eyes reminded Kate of another young woman's gaze: her sister's.

And her own.

She quickly scrolled through Leah's posts. There was a stunning photo of the Perseid meteor shower taken at the Dark Sky Preserve while camping at Kejimikujik National Park the previous summer. A family birthday dinner. Some typical tourist photos of the House of Parliament, the Ottawa tulip festival, and the Rideau Canal. As Kate expected for a cyber security consultant, there was not a word mentioned about Leah's work.

The phone rang. She dug it out from under a pile of papers on Eddie's desk.

"Bent & Lange," she said. It hadn't taken long to get used to her name on a firm letterhead.

"I need to speak to Mr. Bent," a woman said. "The police have arrested my daughter!"

"Mr. Bent is in court," Kate said. "I am Kate Lange, his new partner." *That sounded even better.*

"This is Susan Roberts. I'm the mother of Leah Roberts."

"Mrs. Roberts, Eddie Bent has briefed me on your daughter's case. Did your daughter regain consciousness?"

"Yes."

"Did she understand what the police told her when they arrested her?"

Susan Roberts exhaled. "Yes. I think so."

The arrest was fast. But not unexpected, given Leah was

discovered in the Owen house when she was shot. "I'll be right over. Please tell her to say nothing to the police. That's very important."

She texted Eddie with the news of Leah's arrest, and then rushed to her car.

If this was the life of a criminal defense lawyer…she kind of liked it.

22

THE EARLY MORNING DAMP had burned off hours ago. And suddenly it became summer. With it, came the heat. Aiden crouched under the railway bridge near the bottom of Coburg Road. Above him, the privileged children of Halifax walked, skipped, ran, and biked toward the Waegwoltic Club.

He remembered doing the same as a child. Taking tennis lessons, swimming in the salt water swimming pool, being forced to go sailing. He had hated all of it. He was not an outdoors kid, and it was pure torture to be amongst the kids who were more talented, more able, more *everything*. And they let him know it.

When he was old enough to go to the Waeg by himself, he would take a sharp right before the railway bridge, find one of the many gaps under the fence that closed off the railway cut, worm his way under it, and then run down the steep slope to the tracks. He'd spent many days on the track, hanging out with other disaffected teens, smoking weed, and secretly tormenting his tormentors online.

It was a refuge of sorts, this railway cut. He opened his laptop, seeking an unsecured wireless network on which he could piggyback. A list of available networks popped up on his screen. *Mike123* was unsecured. And it had a good signal.

Thanks, Mike, you doofus. He logged on to the wireless. The first thing he did was check the online news sites. What had the police found? A small smile curved his lips as he read the news coverage. Not much at the Owen house, it seemed. They had found his footprints, but couldn't match them. The K-9 unit had come up empty. They still hadn't found his rooming house. He could breathe a little easier. The police had no clue.

Unless Leah turned him in. He skimmed the news articles, looking for information about her condition. But all the press had been told was that she was in 'serious but stable condition.'

Shit. He could not afford for her to pull through now.

The clock was ticking. If Leah spoke to the police, it would tick in double-time.

He pushed the USB stick into the port on the side of his laptop, and opened the file finder.

Harry Owen's entire computer drive revealed itself. It would take hours, if not days, to go through it. He skimmed through it, noting the subfolder of private memos where Harry had filed the most incriminating files about the data breach.

Not only did Aiden have all of Harry Owen's data on his computer, he had uploaded a key logging program onto Harry Owen's laptop so he could capture Harry's passwords. Emails always revealed more than they intended, and often had juicy file attachments. He was sure that for a man in Harry Owen's position, he would have at least one private email address in addition to his official email.

There were two passwords that Harry had entered since the break-in last night. One was for his work email.

The other was for a private email account.

"Holy crap, Harry Owen, you are one sneaky bastard."

His heart began to pound.

The first email account held emails that Harry Owen had forwarded from the Minister of Public Safety, detailing the nature of the data breach, the demand that no one discuss it, and the strategy for covering up the breach. Harry Owen must have sent the emails to himself as a little insurance in case the whole thing blew up politically.

Smart guy. Aiden had to give him credit. He knew how to cover his ass.

But then he logged into the other account. And he couldn't believe how stupid Harry Owen was.

He was having an affair. With a US Captain.

Harry had written just last week: *I wish we could be together, in public, without fear of the consequences. I wish we had met before you had your kids. I know that you don't want to break up your marriage. But all I can do is think about you. And how our life could be together. I can't wait to see you this weekend.*

Aiden took a screen shot of the email.

Then he texted it to Harry with his own message: *Look what I found, lover boy. For $500,000, this will stay between us.*

He hit 'send'.

Then he leaned back against the concrete balustrade supporting the railway bridge and closed his eyes.

It had been a very busy day so far.

But a very rewarding one.

23

KATE SPOTTED THE VAN for a local television news show as she hurried toward the main entrance of the Greater Halifax General Hospital. So Nat was here. She hadn't seen Nat since before her trip to Italy. Kate grinned. They had a lot of catching up to do.

She strode into the main lobby, taking the stairs up to the fifth floor. She pressed the buzzer to the Medical Surgical ICU.

"Can I help you?" a clerk asked over the intercom. "This is a restricted floor."

"I'm the lawyer for Ms. Roberts," Kate said. "May I come in?"

The door buzzed.

Kate stepped into the ICU. From the large station in the middle of the unit, the clerk watched Kate approach. "She's in bed five," the clerk said, flipping open a file folder.

"Thanks," Kate said to the top of the clerk's head.

She walked toward Leah Roberts' room. The ICU had an unearthly quality to it, vibrating, beeping, and humming around the silent, prone forms of the patients whose own bodies barely kept them alive. Fear showed in the grim lines on family members' faces. Hope moistened their eyes. For whatever reason—whether it was the miracles the hospital touted in their annual fundraising campaign, fate, God, or just pure medicine—the patients lying in these beds were still alive. That was the first, all-important step.

"Ms. Lange?" A dark-haired police officer stepped away from the wall by Leah Roberts' room.

"Yes?"

"I'm Detective Gabriel, with General Investigative Services." She held out her badge. "I'm one of the detectives securing Ms. Roberts' room."

"I'm defense counsel for Ms. Roberts," Kate said. "Were you the detective who arrested my client?"

"Yes."

"I thought she was under heavy sedation."

Detective Gabriel studied Kate. "She woke up."

Kate glanced into the room. Bent & Lange's inaugural client watched them from the bed, her face so pale that even from the hallway, Kate could see the ghostly blue constellations of her veins.

"You advised Ms. Roberts of her right to remain silent?"

Detective Gabriel crossed her arms. "Yes. Her parents were in the room with her, as was a nurse." From the corner of her eye, Kate could see an older couple watch her from Leah's bedside.

"So she said nothing to you?"

"Nothing that was relevant."

Kate paused at the detective's choice of words. "What, exactly, did she say to you?"

Detective Gabriel raised a brow. "That is up to your client to inform you until you receive our disclosure file."

Well, it was worth a try.

She stepped around the detective, walking softly into Leah Roberts' room. "Hello. I'm Kate Lange." Her gaze took in Leah's parents, who gathered protectively around their daughter's bed, and then moved to her client. She was struck by Leah Roberts' size. The young woman's feet came close to dangling over the edge of the hospital bed. Faint smudges of black marred her downy hairline. Tubes ran from her chest, hands and God knew where else.

Harry Owen was a good shot.

The revolver felt so smooth, so sleek. So powerful. Kate's finger tightened on the trigger. "Do it," Kate's oldest foe urged. "Do it." She smiled at Kate. "You know you are just like me—"

"Thank God you are here," Leah Roberts' mother said. She reached out to shake Kate's hand. "I'm Susan Roberts. This is my husband Tim."

Leah's father stepped forward, a large, stooped man with tufting white hair who reminded Kate of a snowy owl. Pain tightened his face, rendering his nose even more beak-like.

Through the window, Kate saw Detective Gabriel lean against the far wall of the corridor, angling herself so that she could observe them.

Kate shifted slightly so that the detective could not read her lips and pulled out a notepad.

"Let's start with a little background," she said. "How old are you, Leah?"

"Twenny-five," Leah mumbled.

"She is twenty-five," Susan repeated. "She has never had any trouble with the law. In fact, she works for a private information security firm."

Kate glanced up from her notebook. "You mean, computer security?"

Tim Roberts nodded. "Yes, she is a cyber security expert." Pride shot with pain radiated in his eyes. "She was recruited straight out of university. MIT."

"Do you know why she was in the house of Harry Owen's parents?"

Tim Roberts glanced at Leah. "We've been trying to figure that one out. As far as we know, Leah never met them."

"What about Harry Owen?" Kate envisioned Harry: tall, athletic build, attractive. He would be about ten years older than Leah, but dating younger women fit his profile. "Could they have dated?"

Susan Roberts pursed her mouth. Kate noted she did not look at her daughter when she said, "I don't think so. She was seeing someone. A guy."

24

"**SHE WAS SEEING SOMEONE**. *A guy.*"

Even through the fuzziness in her head, Leah registered the disapproval in her mother's voice. Her mother did not like Aiden. "I don't trust him," she had said to Leah a few months ago.

That had hurt. A lot. "You don't have to, mom," Leah said, forcing her tone to remain even.

But although she kept her distance from her mother after that, she had never been able to push her mother's words completely out of her mind. They were dust motes floating in her heart—invisible until a particularly illuminating beam of truth about Aiden was revealed.

The first time was when he let slip that his hair had once been very short.

Just the fact that she could curl into his arms made Leah giddy. Aiden was an inch taller than she, and as they lay on her bed, her feet rested on his. Beneath her palm, she felt the rapid thudding of his heart rate as they each caught their breath.

"You are incredible, Leah," Aiden murmured, capturing her hair in his fingers. "You give fairy orgasms."

She laughed. "What does that mean?"

"Your hair is like gossamer and your skin is so pale. You are like a fairy."

A fairy? "A six-foot tall one."

131

"They are the best kind." He nuzzled her, playing with her hair.

She reached for a strand of his hair. It was thick, wavy, almost as long as hers. "When did you start growing your hair?"

"As soon as I got out—"

"Out of where?" She propped herself on an elbow. Her gaze fell on the tattoo on his bicep. It was of a pirate.

He rolled away.

She placed a hand on his back.

He shook his head. His hair brushed his shoulders. "It doesn't matter."

"It does to me."

"Look, I was in trouble with the law when I was a teen. Hacking stuff."

"You were arrested?"

"I went to juvie."

"For what?"

"Like I said, hacking stuff." His mouth twisted. "The feds didn't like that I was smarter than them."

"But what did you do?"

He jumped off Leah's bed and turned to face her. "It's in the past. I don't want to talk about it." He flicked a strand of hair from his face. "But after I got out, I grew my hair. It symbolizes my freedom, Leah." He opened his arms, his hair spilling over his shoulders, his gaze intense. "That's what I'm fighting for, Leah. Freedom."

For some reason, the sight of Aiden naked and fiery should have inspired Leah's own fervor, but instead, his passion rang false to her.

She didn't know why.

She blamed it on her mother's words.

But now she wondered if it was her own gut instinct that had warned her that Aiden wasn't who he seemed. For the lover who had wooed her with compliments and caresses was not the same as the man who pressed a knife into her side at the Owen house—and left her to face the wrath of its occupants.

"His name is Aiden." Her mother's voice once again cut through the swirl of confusion in Leah's brain.

Panic tightened Leah's chest. She needed to think this through. And her brain was so foggy. "Mmmmom."

Her mother reached for her hand. "We have to tell the truth, Leah."

The truth.

That was what this whole thing last night was about: a mission to expose the truth.

She could not formulate the words to capture the intensity of the pain—or the weight of remorse. "I'm... thir...thirsty."

Her father slipped a straw in her mouth and she welcomed the cool, clean water dribbling down her throat. If only it could cleanse her conscience.

Her parents' faces slowly came into focus. Their expressions were identical: concern, fear, stress. These were the two people who had always protected her. And they were doing everything they could to protect her from her most grievous mistake.

She had been so unfair to them.

But she thought she was doing the right thing. She had done what she had been brought up to do: tell the truth.

God, she was so confused.

All she wanted to do was sink into the soft haze shrouding her mind and escape this mess she had created.

"Leah," the lawyer Kate said to her. "Anything you tell me is protected by solicitor-client privilege. If you help the police with the investigation, we might be able to arrange immunity for you."

"Immunity?" Susan Roberts gasped. Hope suddenly brightened her eyes. She took Leah's hand in hers. "Leah, you could get immunity. Just tell Ms. Lange everything you know about Aiden."

Blackness threaded Leah's brain. It was soft, black fluff. Like Spook's fur.

Her mother squeezed her hand. "Leah, tell Ms. Lange about Aiden." Her mother used the tone that demanded Leah respond.

She opened her eyes. "His name is Aiden." The words slurred in her mouth, but she was able to string them together.

"What is his last name?"

She exhaled. "I...don't know."

Her parents exchanged glances.

"Leah, don't protect him. He made you do something that is entirely out of character for you." Her father leaned over her. "Were you there against your will?"

She could tell from the eagerness in his voice that he hoped her answer would be affirmative.

"No...yes. I don't know."

Kate the lawyer's phone rang.

She glanced down at it. "Sorry, I must take this call." She rose with an apologetic look. "We'll finish this as soon as I get back. It should only take a minute."

If only the consequences of this mess would only take a minute.

Leah had the sense that it was more like a lifetime.

Hers.

She closed her eyes and let the blackness cushion her.

But remorse kept stabbing through the oblivion she sought.

25

HARRY SLIPPED INTO HIS hotel room. His phone burned a hole through his breast pocket straight into his chest. His clothing was soaked with sweat. He couldn't catch his breath, the pressure in his chest was so great.

Was he having a heart attack?

He had left the police station, dripping in sweat, believing that the police interview had been the biggest test of mental fortitude that he had ever undergone. His father had been purple with rage as Harry removed him from the interview room. It had taken every ounce of patience for Harry to defuse his father's temper.

"I am going to call Randall Barrett as soon as we return to the hotel, Dad," he had said. "We'll figure out the best course of action."

"There's something wrong with our justice system, Harry," his father said, his voice hoarse, "when innocent victims are prosecuted for trying to protect themselves."

It was pointless to respond, to defend the police's actions—*they have no choice, you broke the law*—because he knew it would further inflame his father.

And he could not defend the unfairness of the situation.

His mother had died from sheer terror and his father was going to be arrested for trying to protect her.

Where was the justice in that?

He quickly flagged down a taxi to take him and his father to the hotel. He leaned against the back seat, staring out the window as the cab negotiated the annoying one-way streets of downtown Halifax.

He was so angry, so grief-stricken, so exhausted, so confused by the turn his life had taken that he was numb. He could not think. He could absorb no more.

And then his phone chimed with a text message.

Thinking it might be Randall Barrett, he had checked it.

And almost passed out from shock.

The text message was as targeted and explosive as a grenade. But it wasn't the words of the sender that caused his heart to hammer. It was his words. The words of a private email, cut and pasted from his secret email account.

Along with a demand for half a million dollars.

His thoughts collided into one another. Was the blackmailer nuts? Where did he think he'd get that money? He was on a politician's salary for God's sake. And a son of working class immigrants. There was no inheritance to fall back on when the going got tough.

But most frighteningly: *Where did the blackmailer get access to his most secret email?*

A thought chilled him. Had the blackmailer stolen his laptop while he was at the police station?

And was he the suspect who got away last night?

Had he and Leah broken into his parents' house to steal his laptop?

Harry's pulse raced, as if the speed of his heart could urge the taxi to drive more quickly to the hotel. But the downtown was bogged with construction, closed-off lanes, and streams of pedestrians.

Once they arrived at the hotel, Harry pushed his father through the throng of journalists who hovered around the entry door.

"Could we have a statement, Mr. Owen?"

"What are the police findings?"

"What is the status of the suspects?"

The questions slammed into him. All he wanted to do was reach the privacy of his room. And check to see if his laptop was still there.

He raised his voice. "We have no statement at this time. Please respect our privacy. We are a family in mourning."

His father shielded his eyes from the blinding flash of the cameras. Harry murmured, "Almost at the elevator, Dad."

They stood, waiting for the elevator, ignoring the television cameras, smartphone cameras, and journalists who hoped to get one last word. But he would say nothing, would never admit to the fear that grew within him until he felt as if his insides were an abyss and his outer self was crumbling in slow motion into it.

Finally, the elevator arrived and delivered them to the penthouse floor of the hotel.

"Dad, why don't you have a rest?" Harry unlocked his father's door.

"I'm not tired," his father said. He had a frantic, wired look in his eyes.

But Harry could not wait one more minute. His phone was on fire. No, it was like acid. Corroding something that had been full of promise and searing it with malice.

"But you need some down time." He couldn't hide the edge of desperation to his voice. He wheeled his father into the living room of his suite, and then pulled the blinds closed. "Try to have a nap. Neither of us have had much rest."

His father opened his mouth to protest, but then something flickered in his gaze. He snapped his jaw closed so hard that it clicked. "Go. You need a rest. I'll be fine."

"Okay. I'll check on you in an hour." Harry opened the door to the hallway, his impatience mounting, anxiety constricting his chest until he could barely speak in a normal voice. "If you need me, just call."

Then he left his father's room and crossed the corridor.

With shaking fingers, he pressed the hotel card against the lock, and pushed open the door to his suite. He strode across the sitting area, flinging open the large wardrobe that housed the safe.

The safe door was as he left it. Locked.

He punched in the code.

The door swung open. His laptop was there.

He slid it out and booted it up.

It appeared untouched.

He sank on the sofa. Then sprang to his feet, opened the mini-bar, and poured himself a stiff scotch, his hand shaking. He drained the glass, pressing it against his flushed cheek.

What the hell?

He didn't understand what was happening.

His phone rang.

He pushed the glass harder against his face, feeling the phone vibrate right against his heart.

Was it the blackmailer?

Rage, fuelled by the fiery alcohol, erupted in his chest.

He wanted to shoot the bastard.

He slammed the glass onto the table and answered the phone. "Yes."

"Harry. It's Randall Barrett." If his lawyer was taken aback by Harry's hostile tone, he hid it well.

Relief poured into Harry. He still had time to puzzle this out. "Hi," he managed. Then a thought made the scotch whoosh into the dark abyss where his stomach used to be.

Had the blackmailer sent the text message to Randall? Was that why he was calling?

Harry's ear was on fire, burning from the contact with his phone, burning with the knowledge that his deepest, most private dream—and his secret, most private shame—might soon be exposed to the entire world. He cleared his throat. "Is everything okay?"

"That's why I was calling," Randall said, his tone somber.

Oh, God. It was a plea, an invocation, a rejection all at once.

"I was calling to see how your interview with Detective Ellis went."

Harry had completely forgotten about it. It was as if it had happened to someone else, a lifetime ago.

He closed his eyes. The text message flashed behind his eyelids. *If only we could be together.* Longing ached in his chest. He opened his eyes. "The interview was fine. I mean, no, it wasn't." He scrambled to collect his thoughts. What had happened again?

Jesus, he was a frigging lawyer. He needed to pull it together. He jumped to his feet and strode to the mini bar. "Detective Ellis had identified the suspect," he said, his heart hammering once again at the thought of Leah Roberts. How could so much destruction be hidden inside that awkward, brilliant brain? Had she any idea how much damage she had wrought?

And did he have any idea how much damage he had wrought?

He didn't know where that thought came from, but he drowned it away with a large dose of scotch. It was fiery, immolating his fears and his remorse. And it fuelled his anger. "Her name is Leah Roberts. She is a cyber security analyst. I knew her."

There was a pause as his lawyer absorbed what he said. "How well did you know her?"

"Vaguely. She worked on a contract for the department. She was tightening our security protocols."

"Why do you think she was in your parents' house?"

"I don't know." He drained the last of the scotch. "My father said he didn't know her."

"It seems the most obvious connection is with you, Harry." There was a slight rebuke in Randall's voice. "And since she is a cyber security professional, do you think she was trying to access your computer?"

He swallowed. "No. I have my laptop. They never made it to my bedroom."

"What about your computer network? Could they have done something with that?"

His head began to swim. He had logged into his parents' Wi-Fi network last night.

And received a text with an email that had been hidden in a private, password-protected email account today.

Had Leah and the unknown suspect somehow hacked into his computer through his parents' network?

It was so obvious that it frightened him that he hadn't thought of it himself. "I don't know."

"We need to alert the police."

"No!" There would be hell to pay if his boss discovered he'd been using a private network.

He thought of the emails he had saved in a private email account as 'insurance.'

And he almost puked.

Jesus. The hackers would have access to those files.

"Harry, is there anything on your laptop that is classified information?"

His admission came out on a long exhale. "Yes."

"Do you think your files have been breached?"

The hacker had only sent him a snippet from a personal email. None of his work emails. Maybe all the hacker wanted was half a million dollars. If he paid him off, maybe that would be the end to it. "No. I do not." He cleared his throat. "Look, this has been an exhausting day. I need to lie down. Can I call you later?"

"Yes, of course. But, remember, Harry: I'm on your side. And I'm here to help you."

"Thanks, Randall. I appreciate it."

He hung up the phone.

Opened his laptop.

He was no techie, but he had been taught how to wipe his computer clean. He remembered joking to the IT staff that it was like getting his computer to swallow a cyanide pill so it wouldn't divulge its secrets.

Within minutes, he had destroyed every file on his computer.

He stared at the empty folders.

His head pounded. His stomach roiled.
His career might just have swallowed a cyanide pill, too.
But maybe, just maybe, it had just saved itself.

26

2:18 p.m.

"HOW CAN LEAH BE arraigned in the hospital?" Kate asked, her voice low. She stood in the corridor outside her client's room, phone pressed to her ear. Eddie had called her during his break from court. "The judge and clerk would have to be here."

Eddie exhaled. Kate guessed he was standing outside the Law Courts, getting his nicotine fix before returning to the courtroom. "It is unusual," he agreed. "But the media are breathing down the backs of the police and the Crown. Leah was placed under arrest, so she must be arraigned within twenty-four hours."

"I thought they'd wait until she was discharged."

"Apparently not. They left a message on my phone, but I only just got it. They said they'd be there by 2:15."

Kate glanced at her watch. "Well, they are three minutes late. I'd better go. I'll call you later." She hurried into Leah's room. Her client's eyes drifted open.

"I just had a phone call from Eddie Bent," she said. "The Crown called to inform him that you will be arraigned, Leah."

"Arraigned? What does that mean?" Tim Roberts asked, moving closer to Leah's side.

"It means that the charges are read in court in front of a judge and Leah enters a plea. Then the judge decides if she should be remanded to a correctional facility."

Leah, if possible, turned paler. Her mother gasped. "How could they do that? She's too ill to be moved."

"I doubt very much that a judge would order Leah incarcerated in her present state."

Tim Roberts glanced around the room. "This isn't a court room. How can they even do this?"

"As long as all the parties representing the judicial process are present, a hospital room can be considered a court room."

Leah's parents had a stunned expression on their face. They were beginning to grasp how bad things were for their daughter.

Kate bent over Leah. "Leah, the judge will ask you how you plead. You need to tell the judge whether you are guilty or not guilty."

Leah's eyes widened. "I don't…know."

"Of course you are not guilty, Leah," her mother said. It was fear, not anger, that caused her sharp tone.

Kate grasped her client's hand. "At this stage, I would advise you to plead not guilty. Once you plead, the Crown will have to disclose their case, and we can discuss your options, especially immunity."

"O…kay." Leah's eyelids drifted closed.

There was a knock on the door.

Kate straightened.

John Hillcroft walked in. Kate's heart pounded a little faster. She hadn't expected that the Chief Crown would be handling this himself. Now, she was up against the best Crown in the province. And the man whom she hoped would hire her at some point.

She could not screw up.

"Kate…" Hillcroft held out his hand. "Good to see you. I'm the Crown for this case."

She shook his hand, her grip firm. "I understand that the

arraignment is scheduled for…now? And here?" she asked. "It's a bit unusual, isn't it?"

"Yes, but Ms. Roberts isn't the first accused we've arraigned in hospital. Sorry for the late notice. Judge Fitzgerald notified us that this was his only availability. We let Eddie Bent know. He's the counsel of record."

"Please add me to the list. Eddie's got a trial that has been extended by at least a week." Eddie had dropped that bomb during his phone call.

"I presume you are now working for him?" His eyes flickered over face. She could not miss the slight nuance in his voice. Kate had not taken his advice to avoid Eddie, and it was duly noted.

"I'm his new partner," she said, her voice brisk. "We have launched a new firm. Bent & Lange."

"Congratulations." There was no irony in his voice.

Kate smiled. "Thank you. Is Judge Fitzgerald on his way?"

"Yes, I believe so." Hillcroft's gaze quickly took in the panic on Leah Roberts' face and the protective stance of her parents. "I'll wait in the hallway." He left the room, flipping through a file folder labeled R. vs. Roberts.

Regina vs. *Roberts*. The Queen—*Regina*—versus this woman who lay at death's door, who had inexplicably broken into the house of a paraplegic and his dying wife, and then was shot at point-blank range.

First case as a bona fide defense lawyer, and it's this one. Into the fire you go, Kate.

Within a minute of leaving, Hillcroft materialized in the doorway. "Judge Fitzgerald and the clerk have stepped off the elevator. We will begin shortly."

It was only an arraignment—a simple judicial process, really, but Kate felt her palms sweat. This was her first legal matter for Bent & Lange, and she didn't want to mess it up.

It's show time.

She bent over her client's bed. "Leah, the judge and the court clerk have arrived."

Her client slowly opened her eyes. "Okay." Her voice was a mere breath.

Kate frowned, concerned. "Leah, how are you feeling?"

"Not too good."

"Do you understand what is going to happen?" That was the test for whether the process would go forward. If her client had capacity, she would be brought before the law.

"I plead not guilty..." she murmured.

Kate studied her client. Should she call a halt to the arraignment? In her opinion, her client was borderline for lack of capacity.

Hillcroft watched their exchange from the doorway.

If she halted the arraignment, the police would still be guarding Leah. Detective Gabriel seemed very sharp. She might ask her client questions that could hurt her down the road. On the other hand, if the arraignment went forward, the custody of Leah would be turned over to the sheriffs, and they weren't part of the police investigation. They were less likely to connect any dots to build the Crown's case against her.

Kate patted Leah's hand. It was like patting marble. "Okay, just remember to say the same thing when the judge comes in."

As if on cue, a robed Judge Fitzgerald strode into the hospital room and took a position by the head of Leah's bed. If possible, the room became even more hushed than before.

The clerk, a young woman with blond-streaked hair pulled back into a ponytail and high-heeled pumps, hurried in behind him. She held a notepad and a Dictaphone. It was an archaic piece of technology, but the judicial system wasn't known for its leading edge approach to anything. The Dictaphone was carefully positioned on a wheeled table, which was pushed next to the judge.

Judge Fitzgerald's gaze flicked over Leah. Dispassionate. Assessing. A dark-robed phantom of Justice looming over the ghost of shattered potential.

"Ms. Roberts, I am Judge Fitzgerald. I will preside over

your arraignment." The judge then nodded to Leah's parents, who watched anxiously from the foot of the bed. "Good afternoon."

Kate stepped forward. "Your Honor, I am Kate Lange, representing Ms. Roberts."

He turned his gaze to her. "Have you explained the nature of the proceeding to your client, Counsel?"

From the corner of her eye, Kate saw Hillcroft lean forward. They had roughly adopted the formation of a courtroom: Judge Fitzgerald stood by the head of her bed, with Hillcroft next to the foot of her bed, and Kate slightly to the back.

"Yes, Your Honor."

He gestured for Kate to come closer, his sleeve flapping. "Counsel, we need to dispense with some of the formalities for the Dictaphone to record this proceeding."

It took only moments for Leah to plead not guilty to the charge of break and enter with intent. "Ms. Roberts, as soon as you are medically discharged from this hospital you will be remanded to a correctional facility to await your bail hearing in two weeks hence," Judge Fitzgerald ordered. "Do you understand?"

"Yes," she whispered.

Five feet away, her mother and father watched the proceedings, mute, their pain palpable.

The judge closed his file folder, and the clerk turned off the Dictaphone. The proceeding was over. Judge Fitzgerald nodded to Hillcroft and Kate. "Good day, Counsel."

As soon as he left, Tim Roberts stepped toward the Crown prosecutor. "Mr. Hillcroft, we would like to express our deepest sympathies to Mr. Owen for the loss of his wife. Could you please let him know?"

Hillcroft surveyed Leah's parents. "I will convey your sympathies. But Mr. Owen may not be receptive to them. He believes your daughter killed his wife."

Susan Roberts gasped. Tim Roberts turned ashen. "But she didn't...Leah's not violent."

"It was my understanding that Mrs. Owen was in a palliative stage of cancer," Kate interjected, throwing Hillcroft a glare. "I believe Mr. Owen's accusation is misplaced. And certainly does not merit criminal charges," she added.

"I agree that there are no legal grounds for his assertion, but Mr. Owen believes that fear stopped his wife's heart, Ms. Lange." Hillcroft's voice was steady. "She was in a fragile state."

Susan Roberts turned away and hunched over, her hands to her face.

"We are so sorry." Tim Roberts' voice was rough with anguish. "Leah would never have done this intentionally."

"Mr. Roberts, the facts speak for themselves." Hillcroft placed the file folder of *R.* vs. *Roberts* in his briefcase.

Leah shifted in the bed, trying to push herself up on her elbow. "I'm so sor—" She abruptly cried out in pain.

The machines hooked up to her echoed her cry, erupting in a frantic cascade of alarms. A nurse rushed in. She checked the monitor and frowned. "You all need to leave."

Leah's parents rushed over to their broken daughter. She had turned convulsively to her side, her hand curled up into her chest. A baby chick in utero.

A surgical resident hurried to Leah's side, reaching for her wrist as he checked her pulse. "Let's get some blood work done," he said to the nurse. Then he glanced at Kate and the Roberts. "Everyone must leave the room. We need to check her dressing."

Tim Roberts gently pushed his wife toward the door. Susan Roberts left Leah's bedside, staring over her shoulder at her daughter's bedside all the while, tears streaming down her face. "It will be okay, Leah," she whispered.

It will be okay. Kate realized that the reassurance relied on two key elements: that the doctors save Leah's life—and that the saved life was defended competently in court.

And, right now, neither of those elements looked so good for her client.

In fact, as Kate gave her client one last, concerned look through the glass door, things looked pretty bleak.

Kate exhaled and headed toward the elevator. Hillcroft caught up to her.

There was nothing for it but to walk together to the elevators.

"She's in bad shape," Hillcroft said. "I'm sorry." He pushed the down button on the elevator panel.

Kate exhaled. "I hope they can stabilize her. It seems like today's proceedings pushed her over the edge."

Hillcroft threw her a sideways look. "The arraignment had to be done. Otherwise, a sharp defense lawyer might try to have the charges thrown out."

Kate's mouth lifted in a reluctant smile. "I had heard that you don't miss a trick, my friend," she said, using the term of courtroom etiquette.

They stood, waiting for the elevator, both of them conscious of the woman fighting for survival just feet away. Hillcroft pulled out his phone and began scanning his messages.

The elevator arrived. Hillcroft courteously waited until Kate had stepped in.

The elevator announced its arrival on the main level with a gentle chime.

"After you," Hillcroft said.

Kate felt Hillcroft's presence right behind her as she stepped out of the elevator.

She knew without a doubt that Hillcroft would be right on her heels for this case. She just hoped that she could keep one step ahead.

But as she watched him stride toward the main entrance, she knew that very few defense lawyers had achieved that feat.

There is no rest for the wicked, Kate.

27

3:05 p.m.

KATE STRODE THROUGH THE hospital doors, stepping to one side to allow a man pushing a woman in a wheelchair to pass by. The woman's IV pole rattled over the sidewalk. It was hard to tell her age, but Kate guessed she was in her fifties. Blankets had been carefully tucked around her, and she wore a pale blue knitted hat. Her face bore the unmistakable pallor of serious illness. She had turned her face to the sun, her eyes closed as she breathed in the warm July air.

"Ms. Lange, Mr. Hillcroft, could I have a word with each of you separately?" Natalie Pitts approached them with an outstretched microphone, cameraman in tow. She was made up for the camera, her dark blond hair smooth and gleaming. If Nat was surprised to see Kate acting on Leah Roberts' behalf, she gave no indication of it.

"As I said, after you, Ms. Lange," Hillcroft said, his face expressionless. Kate knew he wanted the last word, so that he could discount Kate's comments and garner as much sympathy as he could from the public.

Nat glanced at her, her blue eyes flashing at Hillcroft, and then back to Kate again. "Mr. Hillcroft, we'd like the Crown's statement first."

Nat was a pro, and even if she tended to be a little in-your-face at times, she possessed integrity. She also had a knack for digging under the surface of things. It had helped save Kate's defense of Randall Barrett last year.

Kate stood out of camera range, but close enough to hear Nat ask, "Mr. Hillcroft, what is the Crown's case against Leah Roberts?"

"We are still collecting the evidence at this stage, but she has been charged with break and enter with intent." He then added, "More charges might be pending depending on the outcome of the investigation."

His words sent a trickle of alarm through her. What had the police found? It was impossible to interview her client in the state she was in.

She watched Hillcroft deftly deflect the rest of Nat's questions, and then head toward the parking lot.

Nat walked over to where Kate stood. She gestured for her cameraman to remain back. "Okay, this part is off the record." She crossed her arms, head tilted to one side. "What the hell is going on?"

Kate grinned. "Do you mean, how did I end up representing Leah Roberts?"

"Exactly. One minute you were the star associate doing civil law at McGrath Woods and then you come back from Italy and become a criminal defense lawyer overnight? What the hell?"

"While I was away, I decided it was time to start over." She lowered her voice so the cameraman wouldn't hear. "And McGrath Woods had shuffled me back to the family law practice."

Nat's eyes widened. "Seriously? Why?"

"They would rather I was shot by a good-looking MP than attacked by a depraved stalker." Kate shrugged.

Nat threw a glance at her cameraman, who shifted on his feet. "We have some catching up to do. But in the meantime, let's get this show on the road. I have to warn you, I'm going to ask you some tough questions. Your girl is in deep doo-doo."

"I understand, Nat. But remember I can't tell you anything more than I'd tell any other journalist. And anyway, there isn't much to tell right now until I find out the Crown's case."

"We'll see," she said, motioning for the cameraman to come closer.

True to her word, Kate revealed as little as possible, while trying to create some sympathy for Leah Roberts in the face of questions like: "Did your client know when she broke into the house of the parents of Member of Parliament Harry Owen that his father is a paraplegic—the result of being a previous victim of a bungled robbery—and his mother was dying of a terminal illness?"

"Absolutely not," Kate said, clammy sweat pricking her underarms. "At present, my client is gravely injured and unable to give her statement, due to the gun fired point-blank into her chest by our Member of Parliament. A gun, by the way, which is on the prohibited weapons list. A list, I might add, that was approved by the very committee that the Honorable Harry Owen sits on."

Her ammunition spent, Kate ended the interview. The battle lines between the Crown and the defense had been publicly proclaimed.

The adrenalin rushed out of her, leaving her drained.

"How about brunch on Sunday?" Nat asked, packing the microphone into her shoulder bag.

"Sounds good. But take it easy on me. After that interview, I'm feeling a bit bruised." Kate gave a wry smile.

Nat gave Kate the thumbs up sign. "You handled it well. See you on Sunday at noon."

Kate slung her briefcase over her shoulder and walked through the small park toward her car.

She noticed that the man pushing the woman in the wheelchair—*must be his wife, the way he stopped to tuck in a stray corner of her blanket*—had brought her over to a park bench. He sat at one end, his wife parked next to him in a sunny patch between the trees.

As Kate walked by, she saw him pointing toward a man walking a group of dogs on the sidewalk beyond the hospital property. The woman smiled. So did Kate, when she saw the man who deftly managed his posse.

It was Finn, with several of his doggy charges. Foo Dog rounded up the pack, the small pug an unlikely shepherd of several happy-go-lucky Labrador retrievers, and a watchful husky. The pug's jaunty, bossy command of the Labradors was comical. Finn crossed the intersection, heading down Robie Street.

Kate would tell him tonight about how he made the lady in the wheelchair smile. She stepped out of the path of a taxi that had pulled up to the front of the hospital, and walked toward the parkade. As she opened the door leading to the dank interior, she threw one final look at the GH2.

It gave nothing away about the battles being fought in there.

But then the taxi divulged a passenger that she had only just seen on the front page of the newspaper.

It was Mel Owen. And he looked primed for battle.

28

AIDEN HAD AWOKEN FROM his nap by the railway bridge feeling dizzy, thirsty and hungry. He glanced at the clock on his laptop screen. God. He still had hours to go before his meeting with Tr0lz.

It didn't seem fair that he sat out here baking in the freakin' sun when Tr0lz was kicking back somewhere, counting his money. Once Harry Owen came through with the money, it would be Aiden in the power seat.

He checked his phone again for a message.

Nothing.

The bastard hadn't responded.

WTF!

Didn't he get Aiden's text? Why wasn't he transmitting that money as fast as his greedy little hands could hit 'send'?

Maybe something had happened to him. Maybe he had been arrested for shooting Leah.

The thought stopped him cold.

He hurriedly loaded an online news website.

In bold red letters, the site announced: *BREAKING NEWS: Woman charged with break and enter in MP case.*

Shit. Leah had been charged.

Which meant Leah was alive.

And she would talk to the police, he was sure of it.

And if she spoke to the police, then it was only a matter of time before his plan with Tr0lz would be revealed.

Shit, shit, shit.

If she died, it would make everything so much easier.

He stared at the train tracks. What would it take to cause Leah's death? A simple unplugging of a machine? The kinking of an IV? He had read somewhere that injecting air into a vein could kill you. He was sure he could do that. Needles didn't bother him.

But how would he get to her? She was under police guard.

He needed information. And the news reports weren't giving him enough.

Maybe there was an update on the Forum. He logged in. Immediately, Motherdoxxer jumped on him: *What's taking you so long? When are you going to doxx the effer?*

He ignored it. The guy was just jealous. He talked the talk, but didn't walk the walk.

Has WhiteDwarf been online? He knew full well she hadn't.

haven't u heard? PillBaby asked. *she wuz shot*

Oh my God! he responded. *Is she going to be okay?*

WeepingGelsan says she is hurt pretty bad, Motherdoxxer said. *Harry Owen shot her in the chest the mother effer.*

How does WeepingGelsan know how bad she's hurt?
he lives in hali.

PillBaby probably did, too, given she had referenced 'Hali', the popular nickname for Halifax.

A suspicion formed in his mind. He had met Leah's little brother a few times. His name was Jimmy or Joey or something. He was a big Dr. Who fan. In fact, Aiden had watched a Weeping Angels episode with Joey at Leah's place. He couldn't believe he hadn't figured out the connection before.

Okay, he typed. *Keep me posted about her. I'll doxx Harry tonight.* After he pays me half a million dollars, he added silently.

He checked his text messages again. No word from Harry

Owen. Stubborn bastard. He might have to nudge Harry out of his inaction with a tweet from @TruthAboutHarry. He logged into Twitter and tweeted: *Harry Owen haz a secret. All the sexy details revealed 2nite.*

But while he let Harry Owen freak out over Aiden aka @TruthAboutHarry's latest tweet, he needed to find out Leah's exact status.

He scrolled through his contacts until he found the number for Joey Roberts. After two rings, the kid answered, his voice wary. "Hello?"

"Joey." Aiden cleared his throat. It was so dry, he sounded like a frog. "It's Aiden."

There was a sharp inhale. "You left my sister to die!"

"No, it wasn't like that. Didn't Leah tell you?" He needed to know what she had told her family and the police.

"She's barely conscious."

"But the police arrested her."

"She woke up, but she can't speak very well."

Relief rushed through him. If she couldn't speak, then neither Joey nor the police would know what really went down. "I didn't leave Leah to die. I thought she was right on my heels, but then she dropped something and ran back in before I could stop her."

"Didn't you hear the gun?"

"No. The police had a dog chasing me. You know dogs scare the shit out of me."

Joey's voice lost a bit of its hardness. "She almost didn't make it. She's got tubes stuck all over her."

That was good. Tubes meant she was in bad shape.

"Has she said anything to the police?"

"No. Just to her lawyer."

"Her lawyer?" Shit. He hadn't thought of that. "Who's her lawyer?"

"Someone named Kate Lange. She keeps coming to the hospital to check on Leah. I'm hoping Leah won't say anything until after Condor comes."

He froze. "Condor's coming? All the way from the US?"

"Yeah." Joey's voice lowered. "He wants the data on Leah's laptop."

"Why?"

"Because he wants to make sure that everything Leah went through was worth it."

If Condor posted the contents of Harry's computer onto the Internet before Harry paid the half million, then Aiden would get nothing. And he'd be back relying on Tr0lz for his measly handouts. "But I've got it covered. I'm gonna doxx Harry Owen tonight."

"Condor said that if we left the laptop for the police to find, it would incriminate her."

"Where is it now?"

"I took it." Joey whispered the admission, as if he couldn't quite believe he did it.

Aiden couldn't quite believe it, either. The kid had more balls than he gave him credit. It also meant that Condor would find all the files that Aiden had uncovered. And Condor would doxx Harry mercilessly.

Aiden's blackmail would be dead in the water if he didn't stop Condor from getting the files until after Harry paid up. "Where's her laptop? I'm in a safe place. I can look after it for you."

Joey's voice became wary. "It's taken care of. Look I gotta go, someone's coming—"

Aiden made one last-ditch effort. "Where are you meeting Condor? I need to talk to him." If he could find out where they were meeting, he could snatch the computer from them.

"What about?" No question the kid was suspicious of him.

"It's about a special sub-folder I found on Harry Owen's computer. It has all the memos we need to expose the bastard."

"Condor can find them."

"Probably. But it will save a lot of time if we work together."

"The police are looking for you. You're gonna make us a target."

Jesus, this kid was way smarter than he looked. "I'm good at hiding. They have no clue where I am. Just tell me where you're meeting him. I promise you, Condor will be glad you did."

"I'll check with Condor. If he gives the okay, I'll text you." Joey's voice cracked, but this time it cracked from determination.

Aiden wasn't going to get anywhere with the kid. It was time for Plan B. "I know he'll wanna meet me."

"Gotta run," Joey said and hung up.

Aiden stared at his phone. He couldn't believe the kid had hung up on him.

The afternoon air had thickened in the sun. There was no breeze to cut through the heat. His stomach growled.

Screw it. He needed to get some water. Some nice A/C. And a burger with fries. He texted Tr0lz: *I'm going to mall. Meet me there.* Then he put his laptop into his backpack, hiked it onto his shoulder and began the long walk along the tracks toward the shopping mall. The sun beat down on his head.

But Aiden knew all of the discomforts and indignities of the past few years were about to be wiped out.

Along with Harry Owen.

And his father.

29

KATE SPUN AWAY FROM the parkade, and strode toward the hospital doors, fumbling for her phone.

Randall, tellingly, was still on her speed dial. He answered on the first ring.

"Randall, it's Kate." She kept her tone professional. She didn't want him to think she had any other reason to call. "I just saw your client entering the hospital." She stood in the foyer, scanning the lobby.

No sign of Mel Owen.

"Which client?"

Dammit. Mel Owen must have already gotten into the elevator.

"Is it Mel or Harry?" Randall asked.

She found the stairwell and began to sprint up the stairs. "Mel."

"Is he okay?"

"Yes, no, I mean I think he's here to see Leah."

"I'm on my way."

Kate flung open the stairwell door and punched the intercom to the ICU. "It's Leah Roberts' lawyer. Please let me in." The door buzzed, and she strode into the ICU.

Was Mel Owen even here? Maybe she misinterpreted the

expression on his face. Maybe he had gone to the ER for medical attention. She hoped that was the case.

But she doubted it.

She hurried around the central station and down the corridor to Leah's room. Her heart sank and skipped a beat at the same time. Ahead of her, Mel Owen rolled down the hallway, his gaze wild as he headed toward the sheriff who guarded Leah's door.

The sheriff leapt to his feet, hand on his gun. "Stop! Put your hands where I can see them."

"Get out of my way," Mel Owen yelled at the sheriff. "I don't want to hurt you."

Tim Roberts rushed out of the doorway.

The sheriff gestured at him. "Get back in the room. Now."

But Leah's father held out his hands, his gaze conciliatory. "Mr. Owen, please allow us to extend our deepest symp—"

Mel Owen took his hands off his wheelchair and fumbled in his lap.

In that second, everyone in the hallway understood.

Mel Owen had a gun.

Kate lunged for the handlebars of his wheelchair, spinning the elderly man around as he waved the gun wildly.

"Let go of me! Let go!" Spittle flew out of his mouth.

Kate felt Mel Owen's spit land on her jaw.

"Let go of me or I'll kill you!" Then he twisted in his seat, and smashed the revolver on Kate's hand. Kate yelped, snatching her hand back reflexively.

The sheriff grabbed Mel Owen by the throat and threw the elderly man to the floor.

With no functioning knees to break his fall, Mel Owen landed hard. The sound of his bones connecting with the floor made Kate feel sick.

The sheriff handcuffed him. All resistance had left Harry Owen's father. He lay with his face pressed to the cold floor. Blood trickled in a desolate pool by his mouth. His legs, thin and atrophied from years of disuse, lay crumpled under him.

"Please get him off the floor," Tim Roberts said, his voice shaking.

The sheriff began to hoist Mel Owen into his wheelchair. Kate gasped when she saw the unnatural angle of his upper thigh. The sheriff lowered Mel Owen gently to the floor, and crouched by his side. "We need paramedics. Stat," he said to a porter.

Tears and mucus mixed with the blood on Mel Owen's chin. He was pale, sweat dripping down his temples.

The break looked grotesque. Yet Mel Owen did not seem to feel the pain—and Kate wasn't sure if he was aware of what was going on.

She skirted around him toward Leah's room. Mel Owen suddenly raised his head. "You're her lawyer...aren't you?" he mumbled.

Kate straightened, and released the throbbing hand that she had been cradling. "Yes."

"How do you sleep at night?" His eyes bore into hers, bloodshot and glistening with tears.

I don't sleep. But not for the reason you think.

Two paramedics came rushing down the hallway with a stretcher.

Tim Roberts backed into his daughter's room and put his arm around his wife. Susan Roberts put her head on her husband's shoulder, despair and grief in every line of their bodies. They huddled together as if they could provide a physical wall against the forces that conspired to break their family.

Kate moved to the far end of the corridor, away from Mel Owen's thwarted vengeance, away from the Roberts' stunned expressions. She needed to compose herself.

Leah could have been killed.

And Salma Owen was dead.

The Roberts' lives would never be the same.

The revolver pointed at her head. Kate froze. She would be shot point-blank by the woman who had caused her so much pain as a teenager. The dank odor of the storage room filled her nostrils.

Would she die here?

In a room that was so full of hate and evil that her mouth was rank with it?

Spots swam in Kate's vision. She put a hand on the wall. It was cold.

Cold like the surgical table on which she had once been bound. Cold like the blade of the scalpel that had scarred her leg.

Breathe, Kate.

Mel Owen's blood gleamed in a bleak pool under the harsh lights.

She closed her eyes.

Get it together.

"Kate!" Randall rushed toward her. "What happened? I just saw Mel Owen in a stretcher."

"He tried to shoot Leah. The sheriff tackled him and broke his leg. He's going to the ER."

"What?"

"He had a gun. He was trying to get to her room, but I grabbed the back of his wheelchair."

"Did he hurt you?" Randall ran an assessing gaze over her.

She managed a weak smile. "He gave my hand a good whack with his gun."

"Tell me what happe—"

Two police constables sprinted through the doors to the ICU, guns drawn.

"Don't move! Put your hands out in front of you!" the first officer shouted.

Kate and Randall stretched their arms out so the police could see them. As soon as the two constables ascertained that neither of them possessed weapons, one of the officers approached them, while the other stopped in the doorway of each of the rooms and scanned the interior.

"I represent Mr. Owen," Randall said. "And Ms. Lange is counsel for Ms. Roberts. Can we put our hands down? As you can see, my colleague is injured."

The police officer glanced at Kate's bruised, swollen hand. "Yes, put your hands down. Did either of you witness what occurred?"

Kate nodded. "I saw Mr. Mel Owen arrive at the hospital. I was concerned that he might try to approach my client, so I followed him inside. I ran up the stairs while he took the elevator. Once I reached the ICU, I saw him race down the hallway to my client's room. Then he waved a gun, telling the sheriff to get out of the way."

"Did he fire the gun?"

"No."

"What happened to your hand?"

"I grabbed his wheelchair before he could get to the room."

"Did you see anyone else with Mr. Owen?" The constable's gaze darted around the nursing station.

Kate shook her head. "Mr. Owen appeared to be by himself."

The other constable gave a signal that he had finished checking the rooms.

"Ms. Lange needs to have her hand looked at," Randall said.

The police officer nodded. "Go ahead. If we have any further questions, we will call you."

"Of course." Kate cradled her hand. The pain now radiated in deep waves. She felt slightly nauseous.

"Come on." Randall put his hand on the small of her back and ushered her toward the elevator. "I'll take you to the ER." The Emergency Room was located in the lower level of the building.

Kate shook her head. "You need to call Harry Owen. I'm okay." She lengthened her stride so his hand—which felt too welcome—no longer rested on her.

Randall frowned. "You need someone to walk you there."

"Really, I'm fine. It's just a bit sore." She needed to get this relationship back on a professional track, stat. Before she crumbled against him. "Now go. Your client needs you."

30

IT WAS AS IF Harry had gotten off the plane on Thursday night and entered a nightmare. Every day—no every hour—something terrible seemed to happen.

What had he done to deserve this?

The buzzing of the phone had penetrated his nap.

Was it the blackmailer?

He had seen the tweet from @TruthAboutHarry. There was no doubt in his mind that the man behind the avatar was also his blackmailer—and was Leah's accomplice in the break-in of his parents' home.

The bastard had caused his mother to die. And now, to add insult to injury, he was blackmailing Harry.

And it was only a matter of time before the police connected the dots.

The phone rang again. "Harry Owen." Even though he had just woken up, his voice was tense.

"It's Randall. We've got a problem."

Did the police somehow know that Harry had deleted his files?

Were there cameras in his hotel room?

Harry leapt to his feet and paced the small living area, his eyes searching out the nooks and crannies of the room.

He stopped, shaking his head. Good God. He was paranoid. And that scared him, too.

"What's the matter now?"

His lawyer cleared his throat. "It's your father. He was caught in the hospital."

"Caught? What the hell does that mean?" He ran a hand through his hair.

"He threatened to kill Leah Roberts."

"Jesus Christ."

"And he had a prohibited gun."

Harry felt as if he had been sucker-punched in the gut. *Dad.* "Oh, God. Where did he get the gun?" His voice was hoarse. "Didn't the police seize them all?"

"Evidently not." Randall cleared his throat. "Did you know he might do this?"

In the cab on the way back to the hotel, his father had rambled about vengeance. But Harry had other, more pressing matters on his mind—like blackmail. He had left his father in his hotel room and headed straight to the safe.

And his father must have turned around and gone straight to the hospital.

"He talked about vengeance, but I never thought..." He swallowed. "Oh, God."

"He's in a lot of trouble, Harry." His lawyer's voice was soft, but Harry could not miss the warning.

"Where is he now?" Harry grabbed his jacket.

"In the ER. His leg was broken during the arrest."

"Will he be okay?" *Dad.* The pain in Harry's heart was almost too much to bear. "I'm heading there right now."

He hung up the phone and stared at the screen. His inbox had grown at an exponential rate along with his unanswered text messages.

But the one message he longed to receive—the one person he needed to hear from—was silent in the face of all this misery.

Of course, he knew why. The logical part of his brain accepted it.

But in the darkest moment of his life—of which there was no doubt that this was—he yearned for contact with the one person that he knew loved him.

Would it always be like this?

Harry waiting, counting the days, hours, minutes?

Would he always be at the mercy of their situation?

He remembered when their eyes met at a NATO security meeting. *Coup de foudre*. He was smitten, he was lost, he was drowning. And he could not control himself.

His fingers had a will of their own.

He typed: *I need to see you.* He knew that the message would not be seen for another twelve hours.

But he hit 'send' anyway.

31

AIDEN CRAMMED AS MUCH of the cheeseburger as he could into his mouth, his jaw working furiously while he stared at his laptop screen. He was ravenous for food and starving for information. There was nothing more satisfying than having both of those needs met simultaneously, especially in an air-conditioned, neutral environment.

The food court at the mall was busy enough that he didn't stand out to security, so he took his time squeezing a strip of ketchup from the ridiculously small packet along the edge of his French fry. It was a habit he had developed as a kid. No double dipping for him. It kept things neat, and provided an even spread of the condiment. He could not eat his fries any other way. It allowed him to savor each bite.

Just as he savored each byte of data he stole from Harry. He tweaked the angle of his laptop so that it faced the wall behind him. He didn't want the nosy hipster dude next to him to see the text scrolling down his screen. But the guy kept glancing at him. Aiden scowled at him over his French fry.

The tension of the past day lifted a little as the food hit his blood stream, leaving a deep fatigue in his muscles. He still didn't have a place to sleep tonight. His plan was to hit up

Tr0lz when he came. They were about to become partners, right? Even if he had never met the guy before.

He sipped his soda as he scanned the online news.

What the hell?

There had been, "an incident in the Intensive Care Unit of the Greater Halifax General Hospital. An armed man attempted to shoot accused Leah Roberts, charged with the break-and-enter of the parental home of MP Harry Owen."

Who was the armed man?

It couldn't have been Harry Owen, could it?

Was that why he hadn't answered Aiden's blackmail demand?

If it was Harry Owen who attempted to kill Leah again, this might screw everything up. If he was arrested, it would make it difficult—if not impossible—to get the blackmail money from him.

The cheeseburger churned in his stomach. He'd been waiting for years to serve his revenge on Harry Owen, the rabidly ambitious lawyer from Halifax, who made a name for 'protecting' the public and 'keeping citizens safe' when he appeared as the government's witness in Aiden's criminal trial.

"We cannot allow indiscriminate and malicious hacking into our government systems," the Honorable Member said, his voice somber. *"This case was especially egregious, as it not only exposed the vulnerabilities of a key network system of a provincial judicial department, but caused untold harm to the victims whose sealed cases were posted online for all the world to see…"*

Aiden had poked a stick in the eye of the Minister of Justice, the courts, and the police—and they had their revenge. The only thing that saved him from a very long sentence was the fact that he was seventeen, "with tremendous promise" according to his defense lawyer.

The effing judge had viewed it differently. "A young man with every advantage who exploited his intelligence, the high tech computer network gifted to him by doting parents, and wreaked havoc on the courts while causing untold grief to victims of sexual abuse and gang violence, while exposing them to new threats and harassment."

It was true, he hadn't understood the ramifications of what he had done...his victim was supposed to be the government. The *Honorable*—God, that title made him sick— Harry Owen had made sure that the judge knew exactly how terrible Aiden's crime had been. And the judge came down as hard on him as he could within the confines of the law.

This time Aiden would get it right. He would show the hypocrisy of the government, the lies perpetrated in the name of 'public safety'. The citizens of this fair country had no idea what was going on in Harry's department. Or what was going on in Harry's bedroom.

Public safety. What a joke. He squeezed another line of ketchup onto his French fry, imagining he was squeezing Harry's throat. "You really screwed yourself big time, Harry. Didn't anyone warn you that you could be blackmailed for shit like that?"

"Talk to yourself much?" A girl slid into the seat opposite him.

He guessed she was an international student judging by her age and the backpack slung over her shoulder emblazoned with the logo of one of Halifax's local universities. Her accent was impeccably Canadian. But her style was decidedly Asian-street: slouchy cropped grey sweater, tiny flared black mini skirt, and black over-the-knee socks that sported a cartoon kitty cat face outlined in white that appeared to peek above her knees. Her long, black hair had been casually curled below her shoulders. Thick bangs framed an exquisitely heart-shaped face.

He quickly lowered the screen of his laptop. "Do I know you?" Her timing couldn't be worse. He was expecting Tr0lz any minute.

She raised a perfectly penciled brow. "I don't know, AggroBoy...do you know me?" Her low, breathy voice mocked him.

Her large brown eyes challenged him to move past his

assumptions, to get over his initial stumble. She crossed her arms, revealing a delicate tattoo in Asian script on one wrist.

"You're Tr0lz." His voice was low. He hoped his face didn't show how stunned he was at the revelation that this cute, waif-like girl was his new partner in crime.

She grinned, her red lips revealing a set of strong-looking teeth. "Took you long enough, AggroBoy. I thought you were supposed to be the brains in this partnership." Her gaze ran over him, as cool and oblique as a waterfall he had once walked through.

He straightened. "I am." He felt desperately out of his league. It was an unwelcome and unfamiliar feeling.

She shrugged, her expression bored. "We'll see." She reached over and gripped the edge of his laptop screen, neatly pivoting his computer so that it faced her. He noticed how elegant her hands were: long, pale fingers, with nails painted in the palest pink. "Why did you say that Harry Owen had really screwed himself? Did you find something?" She typed a command, her fingers skimming the keys with the grace of a dragonfly.

He leaned toward her. "He's having an affair."

She threw him an amused look. "Welcome to the twenty-first century, AggroBoy."

He flushed. "Read the emails I just loaded."

She tucked a strand of hair behind her ear and scanned the emails. "Did you realize that his lover will be in Halifax tomorrow?"

He squinted at the date in the email and then at the calendar on his screen. "Oh, yeah."

"Do you know what this means?"

He eyed the line of ketchup on his French fry. "He's going to get laid." He felt an erection coming on.

She plucked the fry from his hand. "What it means is that we are officially in business." She delicately bit off the end of the fry. A drop of ketchup smudged the tip of her finger. It was startlingly red against her skin. She slid her finger between her lips and licked it, locking her gaze with his.

His brain was having difficulty processing the implications of what she said when it was bombarded with the suggestiveness of what she just did. It was as if she had taken his chair and spun it in circles until he was so dizzy that the only thing he could focus on was this strange mutant version of the hacker Tr0lz. He was supposed to be an awkward nerd. Not...*this*.

"Do I need to spell it out for you?" She closed the lid of his laptop and leaned toward him. "Harry's lover is a United States Captain. Just imagine the cred we would get if we took his lover out as part of our exploit."

"What? Are you crazy?"

She threw a look around the food court. "Keep your voice down."

He leaned toward her. "What the hell are you suggesting?"

"I'll tell you somewhere more private." She eyed his sweat-soaked clothing with disdain. "Where are you staying?"

He threw a glance over his shoulder. "Nowhere."

"Fine. You can come to my place until we finish the job."

He grabbed his burger from the wrapper and was about to finish it off when he noticed she was staring at him. He held it out to her. "Want some...partner?"

"No." She made a moue of disgust. "I'm vegan." She stood. "Let's go."

He shoved the rest of the burger in his mouth while pushing his laptop into his backpack.

Tr0lz had already begun to wend her way through the tables in the food court. From the back, he discovered that her over-the-knee kitty socks revealed a black cat tail that curled up the back of each of her slim thighs.

He fell into step beside her. "I don't know your name."

She flipped her hair as she flashed him a look. "You do know my name."

"No, I don't. I'm——"

She gripped his wrist. Her fingers had a tensile strength

that shocked and excited him at the same time. She reached up to murmur in his ear. "You are AggroBoy. And I am Tr0lz."

"But—"

"And that is how we will always be. Got it?"

Then she released his arm.

He nodded. But his mind raced.

Tr0lz strode in front of him. The tails on the back of her tights curled confidently.

Or threateningly.

He knew, without a doubt, it was the latter.

32

AN X-RAY CONFIRMED THAT the bones in her hand had miraculously withstood the blow of Mel Owen's gun. Kate left the ER and found an empty bench outside the hospital. It was a beautiful supper hour, the air dry and warm, with enough breeze to lift her hair.

She closed her eyes and breathed deeply. *Just give yourself a minute, Kate.*

But it was no use. Her mind raced.

She straightened, dialed the Crown prosecutor's number, hoping he would still be at work.

"John Hillcroft." His voice was pleasant, crisp in her ear.

"Hi John, it's Kate Lange."

"Kate! I heard about what happened. Are you okay?"

"Yes, I'm all right. Look, I wanted to discuss the possibility of an immunity agreement for my client, Leah Roberts."

His voice immediately became guarded. "Why do you think the Crown would be interested?"

"You have a second suspect on the loose who has not yet been captured. My client might have information about his whereabouts."

"But why would we give up prosecuting Leah Roberts?

172

She was caught in the act, so to speak. And the police might find our guy."

"I suspect there's more to this than meets the eye. Her actions are not consistent with her background or what others say about her."

"You'd be surprised by how many people with the best opportunities in life commit crimes."

Kate gave a wry laugh. "*I* wouldn't be surprised. I may be new to criminal defense, but I was the one attacked by Kenzie Sloane, remember?"

"Right." He cleared his throat. "So you think that the mastermind behind this break-in wasn't Leah Roberts, even though we believe the break-in is connected to cyber security and Leah Roberts is a cyber security analyst?" His tone made her theory sound completely implausible.

Save it for the jury, John.

"I don't know yet. I haven't been able to speak to her. But I would like to present her with the option of an immunity deal."

"If—and this is a big 'if', Kate—we offer her a deal, not only must she give up her accomplice, but we also require her laptop. The police team came up empty when they searched her apartment."

That wasn't good news in terms of portraying her client as a dupe, but it was good news if Leah could tell the police where to find it.

"I will let her know. How soon can I expect to hear back from you?"

"ASAP."

The alacrity with which John Hillcroft was willing to investigate an immunity deal belied his earlier coyness. That only bode well for Leah's prospects—if they could broker the deal before her accomplice was found.

Kate jumped to her feet, and left the summer-scented air for the re-circulated environment of the hospital's ICU.

"The ICU is on lockdown except for family," the clerk said over the intercom.

"I'm Kate Lange, counsel for Ms. Roberts."

There was a muted conversation.

Then a police constable opened the door for her. "We need to pat you down, Ms. Lange. Please step to the side."

Another constable held out his hand for Kate's bag. While one inspected her purse, the other conducted a physical pat down. Over the constable's head, Kate watched the medical staff converse behind the central station. They were tense but calm.

"You may proceed, Ms. Lange," the constable said, while the second constable returned her bag.

"Thank you." Kate headed down the corridor, her mind focused on the interview ahead. She had many questions for Leah. The main one being why was she in the Owen house last night?

And did Leah know Harry's family history when she broke into their house?

Kate hoped not.

She stopped outside Leah's room. Susan Roberts sat on one side of her daughter's bed, holding Leah's hand. Kate wasn't sure who was comforting whom.

Tim Roberts sat on the other side, facing the hallway. He watched Kate approach, meeting her gaze with a look of raw despair.

A teenage boy sat on a chair next to Tim Roberts. Although barely a man himself, his white-blond hair was tied up on his head in a man-bun. He nibbled on the end of a nail. He eyed Kate with a wariness that was striking as she walked into the room.

"Joey, this is Kate Lange. She's one of the lawyers defending Leah," Susan Roberts said. "And we hope she will ensure that Harry Owen and his father are charged for attempting to murder Leah. *Twice.*"

"You need to understand that I can't make the police lay charges, Mrs. Roberts," Kate said. "Only the police decide to do that. The Crown might weigh in on the likelihood of getting a conviction." She wondered what Hillcroft would recommend. He had a near perfect track record for convictions, so he wouldn't recommend charges be laid unless he was certain they would hold up in court.

"But the police will lay charges against that man, won't they?" Susan Roberts persisted.

An eye for an eye seemed to be the flavor of the day. Mel Owen may not realize it, but he had just done Kate's client a huge favor by attempting to shoot her while she was unable to defend herself.

Stop it, Kate. That's cynical.

But true. It would give weight to the argument that this was the second time a member of the Owen family attempted to shoot her client when she was defenseless.

"Mom…" Leah protested.

"Mrs. Roberts, what the police do is out of our control. But I will be discussing the situation with the Crown. For today, let's focus on the charges Leah face. I need to speak to her in private." Kate strode over to the foot of Leah's bed. "Are you up for a discussion, Leah?"

"Yes." Her client eased her hand from her mother's grip. Kate was reassured that her client spoke clearly. The sedation must be wearing off. Or maybe the shock of someone trying to kill her for the second time in twenty-four hours had shaken her from the cocoon of opioids.

Tim Roberts extended his hand to his wife. "We'll wait outside." Leah's father guided her mother out of the room. Joey followed them, hunching deeper into his hoody as he left the room.

Kate pulled out a notepad and sat down in the seat vacated by Susan Roberts. "How are you feeling, Leah?"

"Not good." Tears trembled on her client's lashes. "Everything is spinning out of control. I can't believe Mel Owen wanted to kill me." She took a shuddering breath. "But then again, I can."

"Why were you in Mel Owen's house last night?"

Leah closed her eyes. "You have to understand, I didn't think anyone would be there."

Kate touched her hand. "Leah, you need to look at me. And you need to answer my questions directly if you want me to help you."

Leah opened her eyes.

Kate recalled the photo of Leah with her cat. Those wary eyes with secrets behind them. "Leah, everything you tell me is protected by solicitor-client privilege. I won't divulge anything. But I need you to tell me the truth."

Leah exhaled. "I was there because I wanted to doxx Harry Owen." Her voice was thin and hoarse.

"Docs? What does that mean?"

"Doxxing is when you hack into someone's computer, download files from their folders, and then post all the information on the Internet."

"You mean like what happened to Sony when its internal emails were posted on the Internet by Dark Seoul?"

"Yes."

Kate gave a mental shudder. "Why would you do that?"

"Because I found out that Harry Owen and his department were hiding a massive data breach. The identities of every single traveller entering Canada had been stolen from border security systems."

Kate studied her client. There was a ring of truth in her words. Her gaze was earnest. Anxious. "Seriously?"

"Yes."

"And why did you decide to doxx Harry over that?"

"The government was hiding it. I couldn't let them get away with it. There are millions of people affected. And they decided not to tell anyone."

"Why not?"

"They said it was because they didn't want the 'wrong people' to know the information was floating around in cyber space."

Kate studied her client. "That seems like a good reason."

"Anyone who knows anything about the Dark Web would know that potential buyers would have been contacted by brokers if the information was for sale. It might have even been stolen with a particular buyer in mind."

"I don't understand how a cyber hack resulted in break-and-enter with intent. Can't you just hack through a computer network from the safety of your home?"

Leah threw a glance at the door where the sheriff's broad form could be seen in a chair. "I didn't want the hack connected to me. And it would have been if I had attempted to hack into Harry Owen's computer through work or home. I was on the team that worked in Harry's office. So someone on the Forum—"

"The Forum?"

"It's a group of white hat hackers. People who hack for good reasons."

Kate raised a brow. "People hack for good reasons?"

"They find breaches or vulnerabilities in code and notify authorities. Or they use hacking for social justice causes."

"You mean like hacktivists?"

"Yes. I joined the Forum a few months ago."

"Why?" Kate studied this woman who had achieved so much in her short career. Why risk it all?

Leah hesitated. "I knew someone. And I thought I could make a difference. You know, expose things that were being ignored for political reasons. Or help find information that was hidden on the Web."

"Leah, who was the person who broke into the Owen's house with you?"

"His name is Aiden Boyne."

"Were you lovers?"

"Yes." Pain mingled with shame in her client's eyes.

Nothing worse than discovering your lover has exploited you. Kate gave her a sympathetic look. "So what went wrong last night?"

"Everything."

Kate took several pages of notes as Leah told her exactly how badly everything had gone. "So let me get this straight. You tried to escape out of the window, but he pulled a knife on you?"

"Yes." That admission came out in a whisper.

Leah appeared completely humiliated—but the events provided a light at the end of the tunnel for her client in the form of a nice coercion argument.

Leah gazed down at the sheet covering her legs. "What do you think the police will do about Mel Owen's attack?"

"I think he will be charged. Just like you, he was caught in the act."

She looked at Kate. "I'd rather Harry's father not be charged. I've done enough damage to him."

"It's not up to you, Leah. He was armed with a prohibited weapon, and risked the life of a sheriff. It was very unfortunate."

Tears glistened in Leah's eyes. "Does he have a good lawyer?"

Kate nodded. "He has one of the best. You can't worry about him, Leah. What's done is done. Let's talk about next steps."

"Are they going to send me to prison as soon as the hospital discharges me?"

"Yes, that would be the procedure."

Leah stared down at her hand resting on the bed. Her skin was translucent, every vein articulated and blue.

"I'm hoping we can avoid jail time for you, Leah. Your best option right now is to get immunity from the Crown."

She swallowed. "How do I do that?"

"You become a Crown witness. You give them the name of your boyfriend. You tell the police how to find him. Also, the Crown wants your laptop. The police have searched your apartment but it wasn't located."

Leah's eyes flew to Kate's face. "It was there last night. I left it on my desk."

"In obvious sight?"

"Yes. It was plugged in. And I had it set up to download the data at a certain time. The police should have found it."

This did not bode well. "According to the Crown, they don't have it. Do you know who would have taken it?"

"Aiden, maybe?"

"Did he have a key to your apartment?"

"No. And I guess it doesn't make sense that he'd risk another break in. The data would have also downloaded onto his own laptop."

"Do you have an address for Aiden?"

"He told me he lived on South Street. But I never went to his place. He always came to mine. I don't know for sure if that was his address."

"I'll give it to the Crown and the police will check it out." Kate hoped that the address was real. Leah had been deceived more than once by Aiden Boyne.

She eyed her client. Leah appeared exhausted. "The Crown will want you to testify against him if they grant you immunity. Are you willing to do that? It means you will have to face him in court."

"Nothing would give me more pleasure." The last word came out slurred.

"Get some sleep," Kate said. "I'll let you know if the Crown calls tonight."

"Thank you. You don't know what a difference you've made." Leah's eyes drifted closed.

It was the first time a client had said that to her.

Her phone chimed with a new text message as she entered the hospital lobby.

I'm picking up supper, Eddie announced. *What's your poison?* He added a skull and crossbones emoji.

It wasn't easy to type with one hand. She pecked: *I would love salad and falafel.*

"Kate."

Randall rose from a seat in the waiting area, falling into step beside her. "Let me drive you home." He had removed his tie, the top button of his white shirt unbuttoned.

She became aware of the rise and fall of his chest under his pale grey suit, the warm breath passing his lips, the hint of burnished stubble along his jaw.

Resist, Kate. Resist. "What about your car?"

179

"I'll send Nick to get it. He just got his driver's license." Randall's voice was tinged with pride.

Kate felt a pang at his words. For a brief time, her life and Randall's had become entwined during his criminal case. It had been torn asunder in the aftermath. But life in Randall's household had moved on without her.

Her hand throbbed.

Her heart throbbed.

He was pulling her in, just like he always did. "Thanks, but I can still use this hand to drive." She wiggled her fingers. "See?"

His phone chimed. "Sorry——" he glanced down at it. "It's Lucy. She needs me to pick her up now." He gave her a smile that was too full of tenderness. Why did he have to be so tender? It was making it so hard. "Are you sure I can't drop you off on my way?"

She shook her head. "No. Thanks." She pulled her phone out of her pocket. "I just need to check my messages." It was the only thing she could think of to end this awkward conversation. She knew without a doubt that if she walked with him to the parkade, she would end up in his car, and God only knew where that would lead.

"Of course." She glimpsed hurt in his eyes. "Have a good weekend."

"You, too. Give my best to Lucy."

Please go. Before I change my mind.

He seemed to read her mind, because he turned on his heel and walked through the sliding doors.

Kate wished that her heart had a set of sliding doors that would close as smoothly and surely on Randall's retreating back.

33

6:45 p.m.

"SO I GO TO court for a mind-numbing afternoon of listening to an ill-prepared Crown witness, and you manage to save your client from being killed, get your hand busted, and begin negotiating an immunity deal?" Eddie asked, dipping a piece of pita bread into a bowl of hummus.

Kate swallowed an olive, savoring the salty after bite on her tongue. "That pretty well sums it up. Please tell me this isn't what my life will be like at Bent & Lange from now on."

Eddie chuckled. "Stop complaining. You love it."

"Stop leading the witness, Mr. Bent." Kate popped another olive into her mouth. But maybe she was an adrenaline junkie—and just hadn't realized it.

"By the way," Eddie added, "I think the Crown will offer a deal to Leah. This case is too high profile to risk letting the mastermind off the hook. The media are going nuts."

Her phone rang.

Eddie gave a satisfied smile. "What did I just say? I bet it's Hillcroft."

Kate glanced at the number on her screen. "You guessed right. I guess that's why they pay you the big bucks." She answered the phone. "Kate Lange."

"Kate, it's John Hillcroft. It's a gorgeous evening, so I won't waste your time. We have a deal if your client comes through with our conditions."

Kate caught Eddie's eye and mouthed, "Yes."

Eddie raised a brow.

Kate put down her fork. "My client is prepared to testify against her boyfriend, the suspect who is currently the subject of the police search. She believes he is in possession of her laptop."

"Why does she think he would take it?"

"Before I divulge any more information, John, do we have a deal?"

He exhaled. "If your client is telling the truth that she doesn't know where it is, we are prepared to grant immunity. However, if we discover that she's lied about any of these conditions, the deal will be off. For good. Understand?"

"Yes, of course. The boyfriend's name is Aiden Boyne. His last known address is on South Street in Halifax."

"We will run a check on him and verify your client's information. I'll call you soon." The phone clicked in her ear.

"Congratulations." Eddie handed her a mug of tea. "You just negotiated your first immunity agreement."

"Thanks," Kate said. "But I think the media will claim she got off too lightly."

Leah Roberts was officially the most hated woman in the world right now. So far, they'd been able to keep that fact from her. She was not permitted any laptop or mobile use. But eventually, she would find out about how her actions had resulted in exactly what she had feared: becoming an exile. She might not be forced to flee her country, but her country had expelled her from their good graces with a vengeance.

For a woman like Leah, who had thought she was doing the right thing, the guilt and remorse would be something that she might never recover from. There was no doubt that Salma Owen would forever grip Leah's conscience in her fragile, death-pocked hands, even if Kate and Eddie were able to get Leah off the hook from her criminal charges.

As Kate knew too well, the only way back for Leah was personal redemption.

And right now, it didn't look like that was going too well for Leah.

Fatigue had set in. Kate's body clock was still on Italy time and had been delightfully lulled by a full stomach after their meal. She cupped the tea mug in her good hand, letting the other rest on top of Alaska's head. He had become her shadow since she returned home last night. "How's your new place, Eddie?"

Eddie settled back in his chair, mug in hand, Foo Dog on his lap. The pug had had spent the entire meal sitting on his foot, until Eddie relented and allowed him on his lap. "My place is very comfortable. It's been re-done, like most of the houses in that neighborhood, and my neighbors seem pretty relaxed." He idly scratched the pug's ears. Foo Dog snorted with pleasure.

"Maybe you should get a dog," Kate said. "You've been looking after Charlie for the past year."

Eddie shrugged, scratching the sweet spot by Foo Dog's ear. "Maybe." He cleared his throat. "Elaine's coming for a visit next week."

Elaine was Eddie's ex-wife. Kate knew that Eddie still loved her. But Elaine had made it clear that she could no longer live with his struggles with alcoholism.

"You'll have to bring her over for dinner."

Eddie must have seen the hope spark in Kate's eyes. He raised a cautioning hand. "Don't get too excited. She's staying at a hotel."

But Kate saw her excitement reflected in his gaze. "Still. Bring her over for supper. I'd love to meet her."

Maybe redemption for Leah was a long shot, but she hoped with all of her heart that Eddie Bent would finally get his.

34

6:58 p.m.

"WE'VE GOT A NAME." Cooper slid his phone back into his pocket.

"How?" Lamond looked up from his desk.

"Hillcroft just called. He's negotiating an immunity deal with Leah Roberts. She said her boyfriend broke into the Owen house with her. His name is Aiden Boyne."

Cooper loaded the system that ran criminal record checks. "Let's see if we can run his prints. Maybe he had a key she didn't know about."

Record not found. Cooper exhaled. No Aiden Boyne in the criminal records registry. He tried a few variations on the name: Aidan, Alden, Boyle, Bone, Bowen, with different combinations. But he kept getting the same result.

"Our guy is not in the system. He's not listed with the Registry of Motor Vehicles, either. And I can't find anyone with his name or even close to his name on South Street."

"So he lied to Leah Roberts?" Lamond asked.

Cooper nodded. "I wonder how well she knew him."

"Obviously not well enough."

Cooper opened his Internet browser and loaded Facebook. He searched for Aiden Boyne. "I found an Aiden Boyne who is friends with Leah Roberts." Cooper clicked on

Aiden Boyne's profile picture. It was of a young boy holding a cat. The boy had medium-dark hair, fair complexion, and dark lashes. He gazed at the camera with a strangely unreadable expression.

Cooper scrolled through Aiden Boyne's Facebook profile. It had only been created eighteen months ago. That was the first red flag. The second, bigger red flag was that there was not one personal photo of Aiden Boyne as an adult. His bio indicated he had attended a local high school, but with no graduation year. His friend list was small. And when Cooper cross-referenced them with Leah's, he realized they were mainly Leah's friends, and several others who worked for the same cell phone company. "This is a fake i.d.", he said to Lamond. "Let's get a warrant to hunt this guy down online."

"We need one for this @TruthAboutHarry account," Lamond said. "He just sent a tweet about a 'secret' that will be revealed."

"They must be the same guy," Cooper said. "And I bet he does have Leah's laptop— Hey, Riley, how's it going?"

Detective Riley strode toward his desk, her auburn hair pulled back into a messy ponytail. "I've finished processing the scene." She exhaled. "We couldn't get any prints for the suspects at the Owen house."

"Nothing on the window sill?"

"No."

"How about the computer desk?"

She shook her head. "We went over the equipment a second time once we learned Leah Robert's occupation. She must have kept her gloves on if she handled the computers. We've got Murphy, our computer analyst, going through Mel Owen's system right now."

"Maybe that will give us something. The suspect's name that we got from Leah Roberts is an alias. Nothing is coming up for him." He cleared his throat. "Did you find any signs of weapons that were unaccounted for?"

Riley shoved a strand of hair off her forehead. "You mean other than the one that Mel Owen had snuck out?"

The constables controlling the scene had gotten into serious trouble over that one. The whole afternoon at the ICU had been one almighty screw-up. And even if Mel Owen was at fault, it never looked good for the justice system when a brawny sheriff breaks the leg of a frail, elderly paraplegic who had twice been a victim of break-and-enters. "The weapons were all accounted for with that one exception."

"At least the suspect didn't get his hands on one of the guns," Lamond said. "But Leah Roberts thinks he has her laptop."

Riley shot Cooper a look. "How'd he get that?"

"We don't know. When we executed the search on her apartment at lunchtime, it wasn't there. But she said she left it on her desk last night before she broke into the Owen house. We questioned her parents, her brother, her roommate, and none of them knew where it was."

"Did her boyfriend have a key to her apartment?"

"She says no. And there were no signs of forced entry. So…" Cooper took a sip of the coffee Lamond brought him an hour ago. He noticed Riley eyeing it. "We need to find out from Ms. Roberts who has a key to her apartment. One of her family members might be trying to protect her and took the laptop. Or someone close to Leah who has a key might be connected to the boyfriend and let him in." He looked at Riley. "Was there anything else you found missing at the Owen house?"

She shook her head. "There wasn't any theft."

"Which makes a cyber security crime not only the most obvious motive, but also the most likely one." They needed that laptop. "We're getting a warrant drafted for Harry Owen's laptop, but it has top-security information on it, and the government doesn't want to release it at this point."

"Jesus." Riley grimaced. "They're shooting themselves in the foot."

Cooper refused to let his first GIS case get mired in dead ends. "Let's find out who had keys to Leah's apartment and take it from there."

35

7:08 p.m.

"**I'M GOING TO GET** some fresh air," Joey said to his parents. "Can you text me if…anything changes?"

The fear in the pit of his stomach had morphed—as he knew it would—into anxiety. It filled him—his mind, his chest, his stomach, his limbs. Every part of his body was on high alert, ready to combat all the things in his world that were out of his control.

He longed for the comfort of Spook.

"Are you going home?" his mother asked.

He shook his head. "No, I'll probably go to the Oval and rollerblade." The Oval had been built at the Halifax Commons for the Canada Games speed skating events a few years ago, but had become a popular destination for winter ice skating and summer rollerblading.

"Good idea," his mother gave an encouraging smile. "Are you meeting any friends?"

"Yeah. I'm meeting Kev." Kevin was his closest friend in high school. He'd been texting Joey all day, but Joey hadn't answered beyond telling him that he was tied up for a bit.

He pulled his hood over his head, walking past the armed sheriff, and the police constable standing by the nurses' station. His heart pounded so hard, all he could hear was the blood in his ears.

Had the police figured out that Leah's laptop was missing? Would they guess he had lied to them when he said he hadn't been to Leah's apartment recently?

Would they ask Mike, Leah's neighbor, if he had seen anyone go into Leah's apartment?

The rinsed cat food tin.

He had fed Spook, not even thinking to wear gloves.

Would Maddie realize that Joey had been to the apartment?

Would she tell the police?

Oh, God.

His stomach clenched. He stood at the elevator, waiting for it to arrive. It seemed as if there were eyes drilling into his back.

The elevator had not budged from the top floor.

Screw it.

He took the stairs, arriving in the lobby more breathless than the descent warranted. Within minutes, he was on his bike. His first stop was the gym. He had hidden Leah's laptop in his locker. Heart pounding, he slipped it into his backpack. All he wanted to do was hand it over to Condor.

It was near eight o'clock when he arrived at the library on Spring Garden Road. The modern glass building had transformed the downtown core of Halifax, bringing fresh community spirit to a segment of the city that had once been a vibrant shopping area, but had suffered from the usual woes of dysfunctional urban planning. The fabric of Halifax's downtown was changing, and no one really knew what it would bring. Kind of like Joey's life right now.

He locked his bike and hurried through the main entrance to the stairs near the middle of the library. It wasn't too busy at this hour, so he took them two at a time to the fourth floor.

A series of long white bookcases led to a sitting area of

cubist-style furniture in shades of lime green and citrus orange, placed invitingly in front of the floor-to-ceiling windows.

Near call number 520 stood a man. The man at whose suggestion Joey had become an accessory to a crime that was snowballing into something even worse.

The man stood with his back to Joey, astronomy book in hand, gazing past the expanse of bookcases through the glass window to the nascent evening sky. It was still blue, but the clouds were edged with fiery gold and coral pink.

While the man studied the sky, Joey studied the hacktivist he only knew as Condor. Grey beanie, not very tall, with an olive complexion.

Joey's high-top sneakers squeaked as he walked toward the man who had masterminded some of the Forum's best hacks.

At the sound, Condor turned, throwing him a sideways glance as he pretended to study the astronomy collection.

Joey stopped in front of him. "Condor," he whispered. To his mortification, his voice broke. He felt his cheeks turn pink.

"Call me Matt." Condor aka Matt said. He had a smooth voice, his accent slightly Hispanic. "Do you have it?"

Joey nodded, pulling Leah's laptop from his backpack and handing it to him.

Matt slipped it into his leather messenger bag. "How is she?" he asked, his voice low.

Joey's throat tightened. "She's awake."

Relief flashed through Matt's eyes.

"But Harry Owen's father tried to kill her this afternoon."
"What?"

"Harry Owen's father had a gun and he came to the ICU and tried to kill her as revenge for killing his wife."

The anxiety that had been white noise in his cells now erupted.

Matt looked as sick as Joey felt. "What exactly happened at the Owen house?"

"Leah didn't kill anyone. Mrs. Owen was dying. She had a heart attack." From fear. He could totally relate. He thought his heart was about to shoot up through his throat and out of his mouth this very minute.

"Jesus. Poor lady." Matt's gaze narrowed. "Tell me what happened exactly. When did Harry Owen shoot her?"

"She told me that she was trying to give herself up and he shot her in the leg."

"I thought she had a chest wound."

"Then he shot her point-blank. In the chest."

Matt frowned. "When she was already injured?"

"Yeah. She was on the ground. And he shot her."

"The bastard. What did Aggroboy do?"

"Aggroboy had already escaped." Joey felt rage push against his anxiety. "Her own boyfriend left her to die."

Matt snapped the book closed as if Aggroboy was between the covers. "He left her there? What's the prick's name?"

"Aiden Boyne."

"He's going to regret this." Matt lowered his voice. "But first, I need to see Leah."

"You can't. She's under guard. They are only letting family visit."

Matt ran a hand over his face. Exhaustion darkened the skin under his eyes. But then he grabbed Joey's arm. "Let's get out of here. It's too open. Is there a place where we can look at Leah's machine?"

Joey's mind raced. *I don't know. I don't know. I don't know. Breathe, Joey.*

Matt leaned in closer to Joey. "Are you all right, bro?"

Joey nodded. "Fine." He swallowed. "I'm fine."

"Let's go to my hotel. We can look at it there."

"I just have to let my parents know where I am."

"Call them when we are at the hotel."

"Okay." Joey felt the anxiety ease up a tiny bit.

Matt would take care of this mess.

But then he remembered Leah, lying in that hospital bed with her feet hanging off the edge, tubes stuck in every soft, tender angle of her body.

His throat closed.

Breathe, Joey.

36

8:25 p.m.

LEAH WATCHED HER PARENTS hurry over to greet Kate Lange, who stood at the entrance to her room. Her parents had never looked their age until now. In fact, they didn't just look their age, they appeared older. God. What had she done?

"Ms. Lange, you saved our daughter's life today," her dad said, his voice suddenly choking up. Hearing the catch in his voice made Leah's throat close.

This lawyer was the only thing between her and prison, between shame and redemption. And Kate Lange had not only offered her a sliver of hope, but had literally saved her life. It was funny how a day ago, she had no idea who Kate Lange or her partner were, and now she and her family depended on them for her future.

She sent out a silent plea to the universe: *please let the immunity deal go through*. She couldn't stand what she had done to her family.

Kate gave her father an embarrassed shrug. "I just had good timing." She threw a glance at Leah. "I need to speak with Leah in private."

"Of course." Leah heard the lift of hope in her father's voice. They, like her, were desperate for good news. As her

192

parents left the room, her mother shot a glance at Kate Lange: *Is everything okay?*

But her lawyer's gaze was neutral. After her parents had exited, Kate walked to the foot of her bed.

"Hi." She searched Kate's face. Her lawyer appeared somber. Not jubilant. "Did you hear from the Crown?"

"That's why I'm here. They just called. The Crown ran a check on Aiden Boyne. The name was an alias. He doesn't exist."

Damn him.

Damn him for making a fool of her heart. Pain stabbed through her, but she wasn't sure if it was from the bullet wound or the knowledge that she had thrown her future away for a man who didn't even exist—and perhaps a principle that didn't exist, either. "I should have trusted my gut."

Kate's gaze was compassionate. "If it's any consolation, he's obviously very adept at hiding his identity. The police are having a hard time cracking it."

"What happens if they can't find him?" Leah's heart began to race. The monitor behind her beeped, warning that her one chance at redemption was rapidly slipping through her fingers.

"The Crown made it clear that if there was no suspect, and no laptop, there would be no deal. Do you know any of his friends or family who might know where he is?"

"No. He said that he came from Calgary. That he had just moved here. So he was still making friends." It sounded so weak. But it made sense at the time.

"How about other hackers on the Forum? Would they know where to find him?"

She thought of the hackers: Motherdoxxer, PillBaby, Xstac-I. She was pretty sure none of them would know the real man behind the Aiden Boyne identity.

But what about Tr0lz?

Messages scrolled down Aiden's phone screen. He was in the washroom. She didn't want to snoop, but the rapid movement kept catching her eye. Before she had a chance to read them, he strode out of the washroom and snatched the phone from the bedside table.

"I didn't know you were such good friends with Tr0lz," she said.

"I'm not." His voice was brusque. "He had a question about a SQL code. It was boring, so we took it offline."

She had allowed herself to be satisfied with that response.

But now...

Kate leaned forward. "Leah, you can't protect people any longer. This is all going to come out. Is there someone in the Forum who knows Aiden?"

Leah exhaled. "I'm not sure. He seemed to be buddies with Tr0lz."

"Trolls?"

"Tr0lz is the chat name for another hacktivist. I noticed they messaged a lot offline."

"What about?"

"I don't know. Aiden said it was just coding stuff." At the time, she had believed him...

"Have you ever met Tr0lz?"

"No. I don't even think he lives here. The Forum is global. It has hacktivists from all over the world."

"Do you know Tr0lz's real identity?"

"No. We are careful to protect our identities on the Forum. In case it gets breached."

"Is there anyone on the Forum who actually knows the people behind the chat names? Someone who administers the accounts?" Kate asked.

Leah shook her head. "It doesn't work that way. But maybe Matt could crack their online identities."

"Matt?"

"He's the guy who founded the Forum." Faint color bloomed in Leah's cheeks. "I met him when we were in university."

"You know him personally?"

"Yes." She hesitated. *Why are you hesitating, Leah? This lawyer is the only person who can save you right now. You have nothing left to hide.* "We dated. He's the one who invited me to join the Forum."

"Why?"

"I don't know." She felt heat burn in her cheeks. "I guess he knew I had an interest in social justice."

"And do you think Matt could figure out who Aiden Boyne really is?" Kate asked.

"If anyone could, it would be him. He's the best out there."

"Do you have his number?"

Leah had had his number memorized for a very long time. But she hadn't dialed it in months. Not since she met Aiden. "He's in Florida." She recited it. It was funny how reciting a string of numbers felt strange yet comforting at the same time. Maybe it was the painkillers. "I don't know what his reaction will be when you call him."

"Are you on speaking terms?" Kate's voice was matter-of-fact.

"Sort of." Leah's throat tightened. "He didn't want me to do this."

"Why not?"

"He thought it was too dangerous. He said that the Forum didn't commit crimes."

"Doxxing is a crime, Leah." Kate's tone was mild as she rose to her feet.

"But it had a higher purpose." Or so she had thought. God, she was so confused right now.

"We'll give Matt a call and see what he can do to help."

Help. How ironic that the man whom she had regretted walking away from now was her only hope.

She felt as if her and Matt's past and future were shaped the same as the symbol of infinity. The lazy eight looped back to itself, the paths interconnecting at the critical midpoint, the journey infinite and endless. It was as if she and Matt were on the same lazy eight of existence, but had taken opposing loops. And now their paths had once again connected. Either he would put her back on the right track, or she would remain on the one that would send her to prison, her career in ruins, her life destroyed.

"Could you please tell him I'm sorry?" she whispered.

"Of course." And then her lawyer left.

She lay alone in the bed, the room growing dimmer as the light slowly faded into a dark night, the intermittent beeping of the machines her only company.

37

SO THIS WAS THE city where Leah lived.

Matt wished he had a little more time to look around Halifax, but instead he and Joey walked as fast as possible from the library to Matt's downtown hotel. The sidewalks teemed with people dressed in summer dresses, t-shirts, sandals, and shorts. From what Leah had told him about her hometown, Haligonians knew well enough never to waste a beautiful summer's evening. The winter was always too raw a memory. And judging from the bustling outdoor patios, not a single minute of summer weather was being missed.

Music drifted up from the Jazz Festival along the waterfront. Matt thought about how much fun it would have been to be with Leah, listening to smooth jazz, and having a brew. Instead, he led her little brother to the hotel in which they would complete their doxx of Harry Owen.

He knew he could easily isolate each step that had taken them to this result, but right now, it seemed like he was a hero in a movie where he had been teleported to the future and sees what had happened to his life, and then is sent back to his present to avoid making a huge, life-ruining error.

The problem was, this 'future' was really his present. Leah, the girl he had loved for years, lay with a chest wound

197

and a shattered life in a hospital bed. If she ended up with a criminal record—which seemed a given, in this situation— she would never be allowed to live in the United States. By inviting her to join the Forum with the hope of fanning an old flame, he had actually instigated the circumstance that would now keep them apart.

Why hadn't he stopped Leah from doing this stupid break-in? Everything had gone wrong. Aiden had abandoned her—the fucking coward—and Harry Owen had shot her point-blank. Another fucking coward.

They wouldn't get away with it.

"Is this the hotel?" Joey grabbed his arm.

Matt had almost walked past it, so caught up he had been in his own thoughts. "Yeah. This is it."

It was a nice boutique business-class hotel. The bar was busy on a Friday night, with well-groomed patrons clustering around the tables. He and Joey sidestepped the main desk and stepped into an elevator that had opened its door as they stopped in front of it. Matt punched the button to his floor. The room was on an executive floor. Being a talented and highly paid computer consultant had its privileges.

Including a spacious suite. "We can work over here." Matt said, as they entered the room, pointing to a dark leather sofa. "Do you want anything to drink?"

Joey shook his head. "I need to call my parents."

"Good idea." Matt sank onto the sofa and opened Leah's laptop. For a fleeting second, he fought the temptation to read her text messages to Aiden—did she sign them the way she used to sign them to him?—but then pushed the thought from his mind. No good ever came from that kind of snooping.

He began skimming Leah's laptop, only half-listening to Joey's phone conversation.

Jesus.

Harry's downloaded files revealed a mother lode of classified data that he could not believe had been kept on his personal laptop.

But then he could believe it. Because if it was one thing he had learned, it was that arrogance led people to do some pretty dumbass things. It was always the people who believed they were above the rules who broke them. This was especially true with cyber hacking. It was crazy how many people who held the keys to the information kingdom left the door unlocked.

And what a kingdom Harry Owen's files proved to be.

Hundreds of classified files that had nothing to do with the data breach filled Leah's laptop screen.

Which meant…

That Aiden must have added the code to download those files without Leah's knowledge.

Which meant that Aiden had had an ulterior motive that had nothing to do with doxxing Harry.

And everything to do with the Dark Web.

"That goddamned bastard," he muttered. "No wonder he left Leah there to die."

He'd set up Leah.

He'd set up Matt.

He'd set up the entire Forum.

Joey had turned his back to Matt, hunching over the phone as he spoke to his mother. But certain words started breaking through Matt's concentration: "key", "Leah's apartment", and "laptop." He glanced up. Joey's face was bright red. He twisted a strand of white-blond hair on his finger.

"No, Mom, I told you already that I don't have a key." Joey hunched deeper into the sofa. "Leah asked for it back. She needed to…to lend it to someone." A pause. "I don't know who." Another pause. "I know it's important. But I really don't know who."

Matt could hear the voice of Joey's mother. Then Joey said, "I gotta go, Mom. I'll be home by curfew."

Joey shoved his phone in his pocket and looked at Matt. "We are in deep shit."

If only you knew.

"Why?"

"My mother told me that Leah was offered an immunity deal—"

Matt's heart leaped.

"But she'd have to give up Aiden and her laptop."

Nothing he'd like better than to see Aiden have his head served on a platter to the cops. But he needed to think this through. The Forum might be served along with him if they weren't careful. And if that were to happen, he was going to make sure that they didn't go down in vain. They needed a big finish. One that showed that their entire motive had been for the public good. It might be the only thing that saved their reputation if things kept going the way they were going. "The laptop isn't a big deal. We get the files, doxx Harry Owen, and then dump it somewhere for the police to find."

Joey shot him a startled look. "What do you mean, we doxx Harry Owen? You still want to do it?"

"Yeah. I do. There's a lot of shit going down right now but we can't forget why we started all this."

"No." Joey shook his head. "Leah was almost killed. The police are all over this."

"That's exactly why we need to do this. The police will double down on these files. No one will know why Leah did this. What her true motive was. Have you seen the news? Public sympathy is on the side of the Owens. She's being ripped to shreds by the media. Everyone hates her. And no one knows that she was shot at point-blank range by Harry Owen. If we don't doxx Harry now, he's going to get away with everything."

Matt's phone rang. He didn't recognize the number, but it was Halifax-based. Could it be Leah somehow calling him? "Hello?"

"May I speak to Matt Leon?" It was a woman's voice, low and smooth.

"Speaking."

"This is Kate Lange. I'm defense counsel for Leah Roberts."

Oh, God. Had something happened to her? Fear stabbed him hard in the stomach. "Is she okay?"

"Yes. She's conscious and alert. She gave me your number."

"Why?" Hope uncurled in his heart.

The way Matt said that one word spoke volumes. Matt still had feelings for Leah. But would he put his hacktivist principles above his feelings for Leah? After all, she wasn't his girlfriend now. And from the sounds of it, she had ignored his well-founded advice.

"She needs your help, Matt. But before I explain why, I need your undertaking that everything I tell you will be kept strictly confidential. It can't be posted online or shared with anyone in the Forum." Kate glanced through her kitchen window. The back garden rustled with unseen nocturnal activity. "If any of this is leaked, it's game over for Leah. The Crown will come after her with its biggest guns. You need to understand this, Matt."

"Of course I wouldn't post anything online. I understand that it's confidential. What can I do to help her?"

His offer sounded genuine. Heartfelt. She'd have to trust that this conversation did not end up on the Internet. "First of all, Leah asked me to tell you that she was sorry."

"I know she is." His voice was soft.

"How much do you know about what happened last night?"

"I don't know the full story."

Who ever knew the full story? Even the actors in the story had their own perceptions of what happened.

Was it all an illusion?

She shook her head. *Enough of the existential musings.* "Leah told me that you advised her not to do this. If it gives you any comfort, she had wanted to turn back before even breaking in to the Owen house but Aiden Boyne pulled a knife on her."

"Jesus Christ. I'm going to kill the bastard."

Kate kept her voice neutral. "The Crown have offered Leah an immunity deal if she can deliver the identity and whereabouts of Aiden Boyne, as well as her laptop—"

"We have her laptop."

"You do?" Matt was in Florida, wasn't he? "How did you get that?"

"Her brother Joey took it under my instruction."

She closed her eyes. *Joey*. The not-yet-man with the man-bun. He was old enough to be charged and tried as an adult, in a case that was so sensational that they might have to ask to change venues, and that would have not just the criminal justice system on its ear, but the federal government breathing down their backs.

"Matt, do you realize you just made him an accessory to a crime?" She could just imagine how Tim and Susan Roberts would react if they discovered their other child was also implicated in this crime. Both children facing prison sentences.

God. She'd taken this job to be an advocate for justice, to make a difference in people's lives. Right now, the lines between justice and fairness were blurred into those gray areas where consequences were unimagined, and the guilty were not who they seemed.

Would it be any clearer if she got some sleep?

"I'm sorry, Ms. Lange. I wanted to protect Leah." There was a defensive edge to the hacktivist's voice. "All Joey has to do is stay strong and deny that he was at her apartment. He's been there many times. I doubt they could isolate his fingerprints to his visit early this morning."

"Don't underestimate the police." Kate wondered if he had any idea of the forensic techniques the police employed. "Right now, they are running online searches as well as scouring the area for Aiden Boyne. They've discovered that his identity was an alias. If they find him before we can offer any valuable information, the deal is off. That's why I'm calling you. Leah thought you might be able to crack his online identity."

"I can do better than that." The hope was back in Matt's voice. "Aiden—or whoever he is—contacted Joey a few hours ago and wanted to meet me."

The jet lag seemed to have kept her brain working in a different time zone. "But you are in Florida, correct? Can you get to Halifax quickly?"

"I'm already here. I flew in a few hours ago," Matt said. "I'll get Aiden to meet me."

"Even if he meets with you, how are you planning to find out his identity? He has worked hard to keep it secret."

There was a pause. "He's insecure, Ms. Lange. And when people are insecure, they are easily exploited."

"And easily provoked."

"Ms. Lange, he was the one who wanted to meet with me. He had to have a reason."

The silhouettes of the shrubs in Kate's back garden had melded into the night over the past hour. One minute, easily seen, the next minute, no longer visible.

Just like Aiden Boyne.

"What do you think the reason was? Does he want to hurt you?"

"I don't think he would dare. I think he needs my help. With coding. I'm better at it than he is." He exhaled. "Besides, I need to help Leah. I should have stopped her before she broke into the Owen house. Now that I know he might have a knife, I'll make sure to be extra careful."

"I don't think this is wise, Matt. Aiden seems unpredictable."

"The justice system failed Leah, Ms. Lange. She's a good person. A person who obeys the law and respects it. But the law had continually thrown whistleblowers under the bus. So she felt like she had no choice. And I feel like I have no choice. I convinced her to join the Forum. And if she goes down, so does every other hacktivist who is trying to change things that corrupt people refuse to change. I can't leave her—and everyone else who believes in the principles of the Forum—to pay the price for this."

There was nothing else to say to Matt. She had warned him, cautioned him against his decision, and must now let him follow his conscience. "Time is of the essence, Matt. If the police find him before we do, they have no incentive to give Leah immunity."

"I'll message him now." There was a renewed vigor in Matt's voice.

"Call me after you meet with him. And then I'll come get the laptop." Kate slid her phone into her pocket, her thoughts preoccupied with Matt and Aiden. Matt sounded so confident that he could get the upper hand with Aiden. But Kate wasn't so sure. Aiden had proven expert at manipulation. And right now, every player in this case revolved around his actions. Could Matt be the one to reverse the power dynamic?

The kitchen was quiet, the night peaceful. Her dogs had relaxed against her legs. The warmth of their two bodies soothed her.

Her bed called to her.

Duty called even louder. She dialed Eddie's number. To her relief, he answered on the first ring.

"I've got my first legal ethics dilemma, Eddie."

"Let's hear it." Eddie's voice sounded blurry.

"I spoke to Matt about Aiden Boyne and asked him if he could try cracking his identity."

"And…"

"He told me that he was actually in Halifax, that he possessed Leah's laptop, that Joey took it, and that he could arrange to meet with Aiden tonight."

Eddie gave a low whistle. "What a mess for the Roberts family. Although it's good news that we might be able to deliver the laptop to the police."

"Agreed. But I'm wondering if we have a duty to disclose to the police that we know of a potential meeting between Matt and Aiden Boyne, or would that breach our duty of confidentiality to Leah?"

"An interesting question: the risk to public safety from a"

fugitive versus our duty to our client. First of all, do you know Aiden Boyne's exact whereabouts?"

"No."

"Do you know Matt's whereabouts?"

"No. I think he's in hiding."

"The police would take him in to custody if they could find him. Which could potentially implicate Leah in an elevated charge." Eddie inhaled deeply, a sure sign he was ruminating over a cigarette. "Do you think he's capable of murder?"

Kate stared into the darkness of her garden. "It's hard to say."

"Did you warn Matt about the knife?"

"I told him what happened."

"Did he seem concerned?"

"No."

"Kate, the case law basically lays out three conditions for breaching client confidentiality: there must be a clear and identifiable risk to a person, there must be risk of serious bodily harm or death, and the danger must be imminent. In the case where these conditions were described, the accused had told a psychiatrist about his wish to harm his girlfriend."

"I think the answer to all three conditions is 'maybe'."

"I think have your answer. You aren't obstructing justice if you don't know the whereabouts of Aiden or Matt. And there aren't grounds for breaching your duty of confidentiality if the risk isn't imminent and clear. Aiden Boyne has never threatened to harm Matt, has he?"

"No. Matt says that Aiden needs his help." Kate pushed a strand of increasingly lank hair from her forehead.

"Welcome to the murky world of criminal defense, Kate."

"I now understand why coffee is swilled at midnight."

"Well, this case happens to have more twists to it than the usual break-and-enters. You'll find the daily grind a breeze after this."

"Baptism-by-fire seems to be my *modus operandi*." Kate glanced at the clock on the wall. "Listen, I need to run to the hospital and give Leah the heads up that Matt has the laptop. Maybe she knows why Aiden would want to meet with him."

"I'll come with you."

"It's not necessary, Eddie. Just keep your phone by you in case I have another ethical dilemma."

38

THE ICU WAS HUSHED, low voices, light foot treads, and the muted beeping of machines greeting Kate as she tapped on the door to Leah's room. She was alone.

Leah was so pale that her veins backlit her skin. But she seemed to possess more vitality. Sometime during the afternoon her body had crossed a threshold and left death on the other side. "Did Matt figure out Aiden's identity?"

"Not yet. But he said he'd help you."

"I knew he would." Her client's eyes glimmered, hope in her gaze.

It made it all the more difficult for Kate to tell Leah why she was really here. Could her client physically handle the news? "Matt has your laptop."

"Oh, thank God!" Leah gave a faint smile. "How did he get it?"

Kate lowered her voice. "He asked Joey to take it from your apartment."

Leah flinched. "No." The word came out as a moan. "Why would he do that?" Her gaze searched Kate's.

"He was trying to protect you. I think your brother was, too."

"What will happen to Joey?" Leah shot a panicked glance

207

at the door. "The police are already looking for him. They want to question him."

"That's their job."

"Can you help him?"

Kate exhaled. "It's difficult, Leah. My duty as a lawyer is to you. If I represent Joey, there could be a conflict. I might use different tactics for each of you. And they could be at cross-purposes."

She stared at Kate. "You mean, you'd throw my brother under the bus to defend me?"

"I have a duty to mount the best defense I can."

"What will happen to Joey?" Her eyes were huge in her face.

There was nothing Kate could do but tell her the facts in the gentlest possible way. "If the police find evidence to charge him, he will be arrested as an accessory, or for obstruction."

Leah closed her eyes for a moment, processing. So much to process. It was as if her client had dropped a match and sparked a wildfire of unintended consequences: Salma Owen's death, Joey's misguided attempt to help her, Mel Owen's thwarted vengeance. "However, I'm hopeful that Matt will be able to find out Aiden's identity."

"Do Matt and Joey know that Aiden had a knife?"

"Yes. I told him. Do you think he would use it on him?"

"I don't think so," Leah said slowly. "My gut tells me that he's a coward. I don't think he'd take on Matt." Then she grimaced. "But my gut hasn't been too reliable. I fell for the guy, remember?"

"Leah, we all make mistakes. You're trying to make amends. Not everyone has the courage to do that."

Her words were intended to comfort, but they felt hollow. The encroaching night ushered a despondency into the room.

Kate cleared her throat. "Do you know why Aiden would want to meet with Matt? Has he planned any other exploits?"

Leah shook her head. "I don't think so. Maybe he wants to stop the doxx. It was supposed to happen tonight."

"Why would Aiden want to stop the doxx?"

"To sell the data on the Dark Web. I wonder if he had planned this with Tr0lz." Panic returned to her gaze. "You'd better get the laptop from Matt. Could you give it to the Crown in exchange for Joey's immunity?"

"Leah, you have to understand something. The minute Matt gives me the laptop, I am in possession of evidence of the commission of the crime. It is my duty to hand it over to the Crown, regardless of an immunity deal."

"But you can use it to negotiate a deal for Joey, can't you?"

"I can try. But if the laptop establishes that you have illegally obtained data on your laptop, you will face a whole host of other charges, including criminal harassment and interception of communications." Kate hesitated. "And if the files contain information that could help a state hostile to Canada, and those files have been shared online by Matt— or anyone else—you could be charged with treason."

"Like Edward Snowden."

"Exactly."

"If it means that we can get Joey off the hook, do it." Her voice was weak yet a thread of determination kept it steady. "It's my fault he's in jeopardy. I'm not dragging my little brother into this."

Treason for one, freedom for the other. Yet, Kate would do the same thing if she were in Leah's shoes. "I'll call Matt to let him know that we need the laptop ASAP. I'll review the contents before we hand it over. Then we'll have a better idea of what kind of case the Crown will make against you."

Leah hesitated. "Could you…could you call Matt while you are here? So that I could talk to him?"

The need in Leah's gaze was hard to refuse. But her client no longer operated in the same world as she had a day before. "Leah, I'm sorry. I can't. It would violate the custody conditions."

"Okay." Tears glistened in her eyes. "Could you tell him 'thank you' for me? He must think I'm a monster."

"I don't think he does, Leah." Should she tell Leah that she thought Matt still had feelings for her? No. It was none of her business, and she didn't want to muddy the waters with the crosscurrents of unrequited love. "When I spoke to him, he said he knew that you would never have intended any harm to Mrs. Owen."

"I didn't." Her client's voice was thin with exhaustion.

"We all know that, Leah. Get some sleep. Hopefully, by morning we'll have some better news." She patted Leah's arm. "I'll see you in the morning."

Kate stood, her legs heavy. The adrenaline that had propelled her to Leah's room had been extinguished by fatigue. "I'll take a look at Harry Owen's files. If you think of anything—and I mean any detail that you think would be relevant to Aiden Boyne, Harry Owen, or his parents—tell your parents to call me ASAP."

"I just remembered something." Leah's words were slurred. Kate leaned closer to hear. "Aiden had a pirate tattoo. On his arm. He said he'd been charged with hacking when he was younger."

"Do you know if he was convicted?"

"I think he was."

"I'll give the Crown that information." Finally, a possible break for her client.

"And tell Matt."

"I will. Now get some rest." Leah had been through a lot today. It was hard to believe that she had had surgery just fourteen hours before.

Kate walked through the ICU, her gaze straight ahead, but acutely aware of the people lying behind glass doors. At this hour of night, when the lights were turned down and the staff had completed their rounds, she felt as if she walked through a twilight zone of the unconscious.

Within minutes, she exited the hospital. Dark, gentle warmth embraced her as she stepped from the air-conditioned hospital onto the sidewalk. A breeze lifted the tendrils of limp hair from her cheeks. She inhaled. The air was sweet with the scent of summer. She needed oxygen. She craved sleep.

She dialed Hillcroft's number while she walked. Unsurprisingly, her call went into voice mail. "It's Kate Lange. I have important information regarding Aiden Boyne. My client believes he was charged and possibly convicted of a hacking crime several years ago. Possibly as a young offender."

She hung up. How often did Hillcroft check his messages? He might even be asleep.

She dialed the police switchboard. Within minutes, they had connected her to one of the GIS detectives on the case. "Detective Ellis."

"Detective, this is Kate Lange, counsel for Ms. Roberts. I'm calling with information about Aiden Boyne." Kate had arrived at her car. She leaned against it. Weariness crawled out of her muscles. "My client is offering this information in good faith to honor the immunity agreement."

"Understood. What information do you have?"

"She says he has a pirate tattoo on his arm. And that he was convicted of a hacking crime several years ago."

"In Nova Scotia?"

"She didn't know any more details than that."

"Thank you, Ms. Lange. I'll pass that information along to the team. Do you have any other information you can provide?"

Kate gazed at the sky. The stars were beginning to emerge from darkness, points of brilliant light that hinted of the vastness beyond. "No. That's all. Good night, Detective."

She slid into the car. She had one more call and then she could go home. She dialed Matt's number. It went into his voice mail. "Matt. This is Kate Lange. I need the laptop ASAP. Please call me."

She wished she had asked Matt where he was staying.

But then was glad she hadn't. She needed to keep a certain distance.

The streetlights blurred through the windshield while she drove home. She staggered out of the car, almost drunk from exhaustion.

Neither Hillcroft nor Matt had called by the time she slid under her sheets.

Alaska curled up on his dog bed, his head on his paws, his eyes watchful. He wasn't going to let Kate out of his sight. Foo curled up next to him.

Kate's mind was on edge, trying to piece together a puzzle that seemed to reveal a different perspective every hour.

But her body had hit its limit.

She fell into a deep slumber within seconds of putting her head on the pillow.

39

THE GENIE WAS OUT of the bottle.

And Harry knew this one would be impossible to force back in. The blackmailer had access to his private emails. Who knew how many copies of those files existed, where they were stored, and how many people had possession of them. He could pay the bastard half a million dollars—but there was no guarantee the files wouldn't be plastered over the Internet.

Either by the blackmailer or by someone else.

He poured the dregs of the scotch bottle into a glass and drained it. A room service cart sat by the coffee table. He should eat. The last time he had consumed this much alcohol had been in his law school days, but after two bites of the roast beef sandwich he had ordered, he wanted to puke.

The walls of the room closed in. He listened to the sounds of the hotel. Doors opening and closing, random footsteps. People who were in transit.

It felt as if he would forever be in transit, a purgatory of wishing he had never come home and wishing he could go home. To the home of his childhood, when he was eight. Before his father had been shot by robbers in the family convenience store, before his family had been rent by the

213

pain and bitterness of a crime that had festered in the bullet wound that severed his father's spine.

He needed air. Fresh, unpolluted, uncomplicated air.

But he couldn't leave his hotel room. The media were everywhere.

He couldn't answer his phone. There were too many questions from his bosses, from his publicist, from the police, from family friends who wanted to know when was Salma's funeral, how was Mel, was everything okay?

How could everything be okay? What an inane question.

Pressure pushed against his ribs.

His phone buzzed with yet another text message.

And even though he knew it couldn't be his lover, he looked at his phone.

Because that was the nature of hope. No matter how impossible, how improbable, how implausible, how desperately grim the situation was, hope would make you do something which you knew made no sense.

And yet, you did it.

You hoped.

God dammit.

Ironically, the text message was from his ex-girlfriend Erin. *Just checking in. How are you? How's your father?*

In other words: How's the man whose life you ruined?

He dug his fingers into his scalp but he couldn't erase the image of his father, lying in the hospital bed, his body shriveled, his eyes manic.

He threw his phone at the wall.

Dad. I'm so sorry. What have I done?

He didn't even know.

If he gave his blackmailer half a million dollars in Bitcoin, there was no guarantee—and in fact, it was more than likely—that his personal life or the classified files that never should have been on his laptop would end up on the Internet, the final act of vengeance from a troll who seemed bent on destroying him. And Harry would have bankrupted himself to pay the man who had destroyed Harry's family, his career, his heart, and his soul all in one fell swoop.

Paying the money was not the solution.

Nor was allowing the blackmailer to make good on his threat. Why should Harry and everyone he loved be victimized yet again by this man? He'd destroyed enough already.

Harry's fingers gripped the scotch glass so hard that they turned white.

That's what he wanted to do to his blackmailer. Wrap his fingers around the man's throat until he no longer could threaten Harry, his lover, or Harry's family.

He stared at his hand. His hands had the strength to do what he yearned to do.

But did he have the courage to do it? Could he actually take a man's life?

Just a few months ago, he had objected to assisted suicide when Kate Lange had approached him because he didn't believe in someone having the power to end another's life.

And yet, if he killed his blackmailer...

It would end the torment that had been unceasing and merciless since he arrived in Halifax on Thursday night.

It would give his father a measure of closure for being victimized and robbed of a peaceful death of his beloved wife.

It would prevent his lover's domestic life from being destroyed.

It would save Harry's career.

It would mean that Harry would have the funds to pay for his father's legal defense.

It would prevent national security files from being sold to unscrupulous agents.

Killing his blackmailer would solve almost every problem that had manifested itself in the past twenty-four hours. Every problem that had appeared insoluble, insurmountable, and that had left him alone in his hotel room, a wrecked man, draining a bottle of scotch.

He sprang to his feet—and staggered forward, catching his balance just before he fell into the coffee table.

Where was his phone?

It vibrated on the rug, half-obscured by the sofa.

That phone. That gateway to hell.

He snatched it from the floor.

Before he could think, he sent a message to his blackmailer.

Meet me by the gazebo in Point Pleasant Park at 3 a.m. I will transfer Bitcoin then. Then he added: *I want the laptop.* He needed to give his blackmailer a reason for them to meet in person, even though he knew that getting possession of the laptop was no guarantee of ending the torment from his blackmailer. But he'd let his blackmailer think that Harry was stupid enough to believe that he couldn't be exploited if he gained possession of the hacked files.

Three a.m. was the dead of night. No one should be in the park.

Statistically, it was also the hour when the highest rate of deaths occurred.

He would love nothing more than to make his blackmailer another statistic. Just another number. Just another fucking digit in a computer file.

But first, he had to figure out how to get away with murder.

40

"MY PARENTS SAID THE police are looking for me."

There was no mistaking the panic in Joey's gaze. His mother had sent him at least five frantic texts. So far, he hadn't responded.

Matt stared at the kid. He knew he shouldn't have asked him to take Leah's laptop. It was wrong to ask him to do it. He'd been so freaked out over Leah's situation that he hadn't thought it through.

He had potentially screwed this kid's future. And Leah would never forgive him.

Just like he'd never forgive himself.

"Listen, I'm sorry I got you mixed up in this, bro. I really am." Joey was a wreck: his left index finger sported a hangnail turned bloody from anxious teeth, his hair hung in scraggly strands around his face. If Matt had met Joey before he had asked him to take Leah's laptop, he never would have asked him to take it. Or would he? "But we can help Leah. Her lawyer said that she will get immunity if we can crack Aiden's identity and deliver the laptop."

Joey threw him a wary look. That look alone told Matt that Joey's trust in him was rapidly disintegrating. If he didn't

217

convince Leah's little brother to stay on board, everyone would be sunk: Leah, Joey, the Forum, him.

"He called me earlier," Joey said slowly. "Can we trace his number?"

Relief surged through Matt. Joey was not going to abandon him. Yet. He leaned toward him. "Better than that—you said that he wanted to meet with me. I'm going to text him and set up something."

"Tonight?" Joey gripped the laptop even harder.

Matt swallowed his impatience. Convincing Joey was akin to luring a frightened deer to take a carrot. One step forward, half a step back. But the carrot was one none of them could afford to lose: the immunity deal.

"We're running out of time. If the police find Aiden, they won't go through with the immunity deal. There's too much at stake. The public hate Leah, Joey. This is her only chance to make good." Matt hated to pressure the kid, but they couldn't give up yet. There were too many unanswered questions about what had happened last night. And Leah had almost been killed for it. He wanted answers from Aiden aka AggroBoy.

"Okay. Here's his number." Joey recited Aiden's cell phone number in a voice that cracked on the final digit.

Matt didn't waste any time. He texted: *This is Condor. Meet me at my hotel at midnight.*

The response was immediate: *where r u*

He texted the hotel address, his pulse accelerating.

"What's going on?" Joey asked. "Are we meeting Aiden?"

"He's coming at midnight. We need to find out as much as we can about him. You start going through his social media. I'm going to see if I can find out his criminal history."

They opened their laptops, the only sound in the room the intermittent bursts of fingers hitting the keyboard. Joey suddenly said, "I just don't get why Leah didn't report the data breach when she found it."

Matt glanced up. Joey stared at his laptop screen with a fierce concentration. But Matt sensed that it was to mask the tears that had sprung in his eyes. "She wanted to report the breach. But the government had already decided to keep it under wraps."

"I don't get why the breach was such a big deal. The only person who has been hurt in all this is Leah." Joey's face had turned pink. "Nothing has happened with this data breach at the border. Nobody has complained. Everyone gets their personal data stolen. It happens every day."

That was the battle that the hacktivists fought. The indifference to the loss of private information. "Joey, have you ever gone through border security?"

"Yeah."

"So they have all your passport information. Your physical characteristics. Your address. Your destination. Have you ever heard of the mosaic theory?"

"Isn't that some kind of cryptography technique?"

"Basically, people take all the snippets of information and create a security analysis. So they would use images from CCTV cameras, social network tags, phone records, and any other digital footprint to create theories about corporations, populations, et cetera. Your passport information and biometric data are like the keys to the effing kingdom. In theory, someone could access your health information, your banking account, your tax records, your travel movements. Nothing you ever do would be private. If you went to your doctor for a prescription, it could be accessed. If you sent a private video to a friend, it could be accessed. Someone would be able to know every single thing about you. Everything."

"But a lot of people are like, 'I've got nothing to hide.'" Joey twisted on the sofa. "Until tonight, I was one of them."

"Even more reason to not want some guy in some office knowing everything about you." Matt pulled out a battered paperback from his messenger bag. "Have you read this?"

Joey squinted at the title. "*1984*? Uh, no. I wasn't even born then."

"But you've heard of it, right?"

"Kind of."

Matt tossed the book to him. "Read it. It's all about what happens when we have no privacy. It's not just what happens to us, but to the people in power. How they use that information for their own ends. We need checks and balances, Joey. That's what democracy is all about."

"Yeah, but not when people are afraid of being killed by terrorists and shit."

Bombs were real, data was abstract.

"Joey, think about it. If our government can't protect the data of its citizens what kind of job are they doing protecting our cities from terrorist attacks?" Matt raised a brow. "If they won't admit to their failure to protect our privacy, do you really think they are suddenly going to man up and tell people when they discover that passwords to our missile launchers have been stolen?"

"Of course they will! They'd have to!"

"Maybe. Maybe not. You have a lot of faith in the integrity of your government. Me, not so much." He shrugged.

"So far, nothing the Forum has done has changed anything. Ever." Joey threw a defiant glance at him.

"That's not true. We've had successes in the past."

"But not with this exploit."

Matt could not deny the truth of Joey's words.

They had achieved nothing with this attempt to doxx Harry Owen.

And now they were caught in the system they had tried to expose.

41

AIDEN STRETCHED AND GLANCED out the large picture window of Tr0lz's living room. Ironically, her building was not very far from the dilapidated rooming house where he had lived.

The fact that as a student Tr0lz could afford an apartment on the Halifax waterfront with a living room and two bedrooms was not lost on him. Especially since this apartment possessed nicely-appointed fixtures, high-end appliances, and a killer view of the harbor. The furniture was modern in style, although upholstered in a generic, contemporary gray everything.

Wherever Tr0lz had come from, she had come from money.

Or had a nice side business of something on the Internet. Her computer network was loaded with all of the bells and whistles a hacker could need.

After Aiden got over his initial envy of Tr0lz's living space, he realized it was simply a living space—there were no clues about Tr0lz. No photos, no artwork, no little touches that he would expect such a style-conscious woman to add to her living environment.

He had gone with Tr0lz to her apartment, partly of out curiosity, partly to figure out his next move.

The computer script he had written blurred on the laptop screen. Yet his mind buzzed with the thought of half a million dollars. When Harry Owen had texted him with a promise to pay the money, he could barely hide his glee from Tr0lz. He was so close he could almost taste it—provided Condor didn't doxx Harry Owen before then. Because if Condor doxxed Harry, the MP would be completely exposed, and would have no reason to pay Aiden the money.

The thought made his palms sweat. Just a few hours. That's all he needed. And he would be home free. He could take a cab straight to the airport and catch the first flight out of Halifax. He'd have screwed Harry Owen completely.

And he would be free of Tr0lz. Months ago, he had been excited by her plan to hack into a major transportation system that would not only rock Halifax, but the world. But then she upped the ante.

"I have an idea," she had said as soon as they arrived at her apartment. "Let's take this a step further. Let's hack into the system and cause a collision with Harry's US captain." She had a gleam in her eyes that made his stomach tighten. He had had to cover his shock.

Should he bail on her right now?

Or go along with it?

Tr0lz scared him. She was not what she seemed. And what she had revealed so far sent his juvie-honed instincts into alert.

He sensed she could hurt him.

And she knew he sensed that.

He would play along. After all, he had little to lose. As long as Harry Owen's files remained off the Internet for the next few hours, his blackmail would be successful—and he'd be on a plane at six in the morning with half a mil of BitCoin in his bank account.

And if he could figure out the hack into the GPS system that Tr0lz had set her sights on, he'd settle the score with his father, with Harry, with the whole goddamned world.

So he got to work.

But the hack was complex. Much more complex than he had thought.

As he scanned the code for the umpteenth time, his phone had vibrated in his pocket.

It was a text message. From Condor.

He had read it, his excitement mounting. Condor wanted to meet with him at midnight. Which meant that he could force him to give Aiden the laptop—and ensure that Harry Owen wasn't doxxed before he paid out the blackmail money.

Everything had fallen into place. He couldn't believe it.

Except for the code. Every time he tried to run the script, he got an error. He was so tired, the sequence no longer made sense.

And now, he'd stayed longer than he intended, trying to get it to work.

Tr0lz stood in the kitchen, kettle in hand, making yet another cup of herbal tea. He suspected that was all she existed on. She threw a pointed look at his laptop. This time he could read her expression: *why aren't you working?*

"I'm just going out for a bit." He would just bluff his way out of here. "My head is about to explode."

Her gaze narrowed. "Where are you going?"

He shrugged. "Outside. I need some air. I can't think right now."

For the first time since they met, she appeared agitated. "Don't be too long. We don't have a lot of time. We need to have this all in place for 0500."

"Don't worry. I'll be back in an hour."

She slipped into the seat he had vacated. "I'll work on the code while you are gone. But don't be late."

He hurried from Tr0lz's apartment building. The temperature had cooled since his afternoon on the railway tracks. It was like a different world, standing outside in downtown Halifax on a beautiful summer's night.

Sometimes he forgot what a happening city Halifax could be. He watched beautiful young couples strolling hand-in-hand, millenials in trendy clothes geared for the nightclubs, students in sandals and denim shorts. Why should their lives be so goddamned perfect when his had been one crap thing after another?

They had no idea what was about to come down.

And he wasn't about to tell them.

He slung his backpack onto his shoulder and headed toward his future.

42

MATT HAD BEEN COUNTING down the minutes until Aiden arrived. And now, here he was, with a smirk on his face. Matt could smell the rank odor of Aiden's sweat. The rank odor of his cowardice.

The rank odor of a man who had left a vulnerable woman to die.

He wanted nothing more than to punch Aiden in the face. But instead, Matt had a job to do: he had to cajole Aiden into revealing his identity. Sweat pricked his underarms. "Aiden, thanks for com—"

Aiden shoved his shoulder against the door, causing Matt to stumble backwards.

He held a knife.

"Watch your mouth, Condor. You're not in charge any more." Aiden waved his knife at Joey. "Give me Leah's laptop." It was on Joey's knees.

"Aiden, look we just want to talk to you."

"I don't want to talk to you. Give me the laptop." He pointed the knife at Matt.

Joey threw a panicked look at Matt.

"Aiden, we want to work with you. You obviously have some other exploit going on. We'd like in on it."

225

Aiden stared at him. Matt's offer had caught him off guard. But then Aiden steadied the knife "It's too late, Condor. You missed your chance. Just give me the laptop."

Matt thought of all the times he had dismissed Aiden aka Aggroboy's bragging as all talk and no action. As he stared at the sharp edge of the knife blade, he thought how wrong he had been.

Or had he?

Would Aiden actually use the knife on them? It was two against one. This was typical AggroBoy manipulation. He was a coward. Plain and simple.

"You fooled us all. The best exploit ever," Matt said, a smile curving his lips. "I take my white hat off to you."

Aiden's gaze flickered from the laptop back to Matt. "You have no idea how big this exploit is, Condor. Tr0lz and I are going to fucking blow up this town."

"Got an even bigger exploit planned?" Matt's tone was casual. Hacker to hacker. Talking shop.

"Just give me the laptop." Aiden glared at Joey. The knife did not waver in its target of Matt's chest.

Joey closed the laptop and jumped to his feet.

"No, Joey." Matt shook his head, his gaze never leaving Aiden's. He was not going to watch Leah's one chance at immunity walk out the door. "We aren't giving that up until Aiden lets us in on this exploit he's talking about."

Anger flashed in Aiden's eyes. "You think you're so smart, don't you? But you're just as blind as that stupid girl you're in love with. Tr0lz and me are going to blow up this fucking town. Now give me the laptop," he commanded Joey. The kid froze, clutching the laptop to his chest as if it were a shield.

"Or what? You'll stab him? Like you threatened to do to Leah before you left her to die?" Matt stuck his face two inches from Aiden's. He stared into the heavily-lashed eyes that had beguiled Leah.

He didn't know what she had seen, but he saw a manipulative coward. The rage that had been building in him exploded. "Just try knifing Joey, you bastard!" He gripped Aiden by the throat and slammed him back against the doorframe, pinning the knife against the wall. He tightened his hand on Leah's lover's throat. It felt too good. He wanted to smash Aiden's head against the wall until the smirk left his face.

Aiden shoved his knee hard into Matt's groin.

Matt screamed, pain stabbing into every nerve. He doubled over, his grip on Aiden's knife hand slipping.

From the corner of his eye, he saw Joey rush Aiden, throwing his fist. It landed squarely in Aiden's face. "That's for my sister!"

Blood spurted in a violent spray of red.

"You shit!" Aiden yelled. He ripped his hand away from Matt's grip, whipping the knife across Matt's temple.

Blood gushed into his face.

Joey jammed his shoulder into Aiden's chest, and thrust him out of the doorway. As Aiden tried to catch his balance, Joey slammed the door, jamming the bolt.

Matt pushed himself to his feet.

They heard Aiden's footfalls as he sprinted down the hallway.

Would he drip blood everywhere?

Someone would call security.

"Let's get out of here." Matt's head throbbed. He put his hand to his face. It was sticky with blood. He grabbed a washcloth from the bathroom and pressed it against the slice in his temple while he gathered up his laptop and charger, and shoved it into his bag.

Joey stood by the door. White-faced. Shaking. "What if he's waiting in the stairwell? He's got a knife."

The kid looked as if he'd been hit by a train, and the feeling was catching. The whole thing had escalated crazily in just a matter of seconds.

"He won't be." Matt had no idea if that was true, but he needed Joey to move.

There was a quick rap on the door. "Security," a man's voice said.

Damn it.

Matt peered through the peephole. A man dressed in the hotel security uniform stood outside his door, frowning at the drops of blood on the hallway carpet.

Matt pulled his hat down, held the washcloth to his head, and pulled open the door. "Hello."

"We've had a noise complaint." The security guard stared at Matt's face. "Someone said it sounded like a fight."

Matt smiled beneath the washcloth. "No, sorry, I fell over the footstool and cut my head. I could see I was making a mess on the carpet. So I ran into my hotel room, with my head up like this—" he pointed his chin upwards, "—to try to stop the blood."

The security guard looked at Joey. The teen nodded. "It was my fault. I moved the footstool," Joey added.

Matt tilted his head. "I gotta go to the washroom or I'll bleed all over the floor."

The security guard gave a cursory glance around the room. Given a life-or-death fight had just occurred, the living room appeared untouched. All the action had occurred by the doorway, and the open door blocked the security guard's view of the blood-smeared wall, and the large scrape on the paint where Matt had pinned Aiden's hand.

"Have a good evening." The security guard nodded.

Matt closed the door. "Guess we don't have to leave." He stuck the washcloth back over his cut. The beanie had soaked the blood.

"I can't stay for too long." Joey sank onto the sofa. He held his phone, his fingers trembling. "My parents are losing it. They want me to come home." He glanced at Matt. "And I want to go."

"Joey, I don't want you to get into any more trouble. But if you go, the police will take you into custody. You're their only link to the laptop right now."

"Shit." Joey stared at the laptop, his gaze miserable. "What should I do?"

"Just hang on for tonight. You can stay here. Tell your parents not to worry, that you'll come home tomorrow. Tell them you are trying to help Leah, if that will make them feel better."

Joey shook his head. "They'll freak out."

"Then just tell them you are safe and you'll see them tomorrow."

Joey texted the message, his leg jiggling.

"And now, we need to get back online and find out who Aiden Boyne is. We screwed our big opportunity." Matt's head throbbed. His hands were sticky with his blood and with Aiden's. "I'm going to out him on the Forum. It's time to see if anyone knows about this exploit he's talking about."

43

1:08 a.m.

"YOU STILL AT THE station? It's Riley," she added.

Cooper pulled over to the side of his street. "Yes. I'm here. What's up?"

He glanced through the windshield at his house. The bedroom light was on.

"Don't wait up for me," he'd said, when he called at eight-thirty.

I want to," Steph said. There was no disguising what she meant by that.

"Hon, I'm on a case. I don't know what time I'll be home."

"It's okay. I don't mind waiting."

And she meant it. She'd always been the consummate police officer wife. Understanding of his shift work, undemanding when a case kept him away.

The only thing she minded waiting for was a child.

"Murphy just finished his forensics on Mel Owen's computer. You've got to see this." There was a note of excitement to Riley's voice.

"I'll be there in fifteen." Steph and he had bought a house in the newly-gentrified North End. With a yard. And four bedrooms.

He had never felt at ease in the house. Every time he entered a bedroom with an unoccupied bed, the room recriminated him for not providing a child to sleep in it. And not just any child. His child. Steph's child.

Their child.

He put the car in reverse, turned around and drove to the station. He would sleep at the station.

Eventually, Steph would turn out the bedroom light.

Fourteen minutes later, he swiped his pass in the station's security system. The Forensics Identification Service ran its lab in the basement. He headed downstairs, his feet echoing in the empty stairwell, and opened the door to the FIS.

It always reminded him of his high school chemistry lab. A long, steel table ran the length of the room. One wall contained lockers, stuffed full of lab coats, masks, evidence bags, bottles of chemicals, and God only knew what else.

Riley and Murphy leaned over an older-model computer network that had been set up on the bench. Riley glanced over her shoulder when she heard Cooper approach and smiled.

It was the first time he'd seen her smile. And it almost stopped him in his tracks. He hoped she didn't see him check his stride.

If she did, she didn't let on—or she didn't care. "Murphy is a friggin' genius." She gave a thumbs up.

The computer analyst looked up from the screen, and winked. He had the open features and freckles of Howdy Doody but the analytic brain of Spock. "I know why Leah Roberts and Aiden Boyne broke into the Owen house," he said. "Look at this."

Cooper craned his neck to scan the computer monitor. It was filled with code. "What did you find?"

Murphy practically rubbed his hands together. "This computer was used as a host to spread a virus to Harry Owen's computer. The suspects must have uploaded the virus with a flash drive onto this computer. Once Harry logged in to his parents' computer network, the host computer transmitted the virus over the network to Harry's. He would have no idea that the information was accessed." Murphy shook his head. "It was a genius hack."

"And what happened to the information when it was accessed?" Cooper had already guessed but had learned to never assume anything.

"It was downloaded to two IP addresses. One we believe was Leah Roberts'."

"And the other must be Aiden Boyne's," Riley said. "Has your team made any headway in locating either of the laptops?"

Cooper shook his head. "Not yet. Leah Roberts believes that Aiden Boyne took her machine. And he's still at large. But my money is on the younger brother. We're searching for him right now." Two missing laptops. Two missing men. So far, this case had been kicking Cooper in the butt.

Riley leaned against the computer desk. She had changed into a sleeveless shirt and jeans, and her clothing showed off her triathlete build nicely. Too nicely.

Cooper fixed his gaze on the computer screen. "So the million dollar question is why was it so important for Leah Roberts to risk her career to hack into Harry Owen's computer?"

"She's a computer security analyst hired by the Department of Public Safety..." Riley said. "Do you think she was stealing classified information?"

"You mean to sell on the Internet?"

"Maybe."

"There's a huge black market for that," Murphy added.

"But why would a brilliant woman with the professional world at her feet risk everything to sell data on the black market?" Cooper caught Riley's gaze. Even at this late hour, her eyes were clear and alert. "I'm not convinced that money was the motive. She makes a good salary."

"Well, let's see," Riley leaned against the desk. "Other motives could be blackmail, addiction, espionage, or doing it for love."

"Or doing it for the public good," Cooper said softly.

Riley shot him an appraising look. "That actually makes a lot of sense. It fits with her personality."

Murphy slapped the desk with his palm. "She's the female version of Edward Snowden!"

A slow flush burned in Cooper's chest when he glimpsed the respect in Riley's gaze. "We don't know if that's the motive. I'm going to pin down Harry Owen. He claimed that he didn't know her."

Riley raised a brow. "You heading over there now?"

"Yeah. I want to get him while he's tired and upset." Harry Owen had been through a lot today. He might be at his breaking point.

A perfect time to get information from him.

"Do you need a wingman?" Riley asked with a gleam in her eye.

Murphy flashed her a look of surprise. She wasn't in GIS.

"Let me check with the Staff Sergeant." Cooper was not going to start his new job by pissing off his boss.

Pearson answered on the first ring.

"This is Ellis. I'm with Riley and Murphy. They discovered that the suspects uploaded a computer virus onto Mel Owen's computer to steal Harry Owen's data."

"Jesus Christ. What do you think he has on his laptop?"

"That's what I want to find out. I'm on my way to his hotel. The thing is, Lamond is on patrol searching for Joey Roberts."

"Don't go on your own. You need someone to cover your ass." Not that they were concerned that Harry Owen would be violent. But they knew how smart and how powerful he was.

"Riley said she'd come. You okay with that?"

"Riley? Sure, if she isn't needed anywhere else."

"No one's called her in yet."

"Call me if Harry Owen talks. I'm going to have to micro manage this with the government and the media."

"Will do." Cooper strode back to the FIS lab. "Riley, come on. Pearson has given his blessing." He was about to say, "so you can cover my ass."

But stopped just in time. Somehow, he knew he wouldn't be able to say it the way Pearson had.

44

IT WAS ALMOST TWO a.m. Seven in the morning in Italy.

Kate closed her eyes. She listened to Alaska's deep breathing. Foo Dog's snores rumbled along the floor. She tried her relaxation techniques: *breathe in on one, out on two. Do it for ten. Then repeat.* But her mind kept interrupting. *Had Hillcroft returned her call? Had Matt? Breathe in on eight…no, seven.*

Damn it.

It was one question after another, scrambling around the corners of her mind, trapped in the blind allies of the unknown, adrenalin firing through every cell.

She swung her legs over the bed, and switched on her bedside lamp. Alaska pulled himself to his feet. Foo Dog lifted a bleary eyelid, half-rolled into the warm spot vacated by Alaska, and settled back into his snoring.

Alaska nudged Kate's leg. She reached down to stroke her dog's head. For the first time in a long time, the shadows in Kate's room held no menace.

But then her gaze fell on her closet. Imogen's belongings sat in a closed box in there. Her little sister. The girl she should have protected. But killed through an act of hurt-induced carelessness. Gone in the flesh for sixteen years. But never gone from her heart. Or her conscience.

You faced killers. Stalkers. Face the damn box.

But if she opened the box, she knew she'd not only be flooded with memories of the girl Kate had lost for the rest of her lifetime, but also the woman who had been the catalyst for the tragedy that had befallen the Lange sisters.

Kenzie Sloane.

The woman who tried to save herself from a sadistic stalker by twice putting a Lange sister in his crosshairs.

She understood what had driven Mel Owen to seek out Leah in her hospital bed, gun in hand, vengeance in his eyes.

For she had felt the same urge to kill only a month before.

She drew her legs up to her chest, hugging her knees.

Alaska leaned against her foot. His fur was silky, his body warm.

Her return from Italy had been so fraught with work-related drama that she had been able to avoid thinking about the bomb that John Hillcroft had dropped on her at their coffee date: the preliminary inquiry for Kenzie Sloane. Kate would face her in four days' time. But this time, Kenzie would be in the prisoner's dock. And Kate would be in the witness stand. The thought of seeing those sky-blue eyes made her stomach churn.

Kenzie Sloane had stolen so much from Kate. Her sister. Her peace of mind for the past sixteen years. And then she added more trauma with the involvement of John McNally.

Her gaze slid to the bureau. *The bras had been pushed to one side, the panties tumbled to the other. Two pairs were missing. The lacy ones. The ones she had saved for special dates. The ones that had been taken by a stalker.*

They had never been recovered. The theft of them had robbed her of her dignity, her privacy, and her sense of safety.

And once again, she could lay the blame for that at Kenzie Sloane's artistically tattooed feet.

The anger that Kate had buried in Venice surfaced.

Would she ever be free of this woman?

She sprang to her feet. Sleep was impossible. And staying in her bedroom, with Imogen's box of belongings secreted in her closet, was impossible, as well.

She knew she should just go through the box. Rip off the bandage of her trauma, scour the festering pain, and examine the final remnants of a family that had been irrevocably damaged.

But couldn't face it tonight.

She strode out to the landing, flicking on the light. One glance down the hallway confirmed that Finn had not returned for the night.

I hope you met a nice girl tonight, Finn. Someone who would replace Kenzie Sloane in his affections. For even though the tattoo artist had betrayed his trust, Kate wasn't convinced that Finn was over her. There was something about Kenzie—her wildness, her passion, her daring—that left a certain kind of man helpless in her presence. John McNally had been one such victim. Kate was terrified that Finn was the next. And that Kenzie Sloane would once again succeed in stealing someone Kate loved.

You are becoming paranoid, Kate.

Her phone rang.

She hurried back into the bedroom and snatched it from the bedside table. It was a Florida number. "Kate Lange."

"It's Matt." His voice was strained.

Kate's heart sank at the sound of his voice. "Did you meet Aiden Boyne?"

"Yes. He had a knife. Like you said."

"Did anyone get hurt?"

"No. He tried to steal Leah's laptop. But we locked him out of my hotel room and he ran away."

"So you still have the laptop?" A headache had started to form by Kate's temple.

"Yes. But we didn't find out his real name." Matt's voice was tense with frustration.

Back to square one. "Okay, Matt. But I need to collect the laptop ASAP."

"Won't the immunity deal be off if we can't crack Aiden Boyne's identity?"

"It might be for Leah. I'm going to try to trade the laptop for immunity for Joey."

"Please, give me a little more time to see if I can find out who Aiden Boyne is," he said, his voice low. "We can't let this happen to Leah."

"Leah understands the consequences of this. She wants to protect her brother."

Kate had made a promise to her client that she would secure the laptop. And if she failed to get it, Leah would lose her one chance at redemption. "I'll come to your hotel in half in an hour."

Matt cleared his throat. "Could you bring something to glue a knife cut together?"

"Are you serious? Where did you get hurt? Is Joey okay?"

"He's fine. And I got slashed on the forehead. It's no biggie. But scalp wounds bleed a lot."

"I'll see what I've got in the cupboard."

45

HE HAD TO ADMIT, Riley made a good partner. That is, when she wasn't doing her thing as the best Forensics Identification detective east of Montreal.

She matched Cooper's long stride effortlessly as they walked down the hallway toward Harry Owen's hotel suite. Her gaze scanned the carpeting, the walls, every piece of decorative furniture. He threw her an amused glance. "No one's dead here."

She grinned. "Not that you know of. It's an occupational hazard. It's amazing the stories hidden in carpet fibers."

"You've just convinced me to never buy a shag carpet."

They reached Harry Owen's room. It was almost two in the morning. Would Harry Owen still be up?

Riley knocked on the door.

They waited, listening.

After a minute, the deadlock was flipped and the door opened. Harry Owen blinked. "Detective Ellis."

Cooper and Riley kept their expressions impassive. But the smell of booze came off Harry Owen in waves.

"This is my partner Detective Riley." That rolled off his tongue a little too easily. "Could we have a word, Mr. Owen?"

Harry made no move to let him in. His gaze travelled from Cooper's face down to Riley's. "It's very late. I was just going to bed." He swayed slightly in the doorway.

"We need two minutes."

"Sorry, detectives. I have had a very long day."

And then he closed the door on them.

"Shit," Riley muttered.

There was nothing they could do unless they detained him.

And that wasn't a decision they could make without Pearson's approval. Not when the media would pounce all over it.

They'd be wearing it for the rest of their careers.

46

2:03 a.m.

THERE WERE MANY WAYS to end a life.

Harry had been conducting an inventory of his room service cart to find anything that could be used as a fatal weapon when Detectives Ellis and Riley showed up at the door. He had barely managed to keep it together. Did they know about the blackmail? Was that why they were there?

But, no. It seemed they were on a fishing expedition. And he wasn't about to be hooked again. He was still trying to remove the one that his blackmailer had dug fatally into his family.

Harry mentally ran through the options for murder: gun, knife, poison, suffocation, drowning, strangulation, head injury, or a combination of those things. His problem was that he no longer had access to a gun. The police had seized his father's arsenal as part of the investigation into his father's illegal weapons possession. Poison was not possible. Head trauma was challenging, as he'd need to find a rock or brick to use at the park, and there was no guarantee he would find what he needed in the dark.

It left riskier and more physically violent methods his only choice. His hotel suite did not have any kitchen knives. The bags lining his garbage cans were flimsy at best. If he pulled one over his blackmailer's head, it would be ripped in seconds.

Strangulation was the only option left.

He knew he was strong—daily sessions with a personal trainer guaranteed that. But he had no idea of the size of his adversary. Would he succeed if he tried to choke him with his bare hands?

It was risky.

And he didn't like risk.

Also, that kind of attack would result in a physical struggle, and God knew what kind of forensic evidence Harry would inadvertently leave on his blackmailer's corpse—assuming he was successful.

His gaze fell on the wall outlet. His computer power cord hung from it, useless in the face of the denuded hard drive in Harry's computer.

The computer power cord. That was the answer. The deliciously ironic answer.

Harry unplugged the cord and wrapped it around his hand. Would it flex enough to make a tight grip on his blackmailer's neck? He couldn't tell.

He slipped it around his own neck and wrapped the ends, pulling the cord taut.

His Adam's apple protested at the pressure.

It would work.

He released the cord, leaving it around his neck, like a tie that he had not yet knotted.

He had come home to confess his sins to his conservative mother, and instead shot a woman in cold blood and was about to strangle a man. If his mother were alive, she would tell him to call the authorities.

But he was one of the authorities.

Just another day at the office.

Nausea rose in his stomach.

All that scotch.

None of that food. Should he eat before he went on his date with the devil?

241

He reached for the room service cart. His hand connected too hard with the plate holding his sandwich. The lid tumbled to the ground, the plate tipping over. His sandwich slid to the floor, the slices of bread splaying apart. The mound of beef looked obscene on the carpet. *Au jus* seeped in a brown puddle around it.

"Jesus Christ." Before his brain could convince his body to run to the bathroom, he spewed vomit onto the pinkish slices of rare beef on the floor. The computer cord slipped from his neck. It landed in the foul mess.

There was a knock on the door.

God. Not the police again.

He spun around. And lost his balance. He staggered against the door.

"Harry. It's Randall."

Go away.

Why was his lawyer here in the middle of the night? Had the police called him?

"Harry!" Randall Barrett rapped the door, this time more loudly. "I need to speak to you. It's urgent."

What could be so urgent at this time of night?

"It's about your father."

Harry's legs weakened. *His father.*

He unlocked the door and swung it open.

Shock flashed through Randall's eyes. "May I come in?"

Harry stood back and allowed him in.

Randall's gaze took in the plate that had been knocked to the ground, the computer cord that lay snake-like on the mound of Harry's vomit.

"Sorry about the mess." Harry grabbed a napkin and threw it over the evidence of his alcoholic binge, staggering at the sudden motion.

"Harry, you should sit down." His lawyer put a concerned arm around his back, ushering him to the sofa, waiting until he complied. Then he took the glass of water from the room service cart and handed it to Harry. "Drink this."

He gulped the water. It was cool. But it couldn't eradicate the foul taste of his vomit. "What time is it?" He needed to get to the park. And then he remembered why Randall had come. "Is my father okay?"

Randall sat on the chair opposite him. Although neatly dressed in a navy polo shirt and jeans, fatigue shadowed his eyes. "It's just after two a.m. Your father is asking for you. I came because the hospital asked me."

"Why did they ask you?"

"You weren't answering your phone."

His phone. His damned phone. It hadn't stopped ringing, buzzing, chiming. Half a bottle of scotch hadn't put a halt to it. So he had tossed it into the bathtub and closed the door. And then proceeded to down the rest of the bottle.

"Is my father okay?" Harry barely dared to ask. What if his dad had died—and Harry hadn't been there?

"He's awake. He's refusing sedation. He's asking for you. The hospital wants permission to give him another dose of anti-anxiety medication." Randall's gaze was concerned. "I've been texting and calling you for the past hour."

"I'm sorry." *I was too busy getting rid of the police and planning a murder to come look after my father.*

Randall stood. "Can I drive you to the hospital?"

"What time is it again?"

A small frown creased between Randall's eyes. "It's after two a.m."

And he had to meet his blackmailer in less than an hour at Point Pleasant Park.

Would it give him enough time?

No. He couldn't just appear at his father's side, and then leave. He had planned to be early for his rendezvous with the blackmailer. He needed to watch the blackmailer approach—and then catch him unaware.

"Is my father's life in danger right now?"

"Not that I'm aware of." Randall's frown deepened. "Are you okay, Harry? I'm concerned about you."

"I'm fine." As he spoke the words, his body seemed intent

on making a liar of him. Tiny black spots spun in his vision.

And then receded.

He stood. "Thanks for coming, Randall. I'm going to lie down for a bit and then go to the hospital." He managed to walk his lawyer to the door without lurching.

Randall's gaze met his. "I've been where you are right now. It will get better."

Harry crossed his arms. "How? My mother is dead. Her funeral is next week, but my father is now under arrest in hospital after going out of his head and trying to kill the woman that I shot with a prohibited weapon, almost killing a sheriff in the process. How exactly is this going to get better?"

It might be easier if his father were dead. And then he immediately quashed the thought. He loved his father. He had already lost his mother.

He needed his father.

But the thought of his father being found guilty of assault with a weapon, of spending the rest of his fragile days in prison or under house arrest, was more than Harry could bear.

It might be more than his father could bear, too.

"Take it one day at a time, Harry."

Really. Was that the best his high-paid help could do? Offer platitudes?

"I have been taking it one day at a time. And it's only gotten worse."

"We'll help you. I promise. And you can call me at any time." Randall put a hand on his arm.

"Thanks." He stepped away. Randall's hand dropped. With one last look, his lawyer walked out of Harry's hotel room. Harry closed the door.

Randall's visit had confirmed one thing: no one could help right now.

He lifted the napkin from the mound of vomit, and picked up the computer cord. Then he carefully rinsed the vomit from the cord in the bathroom sink, dunking the cord over and over in the water until all traces of his DNA were removed.

47

AIDEN HAD HIDDEN IN a stall in the men's room of Condor's hotel until it was time to head to the park for his rendezvous with Harry Owen. When he saw his face in the bathroom mirror, he swore. Loudly.

His nose was broken. The tissue around it had already swollen in shades of blue and green. He washed the blood from his face, stuffing his nostrils with paper towel to stop the trail of blood spatter through the hotel foyer. Yanking his hood over his head, he left the washroom, keeping his head averted from the front desk as he hurried from the hotel. As soon as he cleared the hotel entry, he turned into the nearest side street, kept to the dark side of the sidewalk, and began the trek to Point Pleasant Park.

His phone buzzed.

It was Tr0lz. *Where the hell are you?*

It was one of many messages from her, growing angrier and more threatening by the minute.

He could not go back to Tr0lz's apartment. One look at his face, and she would know something was up. Besides, he was almost home free.

He ignored the throbbing of his nose, the labored breathing through his mouth, the dryness in his throat from

245

the exertions of his fight, the metallic taste in his mouth from the blood that still trickled in fits and starts when he moved his face too quickly.

He skirted the waterfront, avoiding the road that ran past the container pier. Although it led directly to the park, it also had twenty-four hour security. He should know. His dad's company was responsible for it.

Aiden hopped over the low stone wall that edged Point Pleasant Park. Darkness rimmed his vision. He pushed off the hood. Cool air wafted over his hair, matted with sweat and blood. Pain throbbed in his face. In his head.

And then he saw the police car.

It cruised slowly, deliberately not fifty feet from he stood.

Harry didn't dare take a cab to the park. He was too recognizable.

Instead, he slipped on his running shoes, and plugged a pair of earbuds into his ears. The headphones were just for effect. He wouldn't listen to music. He needed all of his senses.

The bars had emptied, the sidewalks congested with late night revelers. A large pack of young university students staggered in front of him, laughing and chattering at the top of their voices. He stayed close to the edge of their group, keeping enough distance that none of the young women would feel creeped by him, but ensuring that he had other people around him. It made him less obvious to the police and less easily seen on the security cameras mounted in the windows of the bars that lined the street.

The students veered uphill at Sackville Street. He continued south, his pace brisk as he passed the gracious old buildings and looming condominium towers that had sprung up all over the downtown. The unmistakable smell of weed drifted from the balcony of one of the condos. He kept his head lowered, hoping that whoever was toking a joint above him hadn't glimpsed his face.

His phone rang as he walked past the train station.

It was a hospital number. His heart sank. "Hello."

"Harry." His father's voice sounded so weak. And yet it possessed a strange reediness to it. "Where are you?"

"I'm at the hotel, Dad."

"They're trying to hurt me. You need to come."

"Dad," he tried to keep his voice calm, but panic churned in his gut, "the doctors and nurses are trying to help you. Not hurt you."

"No, Harry! I heard them. They want to poison me."

What was going on with his father? He sounded delirious. "Dad, it's not poison," he said in his most reassuring tone. "It's just medicine to help you sleep."

"I tell you they're poisoning me! You need to come, Harry."

The pleading rent Harry's heart into two. "I'll be there soon."

"I need you now. They're going to hurt me. They took my wheelchair." His father's voice wobbled. "Please come, Harry."

"Dad. I'll be there soon." Harry's throat closed with tears. He hung up the phone, and broke into a jog.

The sooner he dealt with this bastard the better.

48

2:11 a.m.

KATE DIDN'T HAVE TIME to give Eddie's new place more than a cursory glance before she hurried up the front walkway. There were several lights on inside the town house.

Why hadn't Eddie answered the phone?

She rang the doorbell.

No answer.

She pressed it again.

No answer.

Jesus, Eddie. Where are you?

Maybe Eddie wasn't home.

She peered at the front window. Light shone through the crack between the window frame and the blinds.

She texted: *I'm outside your place. Please answer the door.*

Then she waited.

After a few minutes, she texted: *I'm going to meet the hacktivist now.* If Eddie was home, she knew he could not ignore that text.

Two minutes later, the door was unlocked. Eddie stood on the threshold. Hair rumpled, pants rumpled.

Face rumpled.

Ash dribbled down the front of his shirt.

Oh, Eddie.

She could smell the alcohol from where she stood. He swayed slightly in the doorway. "Kate."

"Can I come in?"

"Of course."

She entered his apartment. A black leather sofa sat in front of a television.

And that was it.

The moving boxes were still packed, stacked neatly by the counter of the galley kitchen. And on the counter was a vodka bottle that was only one-third full.

Her heart sank.

Eddie was a recovering alcoholic. He had completely forsworn alcohol.

"You're up late." She walked over to the kitchen counter and leaned by the nearly empty bottle.

His gaze tracked her movements. "Yes."

She loved her friend too dearly to mince words. "Why are you drinking again? Especially with Elaine coming next week?"

Shame, pain, raw anguish flickered in his gaze. "Elaine's not coming. She left a voice mail. I got it when I came home."

Damn her.

And then she realized that wasn't fair. She had no idea what had gone on between Eddie and Elaine. Eddie had freely admitted that he was responsible for the failure of their marriage. And maybe he was.

"Oh, Eddie. I'm so sorry."

He shook his head. "She didn't think it was a good idea. She was concerned it would lead to false expectations."

She was right. It had.

They had both been hopeful.

Kate threw a glance at the vodka bottle. "You can't just drown your sorrows."

He crossed his arms. "Please don't patronize me, Kate."

"Eddie, please." She gave him a helpless look. "Don't do this to yourself."

He shoved his hands into his trouser pockets. "Kate, you should go now."

"Eddie, I'm your friend. I care about you—"

"Kate. You should go now."

He herded her to the front door.

"Will you come with me?" Anything to get him away from the bottle. "I'm meeting Matt. The hacktivist."

Eddie's bushy salt-and-pepper brows lowered. "Tonight?"

"Yes. I'm on my way there." Kate swallowed. "I don't want to go by myself." She didn't need to elaborate why. Eddie knew about her history.

He exhaled. "All right. But I'm not willing to talk about Elaine. Or my drinking habits. Do you understand?"

Habits.

That implied his vodka bottle was not a one-off occurrence.

Oh, I understand. "Of course. But we have to hurry. We have to meet Matt in ten minutes."

Eddie grabbed his house keys and his phone. Kate strode to her car, Eddie hurrying behind her. Three-quarters of a bottle of vodka hadn't seemed to affect him much.

Kate wondered if that was his first bottle of the evening. Or if he'd had another ready in the fridge when he finished the first.

Her heart was leaden. Was her friend so fragile that one disappointment would cause him to topple off the wagon?

No.

There must be more going on that she didn't know about.

Hillcroft had warned her to not tie her career to Eddie. She had brushed that advice aside.

And now she could see first-hand that Eddie was in trouble.

And she didn't know how to help him.

Her hands trembled as she gripped the wheel and turned the car toward the downtown area. She had faced killers, stalkers, and Kenzie Sloane, her oldest nemesis. She had battled for her life more than once. Some would say she had won those battles. She would term it survival rather than victory. Regardless of the semantics, she had made it through those battles.

But her attempt to wrest her sister from the grip of addiction had cost Imogen her life.

Addiction was an entirely different stalker.

And one she had no idea how to beat.

49

HAD THE POLICE SEEN him?

Were they calling in other units to surround Point Pleasant Park?

Where they going to bring in the dog?

Aiden's stomach clenched. He darted deeper into the woods and began to backtrack through the upper reaches of the park. It led to the prime real estate of Halifax's 'deep South End'. He cut through the property of a sprawling home, and headed north toward the railway tracks. At this hour of night, there weren't many pedestrians. The houses were dark, lit by security lights mounted on porches and garage doors. He felt invisible in his black clothing—yet exposed at the same time.

But police vehicles would be exposed, too. That thought comforted him as he hurried along the park side of Francklyn Street, keeping close to the shadows cast by the trees.

Only two cars drove by him as he walked. He had held his breath, hoping he melted into the shadows, wondering if they were unmarked cars. But no police officers materialized.

If the police were searching for him, they were keeping their search to the park.

That'll keep 'em busy. The park was huge.

He turned up Pine Hill Drive. The railway cut ran along the length of the north side of the street. He leapt onto the scrubby border by the chain link fence. It took only a few minutes to find a place to squeeze through. And then he was on the tracks.

Home free!

He needed to make a new plan. It was 0238. Harry Owen should be on his way to the park—

What if the police picked up Harry Owen as he tried to make the rendezvous?

He yanked his phone out of his pocket, his fingers frantic as he texted: *Change of plans. Cops in park. Meet me at airport departure @ 0500.*

He would walk down the tracks until he was near the shopping mall. He should be able to get a cab from there to the airport.

And then he would make the 'exchange' with Harry Owen and take the first flight out of Halifax, with half a million dollars of Bitcoin waiting for him.

———

There were very few people in the hotel lobby at this hour. Business execs and a few well-heeled travellers clustered around the bar, trading the war stories that were generally aired at the time of night when enough cocktails and beer had been consumed to make everyone your best friend.

Kate threw a cautious look at her friend, mentor. Law partner. He walked heavily, sweat dampening his forehead. Should she have brought him?

But how could she have left him?

They rode the elevator to Matt's floor in silence. When they stepped out into the corridor, Eddie cleared his throat. "I'm sorry you found me like that, Kate."

"It's okay."

Was his drinking precipitated by disappointment, or was

it something that Elaine suspected and thus had cancelled her trip?

So many questions.

So few answers.

Maybe that's what bothered Kate the most. Eddie was her go-to guy, the mentor who had a sage answer or an alternative point of view to the questions that Kate could not answer. But now her go-to guy was an unknown.

Just like her father had been.

And every romantic relationship she had. Ethan, Randall…they all left her for good reasons. But it didn't change the fact that they left. And she was alone.

Kate rapped on Matt's hotel door, standing in front of the peephole.

The door swung open. A man with olive skin and wary eyes gazed at her. She guessed he was maybe a year or two older than Leah. He wasn't overly tall for a man—Kate's height—with broad shoulders and a fit build. A dark, mottled wound marked his forehead, partially covered by a gray beanie. The band of the beanie was soaked with blood.

"Matt. I'm Kate Lange. This is my partner, Eddie Bent."

Matt's nostrils flared as his gaze darted to Eddie. He could smell the booze radiating from Eddie. "Come in."

They stepped inside the suite. Matt locked and bolted the door behind them. Kate saw the back of a familiar white-blond head, slumped on the sofa. "Hi, Joey."

Joey jumped to his feet. "Ms. Lange." His hair hung in greasy strands by his ears. His gaze was haunted. Hunted. "How's Leah?"

"She's doing better." Kate gave him a reassuring smile.

"Have you talked to my parents?"

"They are very worried about you, Joey. Why haven't you gone home?"

A flush reddened Joey's cheeks. He threw a quick, revealing look at Matt.

"I told him not to, Ms. Lange," Matt interjected. "The police will arrest him. I told him to wait until we find out

Aiden Boyne's identity. Then we can leverage it to get Joey off the hook."

"The Crown won't add Joey to Leah's immunity deal, Matt."

Joey's gaze became panicked. "You mean I'm going to prison?"

Kate shook her head. "We are going to offer the laptop in exchange for immunity for you."

"But you just said that the Crown wouldn't include me in Leah's immunity deal."

"This is in lieu of Leah's deal," Eddie said.

There was a look of disbelief, of protest on Matt's face.

But he said nothing.

He knows that this is the right thing to do.

"Give Ms. Lange the laptop, Joey." He jerked his chin toward Kate.

Joey hugged it to his chest. "I can't."

"Joey, Leah was very firm in her instructions. Please, give me the laptop." Kate held out her hand.

Joey threw an anguished look at Matt.

Matt gave a small nod.

Joey handed Kate the laptop. "I don't want you to trade this for immunity for me. I wouldn't get much time for being an accessory. But Leah could have a long sentence."

"Joey, we're going to try to get both of you deals," Eddie said. "We'll work on another angle for Leah. The more information you can share about Aiden, the more leverage we have with the Crown. Do you have anything else that they would want to know?"

Matt shoved the beanie back on his forehead, revealing a one-and-a-half inch wound just below his hairline. Beads of red seeped through the skin from the friction caused by his movement. "Aiden bragged about a big exploit. He said that he and Tr0lz were going to blow up this town."

"Jesus." Eddie frowned. "Who's this Tr0lz hacker?"

"Tr0lz was part of the Forum's inner circle. I thought he was a white hat."

"What's a 'white hat'?"

"A white hat is an ethical hacker. I'm a white hat. I hack to expose the truth. But I'm pretty sure that Tr0lz is a black hat."

"What gave him away? His name?" Eddie's tone was dry.

Matt threw him a look. "I thought the name was social commentary."

"Do you think they are capable of a terrorist act?" Kate asked.

Matt exhaled. "I didn't think Aiden was the terrorist type. He only cares about himself."

"But what about Tr0lz?" Kate's gaze swung from Matt to Joey.

"I've never met him," Matt said. "Have you, Joey?"

Joey shook his head.

"So he's a wild card," Eddie said. "And if he convinced Aiden to join him in a terrorist exploit, what kind of cyber hacking would affect the whole city?"

"The obvious hack would be to screw up the city's infrastructure," Matt said. "Electrical grids, communication lines, transportation systems. Does Halifax have a subway?"

Joey shook his head. "Nope. Just buses."

"And trains and planes," Kate murmured.

"What about the electrical grid?" Eddie asked. "How possible is it to hack in to that?"

The trickle of blood from Matt's wound had become several, thicker streams. He used his sleeve to wipe the blood away from his eye. "It's possible. But it's complex."

"What's an easier exploit?" Kate asked. She pulled a pair of sterilized adhesive strips from her pocket that she had found in her cupboard. "I'm going to put this on you. You're bleeding up a storm."

While she tended the slice in his forehead, Matt said, "An easier exploit might be to hack into the communication systems, or the airport flight control system…"

A shiver skittered up Kate's back. "Is there anything in Harry's files which might have triggered this new exploit?"

Matt gave her a wry look. "Harry Owen has so much classified information that it's impossible to narrow it down."

"We can't keep this from the police." She stood back and eyed her handiwork on Matt's forehead. The wound appeared closed. For now.

"Are you going to turn us in?" Matt grabbed his beanie and shoved it back on his head.

"No." She turned to Joey. "But I'll take you home if you want me to."

Joey threw a concerned look at Matt. "Is that okay?"

"Of course it is, Joey."

Kate glanced at Eddie. His eyes were glazed with fatigue. She needed to get him home, too.

"Joey, the police will want to interview you ASAP if they think there is a threat to public safety. Answer them with what you know about Aiden and any potential threat, but I advise you to exercise your right to remain silent about everything else. And ask your parents to find a lawyer for you."

His eyes had widened at her instructions. Poor kid. It was going to be a long night for him. She saw the fear. But she also saw relief.

He was going home.

And Kate would do everything in her power to make sure that it wasn't just a temporary visit.

50

IN TWENTY MINUTES, IT *will all be over.*

Harry half-walked, half-jogged up Inglis Street. The weight that compressed his chest would soon be lifted. Or at least, it would be different. His conscience would forever remind him that he had committed an unforgivable sin: he had taken another person's life, even if the person in question had rained grief and pain on his family's head.

His hand loosely gripped the cord in his pocket. It fit the curve of his hand, smooth, cool, pliant. It felt good there. Comforting and comfortable. It would do the job for him.

Would he be haunted by flashbacks of strangling his blackmailer?

If flashbacks were to be his punishment, he would gladly take it. For the threat of what could unfold for him—and for his father if Harry lost his source of income—was unbearable.

He was ready.

He could do this.

His phone vibrated in his pocket. He read the text message from his blackmailer, his heart hammering.

What the hell? The police were at the park?

And the blackmailer now wanted to do the exchange at the airport in two hours' time.

How could he kill him there?

Damn. Damn. Damn.

He would find a taxi. He would go see his father and put out that fire.

And then he would figure out his next move.

51

"DETECTIVE ELLIS. THIS IS Kate Lange." Kate gazed through the windshield of her car at Hollis Street. It was after three in the morning, and the bars had shut down. The patio tables and chairs had been chained to the fence posts, patrons sent on their merry way. The street was settling into the deepest part of the night. Taking a breather before the early morning risers began their quest for coffee.

She was aware of two pairs of eyes on her. Both were bloodshot. The young hacktivist sat in the back seat, so wired that he strained against his seat belt, his gaze exhausted. Eddie had settled into the passenger seat with his usual ease, but dark bags emphasized the redness in his eyes.

"What's up, Ms. Lange?" Detective Ellis' voice went from groggy to alert.

"I have critical information. But I must have your undertaking that this information will be considered as compliance with the immunity agreement for Leah Roberts." She glanced at Joey's anxious face in her rearview mirror. She had to handle this carefully. She didn't want to implicate Joey in a crime before the police had evidence that he had committed one. "And the accomplice who removed the laptop."

260

"So you are saying that the accomplice is not Aiden Boyne."

"Correct."

"Is it Joey Roberts?"

"Detective, you know I can't answer any questions of that nature." She gave Joey—who appeared to be holding his breath—a reassuring look in the mirror.

"Do you know the whereabouts of Joey Roberts?"

"Yes." She could not evade that question. That truth would come out. "He's in my car."

"What is he doing there?"

"I offered him a drive home."

Joey's eyes were wide. Scared.

She cleared her throat. "Listen, Detective, time is of the essence. I have received reliable information that another cyber exploit might be committed by Aiden Boyne. And it is of a terrorist nature."

"What kind of terrorism are we talking about?" Ellis asked, his voice tense.

She exhaled. "I don't know. We—Eddie Bent and I—only know that it might affect the infrastructure of the city in some way."

"Is it related to the hack of Harry Owen's computer?"

"My source couldn't say."

"Who's your source?"

Kate hesitated.

"Ms. Lange, you can't invoke solicitor-client privilege when public safety is at risk." Detective Ellis' tone was curt.

Kate closed her eyes. She believed that Matt had told her everything he knew. If she revealed his whereabouts to the police, he would face serious charges.

Dammit.

And yet, maybe the police had uncovered evidence that would connect dots of which neither Matt nor Kate were aware.

She exhaled. "His name is Matt Leon."

Joey hissed, "No!"

"Where can we find him?"

She gave Detective Ellis the name of Matt's hotel and then hung up the phone.

"Shit, shit, shit."

"You had to do that, Kate." Eddie spoke softly.

She felt Joey's eyes drill into the back of her head. "Joey," she turned in her seat. "There are too many lives at risk."

"So Matt's and Leah's lives don't matter to you."

"Of course they do. But this has gotten bigger than both of them. We can't keep this to ourselves anymore. Think of your parents. What if they were killed because of this exploit?"

Joey's gaze dropped. There was no answer to that.

They didn't know what was planned or when it would happen.

It was now out of their control.

There was nothing more to say as Kate drove to Joey's house. It was in the west end of Halifax. His home was one of the older wood-shingled character homes, with a lovely stone-walled garden and mature shrubs.

Joey jumped out of the car as soon as she pulled into the driveway. She watched him sprint up the walkway to his house.

A porch light shone down on his head. A beacon. A welcome.

He must have texted his parents on his way home, because the door flung open as he ran up the porch steps. His mother folded her son into a tight embrace, his father wrapping his arms around them both.

Eddie cleared his throat. "He's a good kid. So is his sister."

Kate pulled away from the curb and headed toward Eddie's house. The traffic was light, but it was surprising how many people were on the road at this hour. "I know. And now they are being dragged into a potential terror plot." She threw him a glance. "What do you think will happen to Matt?"

Eddie sighed. "Extradition. If the authorities link him to Leah's doxx, or other evidence of his hacktivist activities comes to light, he could face very serious charges. The US Espionage Act doesn't have a legal exception for public interest, so they might charge him with treason if they find he's posted state secrets. Just like Snowden."

Kate felt sick. "What obligation do I have to deliver the laptop right away? I'd like to see if I can come up with something to get Leah, Joey and Matt off the hook." Kate pulled up to the front of Eddie's house.

"The police can talk to Harry Owen directly, now that they know the threat exists. Harry will have to come clean about what he put on his personal computer. If Ellis finds Matt, they will also have that angle to explore. Ethically, I think you are in the clear."

"Good. I'm going to look at it now."

"Do you want some help?"

"It's a small laptop screen, Eddie. I don't think we both can read it. I'll call you if I find anything."

"Okay." He climbed out of the car and lumbered to his front door. He appeared to have collapsed on himself.

Alaska dutifully met her at the door when she arrived home, but Foo Dog just lifted his head from the dog bed when she placed Leah's laptop on the kitchen table. She put on the kettle. The little sleep she had managed to get last night had run out a while ago.

Mug of tea in her uninjured hand, Kate skimmed the files that Leah and Aiden had stolen from Harry Owen. It blew her mind what he had put on his laptop: memos marked 'Private & Confidential' from the Minister detailing the department's approach to covering up the data breach, as well as information about border security system upgrades, including information about airport safety measures. There were also a series of files about NATO training exercises which included US naval forces, Emergency Management measures involving airport security, and, ironically, cyber security strategies.

But there weren't any memos that screamed 'terrorist target.'

Because they all did.

"Damn." She needed to talk to Leah.

She hurried to her car. She had driven to the hospital so many times in the past twenty-four hours that she was on autopilot.

The clerk was reluctant to let her into the ICU, so Kate called the surgeon. Dr. Kapur was none too happy to be paged, but when Kate explained that she needed access to Leah due to a public safety threat, she was allowed in.

She strode down the hushed corridor, feeling as if she had stepped into a twilight zone where death and life were pitched in eternal battle.

But this time, the battlefield wasn't simply the ailing bodies of the ICU patients.

52

3:20 a.m.

HARRY STRODE INTO HIS father's hospital room, the computer cord in his pocket thudding against his thigh. "Dad," he murmured.

There was no reaction to Harry's voice. His father's eyes remained closed, his mouth slightly agape. *"They are trying to drug me, Harry."*

A nurse hurried in behind Harry.

He spun around. "What the hell have you done to my father?" The rage and pain that had been in his chest threatened to erupt.

The nurse gave Harry a steady look.

Cool down, Harry. But he was furious at himself for dismissing his father's concerns as mere ranting, at the hospital for ignoring his father's pleading. "Did you sedate him against his wishes?"

The nurse shifted on his feet. "Mr. Owen, your father was a danger to himself and to others."

"What do you mean? He's not a danger to others any more. He isn't armed."

"Your father assaulted me," the nurse said, his tone calm.

"What?" *Oh, Dad.*

"We had no choice but to sedate him after that. He also

attempted to leave his bed. He was doing more damage to his leg."

The weight that had been in Harry's chest suddenly became a tightness. He knew why his father had struck out. He had felt trapped.

He had called Harry to advocate for him, while he lay helpless and bereaved in a hospital bed—and Harry had refused to come.

Harry collapsed into the chair by his father's bed. "Dad, I'm sorry," he whispered.

An IV was taped to the back of Mel's hand. Harry touched his father's fingers. Flesh bulged slightly around the wedding ring on his left hand. The joints of his fingers were thickened, the skin tough from years of manipulating a wheelchair.

The murder plan that Harry had hatched just hours before suddenly seemed surreal. Crazy, even.

His father, lying in this bed, in this room, was real. Not the shadowy blackmailer who taunted him on wireless airwaves. Not the man who drank a bottle of scotch, and planned to murder his tormenter with a computer cord.

That man was not real. He was not the son of the man lying in this bed. He was not the Honorable Harry Owen, Member of Parliament. He was not a member of the Nova Scotia bar.

He was not the son of the woman who had taught him to respect his elders, to stand up for the vulnerable, to always obey the law. Tears choked his throat.

She stood at the stove, her long black hair swept up in a knot at the back of her head, her eyes half-closed as she inhaled the fragrant curry. She added a bit more of coriander. Then she smiled. Offered him a spoonful. "You tell me what it needs, Harry."

It needs you to make it, Ma. It needs you to frown in concentration until it tastes the way your own mother made it. It needs you to smile when we declare it delicious. That is what it needs.

That is what I need.

That is what Dad needs.

His father had been through hell. There was no other way to describe it. And if his son were arrested for murder, it would merely add another notch to the tragedies of the Owen family.

Harry rested his cheek on his father's hand. "Dad, please forgive me."

"Harry."

It wasn't his father who spoke his name.

He lifted his face from his father's hand. Randall Barrett stood several feet away from him. How long had he been standing there? "What're you doing here?"

His lawyer gave an awkward shrug. "Mel is also my client. I wanted to keep an eye on things."

"You spent the night here?"

Randall shrugged again. "I thought I'd take a shift until you felt well enough to come."

Read: until you slept off the booze.

Harry felt shame, gratitude—and resentment that his lawyer had done the right thing while Harry ignored his father's pleas.

"Dad's in bad shape." Harry ran a hand through his hair. "I'm not sure how much more he can take. What will happen to him after the surgery?"

Randall exhaled. "At some point your father will be arraigned, and we will ask for bail. Then, we will see what the Crown offers us."

"Do you know Hillcroft?"

Randall shook his head. "No, he's new here. But I will urge him to be compassionate given the circumstances."

He hated that his father's freedom was at the whim of another man, who had no idea of what his father had gone through, had no conception of the rage and pain his father carried. *I'm sorry, Dad.*

"What did I do to bring this down on my family's head?"

Randall put a hand on Harry's back. "I'm sorry, Harry."

That was all anyone could say.

53

3:21 a.m.

AS SOON AS KATE left his hotel room with the laptop, Matt logged into the Forum and set up his trap: *Tr0lz—got some info about AggroBoy. PM me.*

Tr0lz took the bait. Within seconds, he received this message: *Whazzup?*

AggroBoy's playing u.

Pause. *How?*

He tried to steal Leah's laptop from me. Something's up.

You in Halifax?

Yep. Came to fix the mess. And discovered it was a sinkhole.

Is AggroBoy still with you?

Matt frowned. *No. Isn't he with you?*

No.

Another pause. *He's a coward.*

Then: *Want to do an exploit? Will pay $$$.*

Matt exhaled. He had guessed correctly: Tr0lz needed help with the exploit. He knew that Aiden did not possess the hacking skills for the kind of cyber exploit that would create a terrorist attack. And he didn't think Tr0lz did, either.

Don't want $$$. I want Aiden's real name.

Why? The response was quick, the three letters glaring with suspicion from his phone.

It's personal. He screwed with my girl. He thought that Tr0lz would likely be satisfied with that.

You do the code, I'll give you his name.

He smiled as he typed: *Deal. Where u at?*

Tr0lz sent an address that was only a five-minute cab drive from his hotel.

The taxi dropped off Matt in front of a new, bland apartment building in the south end of Halifax. He waited in the foyer, beanie low on his forehead, hoping he was out of range of any security cameras. *Here. Let me in,* he texted.

The buzz of the security lock echoed in the quiet night. He almost jumped out of his skin.

He typed a text to Kate Lange as he walked into the elevator. *I'm at Tr0lz's. He needs me to do code for exploit. He's going to give me AB's real name. Will keep you posted.*

Then he hit 'send'. Just a little protection from the hacktivist who had outsmarted them all.

So far, Matt. So far.

He stepped into the corridor of the fifteenth floor and walked to the end of the hall. The door opened before he could knock. A young woman stood there. He barely knew where to look: the exquisite heart shape of her face? The kitty cats on her tights? The softly curled hair that swung as she stepped back to let him in?

"Condor. What took you so long?" The sharpness of her tone belied the sweetness of her face.

"You're Tr0lz?" He knew as soon as he uttered the words that he sounded like an idiot.

Her raised brow affirmed both his question and his stupidity. She said nothing—barely glanced at the wound on his forehead—merely pivoting on a black-clad foot to lead him into the living room. The apartment was as bland as the lobby, as anonymous as the building, as deliberately disingenuous as the woman who had fooled them all.

Why was he so surprised that Tr0lz was a woman—and a young woman at that? His mind raced through his interactions with her. They were entirely on the hacktivist forum. He realized, to his chagrin, that it was simply her style of speaking online that had led them all to assume that Tr0lz was a man. He felt even more of a fool. So much for priding himself for his lack of gender bias.

Sweat pricked along the back of his neck.

If Tr0lz had been able to fool them all on the Forum, what other deceptions had she practiced?

"Have a seat." Tr0lz gestured to an executive chair in front of a workstation with a massive hi-res computer monitor.

He lowered himself into the chair. It was still warm from Tr0lz's bottom.

Code filled the computer monitor. He studied it, his gaze narrowing. GPS coordinates broke the regularity of the characters on the screen. "So what's this exploit?"

"It's something I came up with to prove our street cred."

"To whom?"

"Buyers online who are looking for the kind of service we can provide."

"We?"

She gave him an appraising look. "I'm creating a new Silk Road, Condor. There's a gap in the marketplace. Perfect for someone with your skills. Do you want to be a millionaire?"

His mind raced. Should he go along with her and learn as much as he can?

Or overpower her and call the police?

But he knew she wouldn't say a word to the police if she were arrested. Tr0lz had proved herself to be a master at deception.

"Everyone wants to be a millionaire, Tr0lz," he said, his tone casual. "I'm in. What's the exploit?"

"I need you to hack this navigation system so we can control a container ship."

In theory, it was a fun hack. *Let's take over a ship! Let's prove to everyone how pathetic the security measures are.* That's what some of the hacktivists on the Forum might do. But Matt sensed Tr0lz had an entirely different reason. "Why?"

"Because it's carrying a special cargo."

Just the way Tr0lz said that made Matt's hands go clammy. "What is it?"

"Do you know what UF6 is?"

It sounded dangerous enough that his stomach tightened even more. "Put me out of my suspense."

"It's an ingredient for a nuclear reactor."

Matt almost jumped out of the chair. "Jesus, you can't cause a nuclear explosion, Tr0lz!" Was this girl completely out of her mind?

"It isn't strong enough to cause an explosion. But it's toxic when exposed to water. It's corrosive." She flipped her hair. "My original plan was to take control of the ship and scare the crap out of everyone. Think of what it would do to the global shipping business!" She grinned. "We could halt shipping in Los Angeles, Shanghai, Rotterdam, anywhere in the world. We would own the sea. We would be pirates. Literally and figuratively."

So, he and Leah's lawyers had guessed right about a hack into a transportation system. But he had guessed wrong about which one. He assumed it would be the airport—because terrorists loved the soft targets of civilians grouped together under one roof.

The fact that Tr0lz had a strategy *and* the cyber code was another story. From what he could see on the computer screen, it was the real deal. And it looked like Tr0lz had fooled him once again: the code looked near completion.

"But then AggroBoy—" she threw a mocking glance at Matt, taunting him with Aiden's chat name because she knew that Matt was desperate to learn Aiden's real name "—gave me Harry Owen's files. And guess what I found?" She shook her head. "Halifax is getting a very special visitor."

"Who?"

Tr0lz grinned, revealing very large, white teeth. "A nuclear class submarine."

"So…?" Matt fought to keep his tone cool.

"And it's going to get a warm welcome from a certain container ship carrying UF6."

"What the hell are you talking about?"

"Have you heard of the Halifax Explosion?"

"No."

I should have called the police before I came.

"It happened about a hundred years ago. A munitions ship collided with a steam ship in the harbor. The explosion destroyed most of the city. It was the largest man-made explosion in the world until Hiroshima." Tr0lz gazed at the dark harbor outside. "And now, thanks to the emails we hacked from Harry Owen's account, we know that a nuclear submarine is arriving in—" she glanced at the clock on the computer "—less than an hour. After the submarine is docked at CFB Shearwater, we wait until the container ship has cleared the shoals by McNabs Island. Then we hack into the container ship and reset its course so that it is steered straight into the submarine." She smiled. "The submarine won't be able to get out of the way. I call it Halifax Explosion version 2.0."

The code blurred in front of Matt's eyes. A nuclear class submarine, a container ship, UF6...

Jesus Christ.

"Now get to work. We don't have much time. Aiden was useless. I'm done with him. As soon as you're finished, I'll give you the information you want."

Matt placed his fingers on the keyboard. He had a plan.

It was a dangerous plan, but if it worked, there would be no frantic scrambling to stop a container ship from ramming a nuclear submarine.

He would subtly sabotage the code.

He pulled the chair closer to the keyboard. Tr0lz carried a dining chair over and planted it behind him. She sank onto it with one leg tucked under the other.

He began working on the code sequence.

Tr0lz's eyes tracked every move.

54

LEAH LOOKED MORE DEAD than alive.

Kate suspected that she probably didn't look much better than her client.

She sat by Leah's bedside, laptop on her knees. The light was low, the footfalls of the staff muted through the glass door of Leah's room.

"Okay, we've gone through all the data breach memos. And the cyber security files. There's nothing there that you think Aiden would use for a cyber exploit?"

"Nothing for a terrorist attack." Leah's words were slightly mumbled.

"Can you think of anything he's said to you about other exploits that could be related to a terrorist attack?"

Leah shook her head. "No."

Kate studied her client. Leah had been given a pain medication a few hours before. They were getting nowhere fast.

Kate opened another sub-folder. Another interminable list of files scrolled down her screen. They blurred in front of her eyes.

Based on what Aiden had told Matt, there was something in Harry's stolen files that triggered the plans for this attack.

But where?

She methodically opened each file. It could be any of them. They were all sensitive, all had to do with public safety. "Damn it."

55

HARRY OWEN WAS A cipher, the consummate politician, unreadable, seemingly unshakable.

And a liar.

So what was he covering up? And why?

He didn't answer his phone.

He wasn't at his hotel.

Cooper strode down the hallway to Mel Owen's hospital room. As he approached, he heard male voices coming from Mel's room.

Bingo.

He stepped through the doorway. Harry Owen slumped in a chair by his father's bed. His lawyer Randall Barrett sat opposite him, tired but alert.

Damn. He hadn't wanted to deal with legal counsel right now.

Both men turned in surprise when Cooper approached. "Mr. Owen, I need to speak with you."

Harry and Randall rose simultaneously. A faint odor of alcohol radiated from Harry. He had changed his clothes and now wore running shoes, jeans, a navy t-shirt and windbreaker.

"I already gave my statement." Harry's tone was as close

to hostile as a Canadian politician in an election year dared get.

Randall threw his client a warning look.

"Mr. Owen, we have received information that Aiden Boyne has planned another exploit."

Harry Owen paled.

"Are you concerned that this exploit involves Mr. Owen's family or his department?" Randall Barrett asked.

Out of the corner of his eye, Cooper noticed the end of a cord hanging out of Harry's jacket pocket. "Yes, in fact we believe it relates directly to data that was downloaded from Mr. Owen's computer."

The nurse stepped into the room. Cooper held out an arm. "I'm sorry, but unless this is life or death, we need complete privacy."

Randall Barrett frowned.

"I was going to check his vitals. I can come back."

"Please instruct the staff that no one is to enter until I give the go-ahead," Cooper added. He suspected his edict was pushing the boundaries of his authority, but there was no time to take Harry Owen to the station for an interview. They needed information now. And he didn't want anyone getting wind of a terrorist plan.

The nurse nodded, backing out of the room.

The Member of Parliament looked as if he might throw up. "What kind of exploit? With what data?"

"Aiden Boyne is planning a terrorist attack, Mr. Owen. And we believe it is some kind of cyber exploit with the city's infrastructure."

"Jesus Christ," Harry whispered. He sank onto the chair.

"We need to know possible targets."

Harry put a hand over his eyes. Then he let his hand fall. No more hiding.

His gaze met Detective Ellis'. "I'm being blackmailed by

Aiden Boyne. And he wanted me to meet him at the airport." The words rang in the room.

He almost collapsed from the release of the weight in his chest.

Randall Barrett gave him a look that was both compassionate and caution-filled.

The detective's gaze sharpened. "At what time?"

"Five a.m."

Detective Ellis checked his watch. "It's 4:01. Were you planning to go to the rendezvous?"

"No. I had changed my mind." He threw an involuntary look at his father.

"Did you tell him you had changed your mind?" Detective Ellis' tone was urgent.

"No. I haven't had any contact with him." And did not want to ever again.

"Mr. Owen, we need you to go meet him. We'll provide back up. We need to know what his plan is."

The detective opened a door that Harry had believed was forever bolted: an opportunity to get out of this mess. Harry leapt to his feet. "All right. I'm in."

Randall Barrett put a hand on his arm. "Harry, you don't have to do this."

"Yes, I do." He brushed his lips over his father's cheek. It was flaccid. But warm. He was still alive. "Good-bye, Dad."

Harry would do everything in his power to make sure that he came back to spend the rest of his father's days with him.

But if he didn't, he would die the way that he wanted.

As his mother's son.

56

4:29 a.m.

SOMETHING VIBRATED AGAINST KATE'S leg.

It was her phone. She fumbled with her back pocket, grabbing the laptop before it slipped off her lap.

"Hello." The inside of her mouth felt as if it had been wiped dry with a towel. She swallowed. She needed to get a bottle of water from somewhere in the hospital.

"It's Matt." His voice was low, tense.

"Is everything okay?"

"I'm in Tr0lz's bathroom."

"What?"

"I only have a minute." She heard a toilet flush. "Have you heard of the Halifax Explosion?"

"Yes."

"Tell the police that Tr0lz is planning version 2.0."

"What—"

The phone clicked in her ear.

She dialed Detective Ellis' number.

"Ellis." His voice was brusque.

"It's Kate Lange."

"Yes?"

"Matt Leon just called me. He says that Aiden Boyne's partner Tr0lz is planning Halifax Explosion version 2.0."

"What?" The police radio was noisy in the background. Ellis must be driving somewhere.

"He says the attack is a new Halifax Explosion." She enunciated her words so that the detective would not misunderstand. "The terrorist attack must have something to do with a ship."

"Ms. Lange, we have Mr. Owen with us. He admitted he was the victim of blackmail by Aiden Boyne. The rendezvous is at the airport."

"Maybe Aiden's trying to stay away from an explosion in the harbor."

"Damn it." Ellis paused. "Do you think Matt Leon is working in partnership with Tr0lz? This could be a diversionary tactic to get us all down to the waterfront while the airport is the true target." It was a genius tactic to send the police downtown while the attack took place miles away.

"Or vice versa."

"How reliable is Matt Leon?" Ellis' tone was urgent.

"I don't know. I just met the guy this evening." Detective Ellis' counter argument was persuasive. Matt Leon seemed genuine, but he also wasn't above breaking the law for his own perception of justice. "But he called me from Tr0lz's bathroom to warn me. He also texted me Tr0lz's address."

"I'll send a team to investigate. What's the address?"

Kate read it out loud while Detective Ellis repeated it to someone over the police radio.

"Don't go there yourself, Ms. Lange."

"Can you also send a team to the waterfront?"

"I'll alert the Coast Guard. Do you know which ships would be involved in this attack?"

"No. I have no idea."

She realized that if Matt was creating a diversion, he had played his hand well. "Are you going to check out the airport?"

"We are fifteen minutes away from the airport with the Serious Incident Response Team to apprehend Aiden Boyne. We have it all under control, Ms. Lange."

"Okay."

"Stay away from the waterfront and the airport until the suspects are apprehended."

A string of commands were fired over the radio. Ellis hung up the phone before she could respond.

"Did you tell the police that Matt called you?" Leah's tone was accusing.

Kate glanced over at her client. Leah glared at her from the hospital bed. Her client's sedation had obviously worn off.

"Yes. He said he was at Tr0lz's."

"Oh, no. Why did he go?"

"I don't know why he went there. But he told me to call the police. He said that Tr0lz was planning Halifax Explosion version 2.0."

Shock flickered across Leah's face.

Kate leaned closer. "Do you know anything about that?"

———

"Leah, have you ever done any work with the Ports?" Aiden had asked one night when they lay tangled in her sheets.

She shook her head. "No, why?" Her finger traced a little circle over his heart.

"I heard that the shipping industry has the worst cyber security in the world."

"Hmmm…maybe…" she murmured, planting little kisses on his shoulder.

"Don't you think it would be cool if the Forum hacked into a container ship one night?"

She raised herself on an elbow. "Why would we do that?"

"Because they transport dangerous things like nuclear ingredients and stuff. That crap comes right into our harbor. But it's all on the downlow. No one in Halifax knows anything about that."

"Are they deliberately hurting anyone?"

"Not yet. But it's just a matter of time." He gazed at her, his expression open. Concerned.

"We can't do anything until that happens, Aiden. The Forum is supposed to reveal wrongs, not cause trouble."

"Why not prevent a wrong? Shouldn't we do that, too? Let people know that our government is allowing scary stuff into our harbor just to make a buck?"

"But we don't even know if it's wrong. They have regulations for handling those materials."

"Leah, the port had a major screw up a few years ago. Remember when the containers of uranium hexafluoride were dropped by dock workers? Those are ingredients for nuclear fuel, for God's sake."

She was surprised at the intensity of his reaction. "Yes, but no one was harmed. It's not very radioactive in that state."

"But if it fell in the water...BOOM!" He made a mushroom shape with his hands.

"Not exactly. It creates highly corrosive gas. But it isn't explosive."

Irritation flashed in Aiden's eyes. "I don't know why you are defending these guys. We could have Halifax Explosion Version Two before we know it."

"That was a century ago. They've never had another incident."

"You know that hackers could take over a ship and make it collide into another one. We should hack into a ship just to demonstrate the risk that exists. And the fact that shipping companies are totally ignoring it."

"You mean a preventative warning?"

He gave a thumbs up. "Yeah. Exactly. We take control of a container ship in the harbor and embarrass the authorities. It will force them to tighten up their systems."

"Hmmm...how would we do that?" She asked partly out of intellectual curiosity, and partly to humor him.

"It's easy for someone with your mad skills," he had murmured.

Then he had told her exactly how to do it: using a vessel's Maritime Mobile Service Identity number to send fake GPS coordinates over the system that provided shipping positions to avoid collisions. The hodgepodge of software applications and platforms used by ships from all over the world left backdoors open for hackers.

His scheme had been persuasive enough that it gave her chills. "It's very risky," she had said. "I'm not sure what good it would do. And what if we grounded a ship and caused an oil spill?"

As she relayed the conversation to her lawyer, she realized that Aiden had set her up. "It required more technical expertise than I think Aiden possessed to do this kind of exploit. He even admitted it to me."

"So how would he accomplish this?"

"I think he convinced me to break in to the Owens' house to give him leverage over me. He wanted to make me write the code for this exploit." And it had been a good plan. But he was wrong about one thing: she would never have written that code for him.

"Do you think that an explosion in the harbor is the ultimate target?"

"It makes sense."

Kate dialed Ellis' number. "My God," he said, when she filled him in. "I'm just outside the city limits. Pearson sent me back to deal with Leon. The Serious Incident Response Team has taken over the airport."

57

4:33 a.m.

MATT GAZED INTO TR0LZ'S bathroom mirror. He hadn't slept in over twenty-four hours. His olive complexion was undercut with gray. He splashed water on his face, smoothed back his hair. *Wake up. You are so close. You just need to get out of here.*

He unlocked the door and stepped into the hallway.

It was dark.

He blinked, the realization slamming into him—*Tr0lz eavesdropped*—at the same moment that something cold and hard pressed into his back.

"Are you done?" Tr0lz asked.

Matt tried to turn. The gun pressed even harder into him.

"You aren't going anywhere, you tricky bastard." He could smell her perfume. It was some kind of lily.

"I haven't finished the exploit."

"It's finished enough."

She was right. He had been bluffing. The exploit was completed enough that it should work. What he really meant was: *I haven't finished sabotaging the exploit.* Tr0lz had not let his code out of her sight.

In desperation, he claimed he needed to use the washroom, and called Kate Lange.

283

"You would have made a great partner," Tr0lz said. "Too bad you turned your back on me. I would have made you wealthier than you could've ever dreamed."

"Uh-huh." Matt didn't bother to hide his contempt. "If I had wanted that, I could have done it myself. You're the one who needs me. I don't need you."

"Actually, Condor, I don't need you."

¡Coño! His body registered the threat faster than his brain, his flesh jerking away from the deadly metal pressed into it.

Tr0lz pulled the trigger.

A stinging pain exploded in his back. He fell to the ground.

He lifted his head from the carpet and looked at Tr0lz.

But she dimmed before him, the cat tails on the back of her thighs swaying into darkness.

His torso exploded into fire.

58

KATE WAS WORKING THROUGH the implications of what her client had told her when Randall knocked on the door of Leah's hospital room.

"May I come in?"

Leah threw him a questioning look. He gave her a brief smile. "I'm Randall Barrett, counsel for Harry Owen."

Her gaze flickered with suspicion. "Why are you here?"

Randall glanced at Kate. "I needed to speak to Ms. Lange. Maybe we could speak outside."

"I didn't expect to see you here this early," Kate said as they left the room. Staff clustered at the central station, so they walked to the other end of the hallway.

"I spent the night with Mel Owen." He looked exhausted—and wired. She suspected she looked exactly the same. Limp clothing over tense body. "And now he's being prepped for surgery. Harry Owen accompanied the police to the airport." His tone softened. "When I left, I saw your car outside and I figured you were still here."

"Have you heard anything from Harry?" Kate kept her voice low.

She hoped that Aiden Boyne had been found, that the threat that had caught them all in its teeth had been extinguished.

285

Randall shook his head. "Nothing."

"Listen, I'm telling you this as a friend, so you can't use it against Leah in the Owen case—"

"Of course, Kate." The way he said that—his gaze steady and his tone steadfast—made her feel foolish for cautioning him.

"—There's a hacktivist named Matt who went to the apartment of another hacktivist named Tr0lz. He's Aiden Boyne's partner. Matt was trying to find out what the exploit was. He called me from the bathroom. He said the exploit had something to do with the Halifax Explosion."

Randall sucked in his breath. "So it's a shipping hack?"

"I think so."

"Do the police know?"

"I told Detective Ellis. He's going to the apartment to verify it, and he called the Coast Guard." Kate exhaled. "He told me to stay away."

A small smile lifted one side of Randall's mouth. "He obviously knows your reputation."

She threw him a reluctant smile. But her tone was serious. "Detective Ellis told me that Aiden had blackmailed Harry."

"Yes."

"If they were going to doxx him, why blackmail him? The files would be all over the Internet."

"There were personal emails that would have caused serious harm to his career."

"Oh. Poor Harry." And Kate meant it. As much as she resented his inflexibility when she attempted to plead Frances Sloane's case, the man and his father had been through hell over the past twenty-four hours.

———

Cooper had picked up Riley at the station after Lamond told him that he was conducting an interview of Joey Roberts in the soft interview room. They grabbed a pair of bulletproof vests from Cooper's trunk, and sped to the apartment building.

Cooper buzzed the superintendent. "Police. It's urgent."

Within a minute, the superintendent ran down the hallway, tying her bathrobe en route, and let Cooper and Riley inside. When she saw the bulletproof vests, she blanched.

"What's going on?"

"We need to secure this building. No one is to leave their apartments." He studied the list of surnames by the security buzzer. "We are looking for a young male, possibly lives alone, would have a lot of computer gear."

The superintendent frowned. "I don't have anyone here like that."

"What about a family with a teenage son?"

The superintendent eyed him. "No. Can't think of anyone. It's mainly young professional couples. In their twenties, who work downtown and are saving to buy a house."

Tr0lz could be any one of them.

"Have any of the tenants sold drugs?" Ellis asked. "Or had regular deliveries of packages?"

The superintendent's gaze shifted from openness to wariness. "We aren't going to arrest you, Ms. …"

"Wilson," she muttered.

"We are trying to find this tenant. It's urgent."

She pushed a strand of hair behind her ear. "Well, we have this international student who specifically requested the penthouse apartment so her cellular signal would not be blocked—"

"Is there only one penthouse?"

"Yes, it's the fifteenth floor," the superintendent said.

"Don't come up there. There will be several backups arriving in the next few minutes. Keep your tenants off that floor. Understand?" The superintendent nodded. "Now I need you to wait in the lobby to let in backup."

They strode into the foyer. Riley tapped Cooper on the arm. "I'll secure the stairwell. You take the elevator."

Of the two of them, she was the triathlete. "Got it."

As soon as he entered the elevator, he dropped into shooting stance. When he exited the elevator on the fifteenth floor, gun ready, he saw Riley was already by the door to the penthouse.

"Police! Open the door!" Cooper yelled.

No sound came from within.

"Police! Open the door!"

It was quiet.

Too quiet.

Cooper aimed his gun at the door lock, fired, and flung open the door. He smelled the blood before he saw the body. Face down, in an alarmingly large pool of red. "Damn it," he muttered, and stepped through the doorway.

Riley followed him, and knelt by Matt Leon. She pushed her fingers against his throat, face intent. Ellis skirted around the hacktivist, and disappeared into the bathroom. It was empty. No sign of struggle. Within seconds, he emerged. He headed into the living room.

It was easy to see that it had been abandoned. There was no clutter, and minimal furniture. His gaze was drawn to the computer monitor, where rows of script raced down the screen.

The code had been launched.

"Damn!" He raced into the bedroom, but there was no sign of Tr0lz. Or anyone.

He ran back into the living room and searched for the 'off' button on the computer. But then he paused. What if he shut down the computer, but the code had been uploaded elsewhere? And they didn't know where?

This computer might be their only chance to abort the exploit.

He yanked his phone out of his pocket and dialed Murphy's number. To his relief, the cyber analyst answered right away.

"The exploit has been launched," Cooper said. "Can you get here fast?"

"I'm still at the airport." Murphy had gone out with the

SIRT team in case he had to override the air traffic control system.

Sweat began to run down Cooper's temples. "Tell me what to do."

"This is complex…" Murphy took a deep breath. "But we can try a few basic commands. See if that aborts it."

But none of them worked.

Cooper shot a glance through a large picture window at the harbor. It was dark. Quiet. Not a single ship, large or small, could be seen. What was going on? "How can I tell which ship is being hacked?"

"I don't know. I've never studied maritime shipping systems, Cooper."

He sprinted over to where Matt lay on the ground. Riley had removed her t-shirt under her bulletproof vest and pressed it against the wound in his side. "He's alive. Barely. The paramedics are on the way."

"Is he conscious?" But he could see for himself that Matt was not.

"No. What's going on with the exploit?"

Cooper shook his head. "It's been launched. And I can't stop it."

"Try Murphy."

"I already did. He's too far away. And nothing has helped."

"What about Leah Roberts?"

———————

Kate's phone vibrated. She pulled it from her pocket, her fingers tensing when she saw the number. "Kate Lange."

"This is Detective Ellis." She mouthed 'police' to Randall. His gaze sharpened.

"Are you still at the hospital?"

"Yes." An orderly pushed a cart by them. Kate stepped to the side.

"I need you to put Leah Roberts on the phone. It's important."

"Detective, you can't question—"

"She needs to help us with the exploit that was just executed. It's urgent."

"Okay. Hold on." She broke into a jog, with Randall on her heels, skirting the orderly's cart. She placed the phone by her client's ear. "It's the police. They need your help."

———

"Hello," Leah said into Kate's phone.

It seemed like an innocuous thing to say to the man who was trying to put her behind bars.

He didn't respond in kind. "Leah, I'm at Tr0lz's apartment."

"Is Matt okay?" Her breath was lodged somewhere between her heart and her throat.

"He was shot, but he's still alive."

Matt. No. She knew why he went there. He wanted to save her.

"Leah, they executed an exploit. And I need you to tell me how to stop it."

Think, Leah. Drifts of black expanded and contracted in her head. She forced herself to cut through it. "Read the code to me."

"Okay." He started reading the code really fast.

Her stomach tightened as she heard the commands. Between Tr0lz and Matt, they had figured out how to hack into the AIS system and put in false GPS coordinates for the container ship. If they could do that, then the ship would change its course.

"What should I do?"

"There's too much to fix here. We need to block the hack."

"You just said you couldn't do that."

"At a macro level."

"What the hell does that mean?

"If the ship already has been hacked, we need to physically block the GPS signal." She spoke more quickly. "A GPS jammer could jam the data transmission from the ship's AIS transponder."

"Are you sure? How do you know that?"

"I looked it up." Aiden had spurred her curiosity when he had explained the ship spoofing, and one night she had done some digging. "You can find everything on Google."

But the detective had already hung up.

59

4:58 a.m.

"REMEMBER, DON'T DO ANYTHING except speak to him."
The SIRT commander's gaze drilled into Harry's. "We need
information."

Harry nodded. "I understand."

The sun had risen over the Halifax International
Airport. Taxis sat at the curb, while cars pulled in
haphazardly to deposit luggage and travellers at the large
revolving doors.

En route to the airport, Harry had received a text from
Aiden Boyne: *men's room. 2nd stall.* There had been a debate
of strategy by the police, as to whether to lock down the
airport or to attempt a sting.

Since they suspected Aiden Boyne was not armed, they
opted for a sting. They needed information. Desperately.
And they needed leverage to get him to cooperate.

"I'm going in now." Harry opened the door of the
unmarked SUV, and hopped out. He knew the airport like
the back of his hand, he'd travelled through it thousands of
times. He walked inside, the bulletproof vest under his
windbreaker providing an entirely different weight on his
chest, a wire taped on the other side of his heart.

He strode past the check-in kiosks, the seafood counter

that packed fresh Nova Scotia lobsters for travel, the gift shop where he often purchased mints and the paper.

These people. All with loved ones.

God. A young child, holding his mother's hand, clutching his blankey and wearing bright yellow boots.

What if the attack was the airport?

Don't think about it, Harry. Just go do your job.

What if Aiden refused to talk?

Just do your job.

He glanced at his watch—4:59—and strode into the men's room.

A man at the urinal zipped up his fly. And then he hurried out to the terminal.

There was no one left in the washroom.

Except for Harry.

And the man in the black running shoes who stood in the second stall from the end.

The paramedics had taken over Matt's care. Riley, her tanned arms spattered with blood, sprinted toward Cooper, a question in her eyes.

"We need a GPS jammer." He dialed the staff sergeant. "I'm going to see if the station has one. And the Coast Guard."

Riley tapped him on the arm. "Tell Pearson to check the evidence locker."

Cooper relayed the information. Pearson kept his cool, but they both knew that the odds were stacked against them. GPS jammers were not standard equipment. And the clock was ticking.

"The Harbor Master has cancelled all arrivals and departures from the harbor as of 0500."

Thank God for that.

Cooper closed his eyes for a second and breathed.

"Cooper. Look at this." Riley stood at the window.

The dark shape of a container ship surged past McNabs Island.

He stood in front of the airport bathroom stall. "Aiden. It's Harry Owen."

The door slowly opened.

And Harry saw the face of his tormentor for the first time. But it wasn't the first time.

Despite the swollen nose, Harry recognized that face.

Tyson Green's eyes had always been distinctive: thickly lashed, changing from blue to green and back again. They drew people in. Made them want to trust him.

Harry had almost fallen for Tyson's pleas of ignorance when he was arrested for the hack into the Public Prosecutions' database of criminal files. But the trauma that he had caused by publishing online the details of the assaults could not be dismissed. Harry had provided damning evidence.

And Tyson had been punished to the full extent of the law.

"Tyson."

"My name is Aiden now." His blackmailer stepped out of the washroom stall. He had a backpack slung over one shoulder. His clothes were black, filthy. Harry recognized the look: Leah had worn similar garb. He fought his instinct to wrap his hands around the man's throat.

Aiden's green gaze mocked him. "But you still go by Mr. Owen. Or should I say the Honorable Mr. Owen?"

"Why are you doing this?" He fought to keep his voice neutral.

"Don't you know already?" Aiden's eyes narrowed. "Or have you conveniently forgotten?"

"I haven't forgotten anything, Aiden."

"Neither have I." He grinned. "And now your family won't, either."

The rage pushed for release. He wanted to wrap his hands around Aiden's neck. *Think of the little boy. Yellow rubber boots.* He took a deep breath. "I've got your BitCoin ready to be transferred. But I need to know what you were working on with Tr0lz."

"That's not part of the deal."

"Then I'm going to cancel the transfer." Harry pulled out his phone and flicked the screen. The site where he had purchased the BitCoin with police funds loaded, the BitCoin ready to be sent to Aiden.

Aiden's eyes darted to the phone. "That's not the deal. I have your laptop."

"I need to know, Aiden."

Aiden's eyes scanned the washroom behind Harry. "You've set me up."

Shit. "No. It's just you and me. I promise."

Aiden shook his head. "You're lying. You've set me up, you bastard!"

He snatched Harry's phone from his hand and sprinted out of the washroom.

Harry lunged after him.

He expected Aiden to run toward the doors, but instead he raced toward the luggage carousel.

Harry forced his legs to run harder, faster.

Aiden had almost reached the luggage carousel's draft curtain, where the conveyor belt traveled through to the other side of the wall. If he got through that, who knew where he could go.

You aren't going to let him get away this time, Harry.

He dove toward Aiden, grabbing his ankles as he crashed into the ground. Harry's head smacked on the tile floor.

Get up. Get up.

Through the fuzz in his vision, he saw black boots running by him.

"Face down on the ground!" one of the SIRT officers yelled.

Where was Aiden?

He raised his head. Four SIRT officers pinned Aiden to the carousel.

Harry let his head sink back to the ground.

Thank God.

He knew he should get up, but he needed a minute.

Just one minute.

"Your boyfriend is toast, Harry!" Aiden shouted, his face pressed against the floor, his arms cuffed behind him. "He's going up in a big mushroom cloud!"

He could barely tear his gaze from the US submarine captain. Rob radiated strength, focus, intelligence, courage.

When they were together, Harry felt invincible.

But those were stolen moments. Rob had been on a deployment for the past three months. Harry hadn't spoken to him at all. Communications were limited when the sub was submerged. And when Rob was able to use the Wi-Fi for personal communications, he contacted his wife.

The thought of her made Harry's heart constrict. She was the unseen force that pulled Rob surely and firmly from Harry's grasp. She and the two children. Rob wanted to end the marriage, but he didn't want to leave his kids.

And he was afraid for his career.

Just as Harry was afraid for his own. Being gay was more accepted than when he first entered politics, but he was in love with a married man. A man who was a captain in the US navy, and whose work revolved around covert intelligence operations—the 'Silent Service.'

No question, if anyone knew about their affair it would torpedo their high-powered careers.

But the pain of not being able to admit who he was, who he wanted, and why he had never fathered a child had begun a physical ache in his heart when it was clear his mother was dying. He carried this ball of pain and chain of fear everywhere he went, until he could barely function.

Then the call came that his mother was palliative and being sent home to die. He decided it was time to tell her. And hope that his conservative, religious mother would still love her only child. He had sinned big time.

He needed her blessing.

And so he had come home on that fateful flight a few days ago, full of hope. Hope that his mother would give him release from his pain, and hope that he might see Rob when his submarine came into port.

His mother had died before he could confess his deepest, most raw secret.

Then he had shot a woman. The first time out of fear. The second, out of rage.

And his father had done the unthinkable and tried to finish her off.

And now, now...

He had made his lover, the crew of the USS Flint, and the entire city of Halifax, a terrorist target.

A SIRT officer helped Harry to his feet and ushered him out of the terminal and into a SUV. As they headed toward Halifax, he placed frantic phone calls to the Defense Minister and a US naval contact that he thought might be able to reach Rob.

Dear God, please don't let him be killed.

His other line beeped. "This is Lt. MacKay, Maritime Forces Atlantic."

"Yes, Lieutenant." He watched the endless trees pass by as they sped to the city. The airport was so damned far away.

"I need to inform you that USS Flint was docked at CFB Shearwater at 0445, sir."

"Can she be moved?"

"Not in time, sir."

"You have to stop the container ship."

"We're doing our best, sir."

"Why can't the captain seize control of the helm?"

The lieutenant's voice was strained. "The hack has undermined the ship's computerized steering systems. It also locked the new coordinates into the autopilot system. Plus the *Petrel* has unusually tall sides that is causing a windage issue. The ship keeps drifting eastward."

CFB Shearwater was eastward.

His heart pounded so fast he could barely speak. "Is the sub evacuating?"

"There is a skeleton crew trying to secure the nuclear reactor in the engine room and neutralize the armaments."

"Call me when you have a plan of action." He hung up the phone.

It killed him to be watching trees rush by his window when all he wanted—all every cell in his body desperately needed—was to be on the harbor, making sure that Rob was safe.

60

5:08 a.m.

"IT'S DETECTIVE ELLIS. I need to speak to Leah."

Kate could hear the desperation in his voice. She glanced at Randall. The police had called less than ten minutes ago to speak to Leah. And now they called again.

She passed the phone to Leah. Both she and Randall made no pretense of listening intently.

"You saw the ship?" Leah asked in response to Ellis' statement.

Kate and Randall exchanged looks.

"No, there is no way to override the hack. It's too complicated. You need the jammer."

A pause. Then Leah said, "No, I don't have one."

Randall jumped to his feet and grabbed the phone from Leah. "This is Randall Barrett. I have a jammer on my boat. It's tied at the waterfront. By Bishop's Landing."

He raced to the door, Kate on his heels.

"Kate, stay here."

"No bloody way."

They ran all the way to her car. Kate drove while Ellis briefed Randall over the phone. Then Randall said, "The jammer has a range of 100 feet. But I've never used it."

Ellis said something, and then Randall added, "I leased

my boat to a company in the Caribbean for the winter. They bought it to use in those waters. They forgot to remove it from the boat."

The waterfront was directly in front of them. Randall pointed to a paved road that ran next to a parking lot. "It takes you straight to the jetty."

Kate jammed on the brakes two feet from the edge of the dock. They flung open the car doors and stared in shock at the harbor. "Oh, my God."

The encroaching dawn revealed a container ship plowing through the water by the northwest tip of McNabs Island. Then it executed a hard starboard turn at the Ives Knoll navigational buoy. A massive wake surged behind it.

It now headed northeast toward Indian Point buoy.

After it cleared that shoal, it would be minutes from CFB Shearwater.

And Ellis was nowhere to be seen.

Randall swung down the ladder to the *Ex Parte*, his feet barely skimming the bars, and jumped into the cockpit. "I'll start the engine. Kate, untie the stern." He disappeared down below to start the engine.

Kate dialed Ellis' number while she knelt by the large cleats and unwound the rope, tossing it onto the deck. Below decks, the diesel engine growled to life.

The detective answered right away. "Ellis, where are you?" she asked.

"I'm five minutes away."

She looked across the harbor. The dark silhouette of the ship neared Indian Point. "We need to go now or it'll be too late. It's getting close to Shearwater."

Ellis exhaled. "Go. But you're going blind. The GPS jammer will jam all cell phone communications. The ship can't communicate with the tug. Maritime Force can't communicate with us. You're on your own until the Coast Guard intercepts you—"

Kate didn't hear the rest because Randall put *Ex Parte*'s

engine into gear. It strained against rope as she untied the final loop.

"Jump now!" Randall called. Kate scrambled halfway down the ladder and leapt into the cockpit, Randall steadying her landing. As soon as she had both feet on the deck, he swung the wheel away from the dock, slammed the engine into top gear and steered the yacht toward Georges Island.

They hunkered down, Randall at the wheel, Kate in the cockpit. There was nothing to do but watch Georges Island loom closer, and pray that they could catch the ship before it was too late. They needed to be within feet of the container ship for the jammer to work.

"I'm going to cut it close to Georges Island," Randall called over the wind and engine noise. "It's more direct."

He steered the yacht so close that Kate wondered if she could jump across to the land, although she knew that the distance was deceptive. They cleared around it, their eyes fixed on the massive ship that plowed—surely, inexorably—toward the Shearwater jetty on the other side of the harbor.

It was as if the early morning sun had lifted the curtain on the harbor's stage. Kate could see CFB Shearwater now. Helicopters rose in the air, as futile as mosquitoes attacking a charging elephant. Trucks pulled onto the dock, lights flashing. A fireboat approached the ship from the Narrows.

The wind blew her hair in gusts around her face. She watched the helicopters, her heart in her throat. A safety boat lowered from the leeward side of the container ship and was set adrift. "The crew are abandoning ship," she called to Randall.

Randall pushed the throttle to its limit. It lurched forward with an angry roar. "That's it." The wind ripped through the rigging, rattling the halyards and slapping the loose ends of the main sail cover against the boom.

The container ship battled the water, creating a massive wake. They neared the ship. The size of it took Kate's breath.

Water sprayed over the side of the boat, soaking their jackets, their pants, their shoes.

"Kate, take the wheel." Randall gestured for him to come back. "I have to set up the jammer." The wheel was large, smooth, stainless steel, and responsive. Kate stood in the rear of the cockpit, feet planted.

Larger than a smartphone, the jammer was a black rectangular unit with four rubber-coated antennae evenly spaced on one end. "Let's hope that it works as well here as it did in the Caribbean."

The broad, high rear of the container ship loomed in front of them. Randall held up the small black unit. "Here goes."

Kate fought the wheel to prevent the yacht from being pushed by the waves into the hull of the ship. The yacht was tiny compared to the behemoth ship.

And yet, a device only a little bigger than her cellphone might be capable of stopping it.

"What happens if we jam the signal?" Kate asked. "If the ship doesn't have any coordinates, what does it do?"

"I think it will founder. Hopefully, jamming the signal will let the Captain regain control."

A large gust of wind slammed into the side of the yacht. The wake from the ship was strong. It had gained speed.

"Why isn't this working?" Randall adjusted the antennae on the jammer. Then he shook his head. "We need to get closer to the ship."

Kate gripped the wheel and turned it toward the ship's hull. The yacht plunged down a swell and almost toppled into the lee of the wake.

"Steady!" Randall shouted. "Ease the throttle!"

Kate gritted her teeth and wrestled with the wheel, her injured hand working overtime while she eased the throttle.

Randall extended the GPS jammer as far as his arm would reach. Against the massive wall of the hull, their efforts seemed Lilliputian.

"Hold tight!" She reached down and pushed the throttle

back to max. The yacht lurched and bucked closer to the ship.

"You're too close!" Randall yelled.

"No! Look! It's working!" The bow of the ship had veered slightly eastward.

Kate used her entire body to steady the wheel as the yacht slammed through the waves. Randall hung off the starboard side of the deck, one arm wrapped around a halyard, the other extending the jammer.

Don't drop it in the water.

The ship veered several degrees more to the east. Kate turned the wheel to keep abreast of it. A wave caught them broadside.

They slammed into the hull of the ship. There was a crunching sound.

Focus, Kate. She righted the wheel, keeping the yacht as close to the ship as possible.

"Kate!" Randall called. "The hull is breached!" Randall pointed to the starboard side where the yacht had hit the container ship.

"Is it bad?"

"It's taking on water."

"We're slowing down!" Kate could feel the drag on the boat. They weren't keeping pace with the container ship.

Randall raced back to the cockpit, still holding the jammer. "I'm going to tie this onto the wheel, and then bail the bilge." He deftly tied the jammer to the wheel, and then scrambled down the companionway into the cabin.

Kate heard a muffled expletive as Randall started the bilge pumps.

We aren't sinking too much. But the ship is getting further away.

Had it changed course at all? Or were they too far away for the jammer to work now?

Kate's phone rang.

Panic hit her. If her phone worked, it meant the jammer no longer worked. She propped the phone in the crook of her shoulder.

"It's Ell—" The signal dropped for a few seconds.

Her heart leapt. *Let the jammer work.*

Then Ellis' voice came back on the line. "...worked...enough, Kate... Captain has control of the ship. He can avoid a collision..." The phone broke up. "It will run aground. You need to get the hell out of there."

"We're sinking." Water sloshed past her ankles. *Ex Parte* was barely responsive now. "We have a hole in the hull."

"Hold on—" Ellis' voice cut in and out. "...coming...you."

The phone went dead. The battery had died. "Jesus."

A wave pushed the yacht into a list. And then another wave hit. Suddenly, water rushed into the cockpit on the leeward side.

"Randall!"

The wheel was completely unresponsive. Kate ran to the companionway and peered down below. Randall lay on his stomach, frantically bailing. Water surged from the hull.

"You need to come up now," she called. "There's water coming in the cockpit."

The yacht shifted over again. "Randall, come now." They were sinking rapidly.

And then the wave hit them.

Randall crashed over to the leeward side, adding more displacement to the beleaguered yacht.

Kate jumped down into the water-filled cabin and grabbed his arm. "Are you okay?"

"I hit my head..." He pushed against the window and got himself to his feet. "We've got to get out of here before she turtles." Kate didn't know what that meant, but she understood the urgency of his tone.

They raced up the companionway. To their right, the container ship had pulled forward and eastward, leaving a safe distance between them and the wake.

"Go back on the stern, Kate." The yacht listed leeward, the bow pitching down at a concerning angle. Randall pulled her up onto the transom. They balanced on the very back of the cockpit, holding onto the lifeline. Randall put his arm around Kate.

Ahead, the tug nudged the ship's stern. More crew members climbed into it, followed by the captain. She was about to hit the rocky shore of Eastern Passage. A helicopter kept a discreet distance overhead, watching the ship's progress.

And if the UF6 containers breached, or the oil spilled, or any other maritime disaster occurred, Kate and Randall were within range of it.

Kate studied the choppy waters surrounding them. Her hand found Randall's. "On the count of three!"

Randall pointed across the water. "Sorry to ruin your fun, but I can see the police."

A police boat raced toward them, spray flying around its bow. Detective Ellis raised a hand in greeting. The boat slowed as it neared their yacht. Within minutes, Kate and Randall had transferred from the *Ex Parte* into the police boat. It quickly did a 180 and went into full throttle, away from the container ship.

Kate and Randall sat in the cockpit of the police boat. They were wet. The wind was surprisingly chilly, maybe because the harbor water was so cold. Randall put his arm around her.

"Would you like a blanket?" Detective Ellis held out a reflective blanket.

"Thank you." Randall unfolded the blanket and wrapped it around Kate.

"We can share this, you know." She unwrapped one end and tucked it around him. *Two peas in a pod.*

"How's Matt doing?" she asked Detective Ellis. She felt Randall's solid breadth next to her.

"He's in surgery. Critical but stable condition."

"And what about Joey?"

"He's at the police station. We are holding him there until his arraignment."

"You wouldn't consider dropping the charges? He did surrender the laptop."

Regret gleamed in Detective Ellis's eyes. "You know I can't do that, Ms. Lange. But I can provide a statement to the Crown when you negotiate his plea. It will be favorable."

Kate nodded. The detective seemed like a reasonable guy. "And what about Leah Roberts? She was instrumental in averting a massive, national disaster." She knew she had plied a little hyperbole, but she wanted to use whatever she could to help her client.

"True, Ms. Lange." Detective Ellis exchanged a look with a small, wiry auburn haired police officer. "Her assistance has been duly noted and I will also provide a statement to Hillcroft to that effect."

"Thank you."

Under the blanket, Randall squeezed her hand.

61

THE DOORBELL RANG.

Kate sprang up from the sofa. It couldn't be Randall. He had gone to Prospect to pick up his children from his mother's house.

Still, she smoothed her hair before swinging it open.

Eddie stood on the doorstep. Behind him, news trucks lined the street. A reporter hurried up the walkway when she saw the door had been opened.

"Quick!" Kate said. "Get in!"

He hurried over the threshold, and Kate bolted the door behind him. He held a box wrapped in a ribbon. "I bought you these," he said, handing the box to her.

The box held an exquisite collection of macarons from Le French Fix, Kate's favorite French pâtisserie in downtown Halifax.

"Thank you." Kate's throat tightened. "Come into the kitchen, Eddie. I'll make tea."

Eddie followed her, sitting at the table. How many times had they shared a meal at this table over the past year? Kate had lost count.

"I'm glad you're okay, Kate." She felt his gaze on her as she arranged the macarons on the plate. The delicate colors soothed her after the craziness of the past forty-eight hours.

She put the plate in front of Eddie. "I'm more worried about you."

He nodded in acknowledgment of what was unspoken between them. "I'll be okay."

Kate sat down opposite him. "Listen, I thought long and hard this afternoon about our partnership."

His eyes met hers. She saw resignation, pain, and something else in there. "I understand if you want to leave, Kate."

"I don't want to leave. But if we're to be partners, I need to trust you."

Wariness replaced resignation. "What are you suggesting?"

"I need to know that you are seeking help for your addiction."

"I have been going to AA, Kate. You know that."

"But last night—"

"—was a big mistake. I plan to attend AA tonight and reset things with my counselor."

Relief surged in Kate. "I'm so happy to hear that."

"But, Kate, I'm not accountable to you. I'm only accountable to myself."

"I know." Kate poured water into the teapot. "I don't want or need a blow-by-blow of your recovery, Eddie. I just need to know that I can rely on you as my law partner."

Her words settled between them.

Eddie exhaled. "Fair enough." He bit into a macaron. "I will do my best to fulfill my obligations in that regard. In the meantime, what happened while I was sleeping?"

His reassurance didn't put her fears completely to rest. But she went along with the change of topic.

While she filled him in, her cell phone vibrated on the table. Her gaze followed his. "It's the media. They are incessant."

"I'd forgotten that you tend to attract the media, Ms. Lange. You are the proverbial nectar to the bee."

Her phone buzzed again. Kate glanced at the number. "It's Hillcroft." She hurriedly swallowed her mouthful of macaron. "Hello, John."

"Kate! I wasn't sure if I'd reach you. The media are staked outside your house." He chuckled. "Although, that's probably not new for you. I'm glad you are okay. The Owen case went in a direction no one had anticipated."

"That's one way of putting it." She straightened. "Have you been briefed by the police investigators on the role Leah Roberts played in averting disaster?"

Eddie gave her a thumbs up.

"You don't waste much time, do you?"

Kate shook her head. "That's one thing I've learned from the past few years, John."

"Understood."

"You can't put Leah or her brother away. They're good people."

He sighed. "They both committed crimes."

"But for the right reasons. Leah Roberts wanted to expose a serious, criminal data breach by the government. And Joey took her laptop for the purposes of protecting her. He did it out of love, John."

"Two wrongs don't make a right."

"Leah was afraid of being treated like Edward Snowden. You have to acknowledge that the law does very little to protect whistle blowers."

"Yes, I agree. But she broke into Mel Owen's house, Kate. It wasn't just a computer crime. It was break and enter."

Kate tapped her fingers on the teapot. "She also freely provided the police and myself with the information to stop the container ship. And she wasn't responsible for the hacking of that ship. You can't blame her for that. She lacked *mens rea* regarding the theft of those files from Harry Owen's computer. She was tricked by Aiden Boyne and that hacker Tr0lz."

There was a long silence. Finally, he said, "Here's what

the Crown will offer for Leah Roberts. We will reduce the charge to trespass. And for Joey Roberts, his charge would be accessory to Leah's trespass. Both of those charges have miminum sentences that can be carried out in the community."

Should she push him harder? Kate caught Eddie's eye. He gave a small shake of his head. "Deal." Before John Hillcroft could hang up, she added, "Don't forget Matt Leon. He should have leniency, as well. He risked his life to uncover the exploit."

"The US wants to extradite him, Kate."

"But the events took place on Canadian territory."

"He is suspected of other online activities with his hacktivist forum."

Her heart sank. "Can't you do something to help him?"

"This is out of my jurisdiction, Kate. I'll talk to you on Monday. Get some rest." He hung up.

"I heard that part about Matt Leon," Eddie said. "So the Crown has washed its hands of jurisdiction?"

"Yes." Kate thought of the hacktivist. Matt barely clung to life. He had risked so much for Leah—and for the city of Halifax.

"I'm calling Harry Owen."

"That's the spirit." Eddie bit into another macaron.

Kate dialed Harry Owen's number. His voice mail answered. "Harry, this is Kate Lange. I'm getting straight to the point: all of your constituents owe Matt Leon, as does the Government of Canada. You better do your very best to get him off the hook with both the Canadian and US governments. I would hate for this to become an election issue." She hung up. "Do you think that'll work?"

Eddie nodded, brushing a crumb from his shirt. "It just might. Now call your actual clients with the good news."

If the war room had buzzed before, it now vibrated with energy. Pearson strode into the room, wearing his uniform, his gaze focused. "I need a debrief. Press conference in thirty minutes. But before I start, I want to thank you for your quick actions today. The containers on the *Petrel* have been secured and as of 1700, there is no risk of a breach. I want to commend you on the excellent team work, especially Cooper, Riley and Lamond. Some quick thinking there."

There was a quick round of applause. Riley shrugged. Lamond grinned. Cooper relaxed back in his chair. He was now part of the team.

"Okay. I need a status update. Cooper, where are you with the APB on Tr0lz?"

Every major city in Canada, as well as US cities on the Eastern Seaboard, had received an APB for the hacker Tr0lz. "We've sent one out across Canada, as well as the US."

"Have you found a photo to use?"

"No. We have sketch based on descriptions from Matt Leon." He had regained consciousness a few hours ago. "There have been no sightings as of 1700."

Pearson did not appear surprised. "Keep on it. And flood social media. Riley, was FIS able to find anything before CSIS showed up?" Canadian Security Intelligence Service had sealed off Tr0lz's apartment. Rumor had it that they had uncovered her connection with the Port of Antwerp's recent hack, as well as contacts that had created 'great concern' for the government.

Riley shook her head. "I dusted her computer for prints, but CSIS has taken all the evidence."

"We'll have to wait until they release it." *If ever.*

"How could she have disappeared?" Lamond asked. "We were at her apartment within minutes of Matt Leon's phone call."

That was still something the team was trying to figure out. But with CSIS now on the scene, that might remain unanswered.

Pearson's phone rang. "Okay, I've got to go. But one more thing," he said, as he strode toward the door. "Someone get us a damned GPS jammer."

"Make that two," Lamond muttered.

62

"KATE." FINN'S VOICE BROKE through her nap. "Enid and Muriel are here. Do you want me to tell them to come back?"

Kate lifted her head from the sofa. "No. I'm awake."

Finn grinned. "So to speak."

She threw a pillow at him. "What time is it?"

Finn caught the pillow and tossed it onto the sofa. "Eight-thirty."

"Oh, no. I'll never sleep tonight." She felt a stirring of panic.

"Kate!" Enid rushed into the living room. Finn followed with Muriel on his arm. The elderly lady had a delighted smile on her face and kept patting his arm. *There was no substitute for human contact,* Kate thought.

Alaska nosed her knee. Foo Dog squeezed himself between the husky and her leg, sitting on her foot. *Canines are the exception.*

Enid's bright robin's gaze swept over Kate. "I was so worried about you." She leaned down and gave Kate a kiss on the cheek.

"I'm fine," Kate said. "Just got a little wet."

"It's not a joking matter, Kate."

313

Finn gently led Muriel to the opposite love seat. She sat down, but did not relinquish his arm. He settled next to her, his hand held in Muriel's strong grip.

"Please have a seat, Enid." She sensed how upset her friend was, and it worried her. "You need to make sure you don't get your heart rate too high."

Enid perched on the sofa next to Kate. "You need to stop taking so many risks." Enid gave Kate a fierce look. Tears made her eyes even brighter.

Kate patted her friend's bony knee. "I will try to live a boring life from now on."

Finn snorted.

Enid shot him a wry look. "You aren't helping matters."

Finn stood. "And on that note, I must excuse myself. I am meeting some friends downtown." He grabbed his keys. "Don't wait up for me, Kate. Good-bye, ladies." He smiled, and strode out the door.

"I just remembered something." Kate jumped to her feet. "I brought a little something from Venice for you both."

She ran up the stairs to her room and retrieved two small white boxes.

She carried them carefully downstairs. "This one is for you, Muriel," she said, placing it in the elderly lady's hands. The look of pleasure on her face was worth the hassle to bring the gift home.

"And this one is for you, Enid." Kate smiled. "Open them together."

Kate stood next to Muriel to help her open the small white box and remove the fragile gift.

Enid gasped. "It's lovely!" She held a small hand-blown glass elephant with a trunk that waved up in the air. It had streaks of blue that were exactly the shade of her eyes. Kate had bought Muriel a similar elephant, but its body was dabbed with the color of her favorite heather green sweater.

"I bought one for myself, too." A tiny cream-colored elephant with delicate flecks of gold.

"We are officially a herd, then." Enid smiled, hugging Kate.

314

But when she tried to speak, tears closed her throat. She nodded.

The two sisters packed the boxes with great care, Enid placing them in her purse. With a promise to have tea the next day, the sisters went home.

The house seemed so empty after they left.

Kate thought of the suitcases still waiting to be unpacked.

She thought of the box in her closet.

It's time, Kate.

You are going to have to face this in a few days, anyway, when the preliminary inquiry is held.

She climbed the stairs, a white dog on one heel and a black dog on the other. They settled on the dog bed, curved around one another. Foo Dog yawned, his tongue endearingly pink against his black muzzle.

Kate strode to the closet and opened the door with more force than she intended. It banged against the wall.

The box sat on the floor of her closet.

It was dingy, a document box that had sat in storage for too many years.

She knelt in front of it.

Lifted the lid.

Blood stains marked one side.

Her blood.

She felt her stomach revolt.

Her cells crawl.

She forced herself to stare into the box. *You can do this.*

Imogen's purple Language Arts binder sat on top. Purple had been her favorite color. Kate lifted it out. Under it was the pencil case. Kate unzipped it and pulled out three pencils, and one pen with the little buttons that changed the ink tube so that one could write in different colors. Imogen had loved that pen. Kate held it in her hand. Her fingers curved around the smooth plastic where Imogen's once had been.

There had been a necklace that Imogen had received for her thirteenth birthday, a gift from Kate and her mother.

Kate felt around in the box, discovering it in a crumpled heap in the back corner. As if it had huddled in fear when Kate was attacked.

She scooped the necklace into her palm. The hard edge of something brushed her hand.

A photo.

Her heart pounded. Maybe it was a photo of her and Imogen. One that she could frame.

She held it up to the light. A man smiled at the camera, his arm around a gangly twelve-year-old Kate and a round-eyed ten-year-old Imogen. He was of average height, with brown hair and amber eyes.

Her father.

She threw the photo into the box.

It fell, face down.

She might have no choice about facing Kenzie Sloane next week, but she didn't have to see her father again, regardless of the form it took.

She placed the lid back on the box and put it in her closet. It took a few minutes to unknot the fine gold chain. She fastened Imogen's necklace around her throat.

The small medallion of the letter 'I' was warm on her skin.

She climbed into bed. "Come on, boys."

The two dogs didn't need to be invited twice.

They jumped on her bed and curled up next to her legs.

And she fell asleep, the light shining bright on her side table.

63

OVER THE PAST FEW years, the waterfront had been developed into a well-appointed boardwalk that connected the downtown core between Purdy's Wharf on the north end, and the Seaport Market on the south end of the waterfront. It was a popular Sunday morning spot for walkers, runners and, of course, tourists, especially after the events of the day before.

Across the harbor, the uneven silhouette of the *Petrel* could be seen, listing to one side where it foundered on the shore. Crews had been working around the clock to ensure that the UF6 containers remained intact.

Harry pulled his ball cap more firmly over his forehead, plugged in his earbuds, and began to run.

He moved forward—*forward, not back, Harry*—his feet urging him toward the open mouth of the harbor.

Part of him longed to keep going: past the tourist-friendly boardwalk, past the eco-hip farmers' market, past Pier 21 which had once welcomed his parents to the country, past the Port of Halifax, where the container ships silently approached with their full bellies.

The lights of the navigation buoys marked the surface of the harbor. But the water beneath was dark. When he was younger, he had been terrified of the water. He did not like swimming in the ocean, and had no desire to scuba dive. The water was cold, black, full of strange creatures and unfamiliar flora.

But then the water had become a source of promise for him.

Because it carried the man he loved.

He watched the water slice over the gleaming back of the submarine as it maneuvered past McNabs Island. A Canadian Navy Auxiliary Vessel kept a respectful distance, guiding it around the navigation buoys, leading it toward the outer harbor.

People stood on the waterfront, waving at the sleek tube of steel until it melded with the horizon.

He turned around and ran back to the hotel.

The weight in his chest was different. But it no longer crushed him.

He showered and drove to the hospital. He ran up the stairwell to his father's room.

"Harry." His father sat in a chair, a hospital robe belted around him, one leg in a thick, white cast.

"Hi, Dad." Harry pulled up a visitor's chair and sat next to him. "How are you feeling?"

"I'm fine."

It was the usual response from his father. But his demeanor seemed calmer.

"I brought you something." Harry handed a photo frame to his father.

His dad held it up to the light. It was a picture of Salma from his parents' wedding day. Her dark eyes were bright, her lips bold, her beautiful thick hair coiled into a heavy chignon under the veil.

This was the second wedding. It had been arranged by Mel's parents, several weeks after the ceremony in India. The photo of Salma had been on Mel's bureau ever since their wedding, until today.

He closed his eyes, his hands holding the framed photo that lay in his lap. His face worked.

"Dad," Harry said, his voice low. "I'm sorry. I didn't mean to distress you."

Mel opened his eyes. "I can feel her here, Harry."

"Me, too." He took a deep breath. "Dad, I'm leaving politics."

"No, Harry, you can't do that." But there was hope in his father's face. "Why are you leaving?"

Because I can't live the lie one more day.

Pain welled in his chest. Harry knew deep in his heart that Rob would say good-bye after what had happened. The near loss of life put everyone's priorities into perspective.

For Rob, it was his family.

For Harry, it was his family. But Harry's family was his father. That was all he had left.

This wrecked man.

Who had done his best for Harry, over and over again.

"I'm leaving because it's time, Dad." It wasn't exactly true. He was in hot water with the Prime Minister, but his actions to stop the terrorist attack had lifted him out of the depths of public depredation. His career might just be salvageable. "I want to live in Halifax." That didn't exactly ring true, but he tried.

"Harry." His father reached over and took Harry's hand. Harry was surprised at the strength of his father's grip. "I know what you're doing, but you can't give up your career."

"I have to, Dad," Harry's voice was choked.

"Why?"

And then the secret that had brought him home just a few days ago could be contained no longer. "Dad... I'm gay."

Mel looked at him. Then he gazed down at the picture of his wife. "That's why you came home early. To tell Salma."

"Yes." Harry knelt by his father's chair. "Do you think she would have given me her blessing?"

His father stared into his dead wife's eyes. "She loved you, Harry."

A shuddering sigh escaped from somewhere in the

deepest, most locked place of Harry's heart. "I'm so sorry about what happened."

"It's not your fault, Harry."

"Dad, it is my fault."

"Harry, you're not responsible for the actions of others. You are only responsible for what you do. And you're fortunate to be in a position where you can do a lot of good, protect a lot of people."

Was this his way of telling me to smarten up?

"I want you to go back to Ottawa, Harry. That's where you belong. But it would be really nice—" Tears choked his voice. "It would be really nice if you kept coming home like when Ma was sick."

"I want you to come with me to Ottawa." And as Harry said the words, he realized it was true. He wanted his father near him. And thanks to Detective Ellis, the police had decided not to lay any charges with a mandatory prison sentence. Mel could serve his sentence in the community.

"Ottawa is so far away," Mel said. He gazed at the picture of Salma.

"It's not that far. Look how far Ma came so she could live in Canada."

Mel exhaled. "I suppose I could go. But just until my leg heals."

A tear fell onto Salma's picture.

It wasn't Mel's.

64

KATE RAN THROUGH THE gates of the upper parking lot at Point Pleasant Park. Alaska loped beside her, a smile on his face. It was their first Sunday morning run in a month.

They had run along the water. With the exception of a more conspicuous police boat presence, it appeared as immutable as ever. The sun had performed a hat trick, shining for the third day in a row, and the water undulated under a silvery cloak.

The feel of her body aligning itself until every step was a tour de force of synchronized muscle, blood, tissue and oxygen elated her. She sprinted up Serpentine Hill, knowing without a doubt she would regret it later, but uncaring.

Because it felt damn good.

She slowed down to let a car pass as they reached the intersection of Point Pleasant Drive and Young Avenue.

And then her feet decided to turn down Randall's street.

Or was it her heart?

She hadn't seen Randall since yesterday, after they climbed out of the police boat. Detective Ellis dropped them each home. Randall told her that he needed to collect his children from his mother's house in Prospect. They both knew that Lucy would be distressed by what had transpired, and Randall would need to spend the rest of the day with her.

Alaska began to pull on his lead when he saw Randall's house. "You guessed right, boy," she said. They jogged up the stone steps, Kate admiring the full-blown roses that billowed by his front porch.

The door opened before she even used the knocker. Charlie yelped in delight, throwing herself in delirious circles. "Kate." Randall gazed at her with as much delight. "I should have guessed it was you. Charlie was going nuts in here." The Lab rushed over to Kate, licked her hurriedly, and then danced around Alaska. "Please come in." He held open the door.

Kate walked past him, suddenly aware of the patch of sweat between her shoulder blades.

"How are you? Did you get some sleep?"

For once, she was able to say, "Yes." She smiled, wiping the sweat from her forehead with the hem of her shirt. "It was a bit hotter than I realized."

"Let me get you and Alaska some water." He turned toward the kitchen. She followed him, as familiar with his kitchen as he was. He filled a crystal glass with chilled water and handed it to her. Alaska found Charlie's water bowl and helped himself. "Did you have a good run?"

"Yes." She gulped the water. "It was glorious. I needed to clear my head. It's been a little nuts." She threw a sideways glance at him. "I negotiated a plea deal for both Leah and Joey."

"Nice work. I did the same for Mel Owen." Randall smiled. "Ellis was extremely compassionate toward him. Especially since this was the second time he was a victim of break-and-enter."

"Leah's charge has been reduced to trespass," Kate said, holding the chill glass to her cheek.

Randall raised a brow. "Well, good for your client. But not entirely accurate."

"Hillcroft recognized that the law doesn't protect whistle

322

blowers, so he was willing to recognize the desperate measures Leah took to inform the public. Although part of the deal was that Leah not publish the files."

Randall leaned against the counter top. "All those lives damaged, and the files remain top secret."

"Pretty top secret." She grinned.

"What do you mean?"

"Our intrepid journo Nat sniffed a story and has dug up some interesting information about a data breach."

Randall raised a brow. "So maybe not entirely in vain."

Kate shrugged. "I don't know. I guess it depends on what you view is a just result. That hacker Tr0lz seems to have disappeared."

"What do you think is a just result, Kate?"

She shook her head. "You know I wanted to be a prosecutor because I felt I could help victims. But in this case...there were too many victims and too many crimes."

"The many faces of Lady Justice." Randall's gaze rested on her face. "Do you think that this case has changed your mind?"

"It's given me another perspective. But Hillcroft told me that Kenzie Sloane's preliminary inquiry is on Wednesday." She looked past Randall, through the window. A white butterfly fluttered above a stunning indigo delphinium.

"That's sudden."

"I know." Kate shrugged. "They want to have it before the judge goes on vacation."

"How are you feeling about it?"

Tears pricked her eyelids. "Fine."

"I don't think you are feeling fine." He stepped closer to her and took her injured hand.

She swallowed. "I don't want to face her."

"I'd feel the same way."

"She's claiming self-defense."

He drew her against him. "No one will believe her."

"I don't want to have to answer all those questions and see her watching me from the prisoner's dock."

He smoothed her hair. "You are the strongest person I know. You can do this."

She shook her head. "Not with her, Randall. It's like she's this virus I can't shake and that I have no immunity against."

"You have already beaten her, Kate."

She thought of the box in her closet.

"No. I haven't."

She pulled herself out of his arms and turned to the window.

The butterfly was gone.

"Kate, why are you so scared of me?"

She turned around. "I'm not."

He stepped closer. She smelled his fresh scent, the tang of sweat, a hint of coffee. "I don't believe you."

She would have backed away but the windowsill was behind her. "I'm not scared of you."

He recaptured her injured hand and placed it against his heart. "Why did you come today?"

She felt his heart thud against her palm. His heartbeat pulsed through the vein in her wrist all the way to her heart.

"I'm here because…" Heat flushed her cheeks.

"Because?" His heart now beat more quickly.

And so did hers.

She shook her head. Tears sprang into her eyes. She tried to pull away.

"No, Kate."

"I can't," she whispered. "I'm sorry."

"Dance with me."

"There's no music." But she didn't move away.

"That's easy." He pulled his phone out of his pocket. Within a second, an electric bass began a rhythmic beat. And then David Bowie's and Freddie Mercury's duet filled the kitchen.

Kate gave him a wry smile. "*Under Pressure*. I wonder why today of all days you were listening to that."

"Shhh…just dance with me."

He took her hand. This time, she did not pull it away. His

other hand slid over her hip.

He began to sway to the music, Kate's hand cupped in his, pressed against his heart.

His breath in her ear, his heart under her hand, his hips moving against hers.

She closed her eyes.

The song built to its climax. Randall softly murmured the lyrics in her ear.

He had a nice tenor.

Loss filled her. Longing swept through her. The song always had that effect on her.

She longed to not be afraid any more.

I can't be afraid any more.

She curled her fingers around his.

The song finished. Randall lifted his head. His eyes—so brilliant, so tender—gazed into hers.

"Why can't you give our love a chance?" he asked, subtly altering the song's lyrics.

She could think of only one response.

And it didn't require any words.

THE END

Author's Note

When DAMAGED was first released, I participated in a panel at Thrillerfest, the International Thrillers' Writers annual conference in New York. Our topic was "Are Thrillers Society's New Conscience?" It remains my favourite conference panel, because it encapsulates the reason that I am drawn to writing crime fiction: exploring the gray areas between the black and white of the law.

I wanted to write about a whistleblower, a person who felt that she had no other option than to commit a small crime in order to reveal a wrongdoing. I also am fascinated by the shift in societal acceptance to the erosion of our privacy, and the unknown consequences that are attached to that.

I decided to write about shipping after an incident that occurred in Halifax several years ago with the unloading of a shipment of UF6 containers. It received front page local media coverage, partly because so few people realized that our port received these kinds of hazardous materials.

At its deepest level, EXPLOITED explores the consequences of how we react to change.

If you enjoyed EXPLOITED, please consider leaving a few words and a rating on the site where you purchased it. A recommendation from a reader means so much!

With my thanks,
~ Pam

Acknowledgments

I am indebted to the experts who so generously shared their expertise with me:

Detective Sergeant Mark MacDonald, Halifax Regional Police Department, who is always willing to explore the scenarios I create;

Chief Crown Prosecutor Paul Carver, who patiently answered my questions about the Crown's criminal justice process;

Senior Crown Prosecutor Susan MacKay, who gave me an inside look at her work—and made me admire her even more;

Defense lawyer Michael Aaron Crystal, who offered guidance, wisdom and encouragement; and

Defense lawyer Michelle James, who was gracious enough to meet me and provide her insights and experience.

Any and all mistakes are mine, and I apologize in advance to those who shared their expertise with me.

My thanks to Nancy Cassidy of The Red Pen Coach, who gave EXPLOITED its first read-through.

I am deeply grateful to Julia Carver, who provided invaluable insight about the character and plot arcs of this book. She helped reset my course. If that weren't enough, she conceptualized and produced the most fantastic book trailers for the re-launch of my series.

On a personal note, in 2013, I was jogging at Point Pleasant Park when a large dog took me out at the knees in a "football tackle." It has been a long recovery from that accident, and I was still receiving treatment throughout the writing of EXPLOITED. The compassion and care that has been shown to me has moved me many times. I give my deepest thanks to:

Dr. Gina Burgess;

David Kachan;

Dr. Michael Gross;

Dr. Scott MacLean;

Dr. Wayne Maillet;

Dr. George Majaess; and

Jacinte Armstrong, my Pilates trainer, who has kept me able to write.

I am truly grateful.

As I am to my friends and family. Thank you. From the bottom of my heart.

The Kate Lange Thriller Series

"Do yourself a favor and jump in the middle of these amazing books. You won't be able to put them down until the final page."

— Fresh Fiction

DAMAGED
Book 1
(2nd edition, April 2016)

INDEFENSIBLE
Book 2
(2nd edition, April 2016)

TATTOOED
Book 3
(2nd edition, April 2016)

EXPLOITED
Book 4
(November 2016)

PAMELA CALLOW, JD, MPA, is the bestselling author of the Kate Lange legal thriller series. With over a quarter of a million copies sold, Pamela Callow's critically-acclaimed series has been compared to works by Robin Cook, Tess Gerritsen and John Grisham. DAMAGED was a "Need to Read Pick" with Top Ten Bestseller placement everywhere books were sold across North America. The series has been translated and published in eight countries.

A member of the Nova Scotia bar, Pamela Callow holds a Master's degree in Public Administration. Prior to making writing a career, she worked as a Strategic Services manager with an international consulting firm.

She is currently working on the next release of the Kate Lange thriller series. She would love to travel to all the places where her books are published, but in the meantime, she drinks coffee, spoils her pug, goes for walks and occasionally burns supper. She recently joined a barbershop chorus.

Visit www.pamelacallow.com for more information about her series, behind the scenes peeks, photos, events, newsletter and more!

64531087R00201

Made in the USA
Middletown, DE
14 February 2018